"Miss Molly, look. I'm wearing my favorite pink ribbon. It's Pa's favorite, too."

Sarah's gaze skittered around, searching. "I wore it just for him."

The twins had gotten it into their heads that Ned would show up at church today. CJ wasn't as confident.

Molly pasted on a cheery smile. "Why don't we wait inside the tent?"

"No," Anna said. "I want to wait for Pa here."

"What if Pa doesn't come back?" Sarah's eyes grew wide. "What if, like Mama, he *never* comes back?"

Anna burst into tears.

Molly pulled the children into her arms. "No matter what happens here today, you will always have me."

"And you'll always have me." CJ looked from one precious face to the other, his resolve growing. These girls were his responsibility now.

He risked a glance at Molly. He remembered what she'd said earlier. *We're in this together.*

Eyes never leaving his, she took Sarah's hand. CJ reached for Anna's.

Together, they guided the girls into the tent.

* * *

**LONE STAR COWBOY LEAGUE:
THE FOUNDING YEARS—**
Bighearted ranchers in ~~~~

Renee Ryan grew up in a Florida beach town where she learned to surf, sort of. With a degree from FSU, she explored career opportunities at a Florida theme park and a modeling agency and even taught high school economics. She currently lives with her husband in Nebraska, and many have mistaken their overweight cat for a small bear. You may contact Renee at reneeryan.com, on Facebook or on Twitter, @reneeryanbooks.

Books by Renee Ryan

Love Inspired Historical

Lone Star Cowboy League: The Founding Years

Stand-In Rancher Daddy

Charity House

The Marshal Takes a Bride
Hannah's Beau
Loving Bella
The Lawman Claims His Bride
Charity House Courtship
The Outlaw's Redemption
Finally a Bride
His Most Suitable Bride
The Marriage Agreement

Visit the Author Profile page at Harlequin.com for more titles.

RENEE RYAN

Stand-In Rancher Daddy

HARLEQUIN® LOVE INSPIRED® HISTORICAL

Special thanks and acknowledgment to Renee Ryan for her contribution to the Lone Star Cowboy League: The Founding Years miniseries.

Recycling programs for this product may not exist in your area.

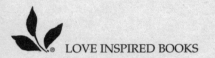

LOVE INSPIRED BOOKS

ISBN-13: 978-0-373-28366-8

Stand-In Rancher Daddy

Copyright © 2016 by Harlequin Books S.A.

www.Harlequin.com

Printed in U.S.A.

Now faith is the substance of things hoped for, the evidence of things not seen.
—*Hebrews* 11:1

I dedicate this book to Louise Gouge
and Regina Scott, two incredibly talented authors
who made writing this book easy. It was a joy
and honor to work with you on this series.

Chapter One

Little Horn, Texas, June 1895

A full hour before the sun peeked over the horizon, Molly Carson Langley slid out of bed. Ranch work started early in Texas Hill Country. If she wished to make her morning journey before the sun rose, she must hurry.

With fast, measured steps, she padded through the room. The hardwood floor was polished to a smooth patina and felt warm beneath her bare feet. A muffled sigh slipped past her lips. After three years of marriage and successfully managing her own household, she didn't belong in her childhood home anymore.

She wasn't sure where she belonged. Until she figured it out, a pair of motherless four-year-olds needed her. That mattered. It had to matter. *Of course* it mattered.

Jaw set at a determined angle, Molly stuffed her feet inside a pair of ankle boots and put on her favorite calico dress with the lavender floral print. She wound her blond hair in a loose braid down her back, then packed a small bag with personal items from her dresser. A hairbrush, a rack of pins, several ribbons in colors she hoped the girls would like, and her worn Bible with the pages crinkled at the edges.

One glance out the window told her the morning sky was shifting from black to deep purple. Dawn was drawing near.

Hurry, Molly.

She made her way toward the door. The other occupant in the room slept peacefully, her soft, feminine snoring the only sound cutting through the still, humid air.

Without breaking stride, Molly smiled down at her sister. At sixteen, the dreams of youth were still fresh and untarnished in Daisy's young mind. Seven years older, Molly could hardly relate to the girl. The death of her husband eleven months ago made it all the more difficult.

Her feet grew heavy as stone and, for a brief moment, despair filled Molly's heart. She'd lost more than her husband. So. Much. *More.*

No. She would not feel sorry for herself. If he were here, George would tell her that the good Lord had a plan for her life. No matter how dark it seemed right now, the particulars were already worked out. She just needed to have faith.

Molly wasn't as faithful as her preacher husband had been. Not anymore. Perhaps she never had been.

At least she'd had somewhere to go after George's death. Molly would concentrate on being grateful her family had welcomed her home.

Her future might look bleak, but she was still young, still vital, still necessary to a family facing their own tragedy. When she'd returned home, she'd never expected her best friend to die suddenly and leave behind twin daughters. Molly would take care of Penelope's children until she was no longer needed.

Resolve firmly in place, she slung the satchel over her

shoulder and tiptoed into the empty hallway. She entered the kitchen, took two full steps and froze.

A pang of guilt whispered through her.

"Good morning, Mama." Molly adopted what she hoped was an airy tone. "You're up early."

"I was going to say the same about you." The soft, musical lilt was in stark contrast to the concern in her mother's eyes.

Even after birthing five children, Helen Carson remained a beautiful woman. Her blond hair, streaked with silver strands, was pulled back in a serviceable bun that revealed a face nearly identical to her two daughters. Save for a few lines and wrinkles, the high cheekbones were the same, as were the straight nose, pale blue eyes and stubborn set of her chin.

"Well, I'm off to the Thorn ranch." Molly attempted to shift around her mother.

"I'd like a word with you before you leave."

Molly tried not to sigh. This was the reason she'd woken early: to avoid a difficult conversation with her mother.

Helen Carson was fiercely protective of all her children, and that included her oldest daughter. What she refused to understand was that Molly was a grown woman capable of making her own decisions. "There is nothing you can say that will change my mind."

Her mother's features showed distress and something else—not censure, precisely, but close. "It's been nearly a year since your husband's death. George wouldn't want you hiding from the world."

"I'm not *hiding* from the world." Molly blew out a frustrated burst of air, hating the defensive note in her voice. "I'm serving a family in need."

George would understand. He would even encourage

her. An itinerant preacher, his personal mission had been to help the less fortunate. Before he'd contracted the fever that ultimately killed him, George had shared a love of serving others side by side with Molly.

Her marriage had been a happy one. Until Molly failed to provide her husband with the one thing he wanted most—a child. She'd been bitterly disappointed over her failure as a wife. George's resentment had only added to her shame.

If her mother knew the truth, Molly was certain she'd give her words of comfort, the kind meant to heal her troubled heart. But Molly didn't want sympathy. She certainly didn't want to discuss her secret shame.

Anything but that.

She stood straighter, lifted her chin and attempted a second time to step around her mother.

Helen Carson moved directly into her path. "It's been six months since Penelope became ill and died. Surely there is someone else who can care for her daughters."

"There is no one else."

Besides, Molly had given her friend her word. Even if she hadn't made a promise, the twins needed a woman's influence in their lives. They had their father, yet even after six months he was still absorbed in his own grief. And lately, Molly had noticed him distancing himself from his daughters, barely going through the motions of being a parent.

Their uncle sometimes stepped in and filled the void. Molly admired him for that—oh, how, she admired him—but CJ had his hands full running the Triple-T ranch.

"If you won't listen to reason," her mother said, "then at least consider taking Daisy with you."

"You need her here."

Her mother opened her mouth to argue.

Molly cut her off. "Please try to understand. Until Ned marries again, or another solution presents itself, I will honor my promise to Penelope. If our roles were reversed, she would do the same for me."

"I can't help but think there's something you're not telling me, some reason you're not sharing with me."

"The twins need me." What woman didn't want to be needed, especially one who couldn't have children of her own? "I should think that reason enough."

"Molly, won't you please be honest with me?"

"It's nearly dawn." She looked pointedly at the band of gray riding low on the horizon. "The girls will be awake soon."

This time, when Molly made for the back door, her mother pulled her into a fierce hug. "As soon as you're ready to tell me what's troubling you, I'll be here to listen."

"There's nothing troubling me." She stepped out of the embrace. "Other than my concern for two small children."

With her mother's sigh of resignation ringing in her ears, Molly hurried out of the house. She made quick work of saddling Sadie, the ten-year-old gray mare born the same year as Molly's youngest brother, Donny.

Halfway between her family's large spread and the much smaller Triple-T ranch, Molly felt the tension in her shoulders melt away. A soft flutter of air stirred the leaves of the Texas oaks nestled in a small grove on her left. She breathed in, smelled the faint scents of sassafras and wild cherry.

Molly loved this time of morning, when night slowly surrendered to day and everything felt new again. When possibilities stretched before her and the future didn't feel so hopeless.

Rolling Hills ranch was the largest cattle operation in the area. Tall, rugged bluffs peppered the landscape as far as the eye could see. The green leaves of cottonwood trees shared space with large granite and limestone rocks. The sound of water sloshing on the lakeshore near the edge of her parents' property accompanied a bobwhite's distinctive whistle.

A movement in the distance caught her attention. Narrowing her eyes, she watched a horse and rider race across a flat patch of land. The man's slouched posture was at odds with the magnificence of the black stallion beneath him.

Molly's stomach dropped.

She knew that horse, and the rider. But the two did not belong together. Why hadn't Ned taken his own gelding? What was he doing with his brother's horse?

No one rode Thunder but CJ. The animal was too valuable to be mishandled and...

Molly had a terrible, awful feeling about this.

Please, Lord, let me be wrong. The evidence suggested otherwise. She should have seen this coming.

Why hadn't she put the pieces together before now?

Ned had become increasingly morose in recent weeks, muttering things under his breath such as "What's the use?" and "I can't keep doing this." Molly hadn't thoroughly understood what he meant and she certainly hadn't wanted to overstep her bounds. After all, she was helping out the Thorn family in a temporary capacity.

Another unsettling thought occurred. Surely Ned hadn't left the twins alone in the house.

What if he had?

Molly wrapped her arms around Sadie's neck. "Come on, old girl." She gave a gentle kick to the mare's ribs. "I need you to run faster than you ever have before."

The horse responded with a burst of speed. Once they were on Thorn land, Molly urged Sadie to a trot, guiding her past the outbuildings, around the corral and on to the main house, a simple, one-story, whitewashed clapboard structure.

Out of the corner of her eye, she noticed smoke coming from the bunkhouse, a sure sign Cookie had already started making breakfast for the handful of ranch hands CJ employed.

Was CJ eating with the hands, as he did every morning? Was he even aware his brother had left the main house?

Molly pulled Sadie to a halt and scrambled off the horse's back. She hurried onto the porch she and the girls had swept clean yesterday afternoon. Without bothering to knock, she rushed inside the house.

Thick gloom closed in around her. The silence was so heavy she decided the children were surely still asleep. *The children.*

Molly must get to Anna and Sarah. She must ensure they were safe. She moved deeper into the house and froze when she caught a faint whiff of whiskey. *Oh, Ned.*

The situation was far worse than Molly had feared, and certainly explained Ned's increasing unpredictability. Her friend's husband had evidently turned to the bottle to swallow his grief. Unfortunately, consuming alcohol was not a wise solution.

Heart in her throat, Molly blinked through the darkness. Her vision slowly cleared, then locked on the tall silhouette of a familiar figure.

A ripple of longing flowed through her before she ruthlessly shut it down.

CJ Thorn stood before her, silent, his eyes on the piece of paper in his hand. His features were inscrutable in the dim light cast by the lamp on the table beside him, but Molly knew every line and curve by heart.

She knew every precious angle of his handsome face, the strong, square jaw and the dark eyebrows slashed over eyes the color of freshly brewed coffee. He was more than merely good-looking. He was a man of integrity and one who'd worked hard to keep his brother from following in their father's footsteps.

Ned had taken to whiskey, anyway. CJ must be so disappointed.

"CJ?" She gently touched his sleeve.

He looked up. Blinked. Then blinked again, as if he hadn't expected to find her standing so close.

"I saw Ned riding away from the ranch." She waited a beat, then supplied the rest of the bad news. "He was on your horse."

Surprise flared in his eyes. "Ned took Thunder?"

She nodded.

Anger replaced the earlier shock, followed by such sorrow Molly could actually feel the weight of the emotion in her own heart. The vulnerable expression made him more compelling than usual.

CJ Thorn was not a man who needed to be more compelling than usual.

The children, she told herself. Anna and Sarah must come first. With the twins in mind, Molly released CJ's arm and stepped back.

In the predawn gloom, CJ tried to focus on the woman standing beside him. But his mind kept returning to Ned and the terrible choice his brother had made.

No matter how hard CJ fought to keep his breathing steady, his gut roiled with regret. This was the moment he'd been dreading for weeks, when his brother gave up completely.

Rage boiled into something CJ couldn't begin to name. Ned had not only made his escape on CJ's prize stallion, he'd not only abandoned his own children, but he'd left the girls alone in the house. Any number of things could have happened to them.

Even for Ned, that was an all-time low. What was next? Cattle rustling? Bank robbery?

For months, CJ had held out hope that the worst of Ned's grief was behind him. He'd prayed that his younger brother was on the brink of returning to the man he'd been while Penelope was alive.

Obviously, that had been wishful thinking.

All the emotion CJ had been holding back threatened to spill over, filling him until he thought he might explode.

"Is that a note from Ned?" Molly's voice seemed to come at him through a thick wall of water.

He gave a brief nod before returning his gaze to the hastily scrawled note. The handwriting was messy, the message even messier.

Ned had always preferred the easier tasks on the ranch, but he'd been a decent man at the core. Penelope had brought out the best in him. Since her death, Ned had slipped deeper and deeper into despair.

CJ thought he'd be able to save Ned, given time.

Time had just run out.

"CJ, did you hear me?"

He lifted his head and glanced once again at the woman he'd grown to rely on far more than he cared to admit. "Ned took off."

"Yes, I know."

His heart began to thump harder.

Five years peeled away and he was twenty-two again, meeting Molly for the first time. She'd been full of light and goodness back then, the same as now. Just being in her company made him wish for…more. But he knew he could never reach so far above his station in life. He'd learned that cruel lesson from another woman and her upright, proper parents.

"Talk to me. Tell me what's happened."

He handed her Ned's note.

Feeling oddly nostalgic, he held silent while she read. During Ned and Penelope's courtship, Molly had acted as chaperone. CJ had been attracted to her from the start. But he'd never let her know. Lillian's harsh words had taught him a valuable lesson. No decent woman from a respectable family would have a man like him, a man with the last name Thorn.

Penelope had taken the risk and married Ned. Look how that had ended.

"Oh, Ned." Molly's hand flew to her mouth. "How could you?"

"I've been asking myself that same question."

How could his brother surrender custody of his own daughters to CJ?

Eyes shadowed with sadness, Molly returned the piece of paper. Her fingertips grazed CJ's knuckles. The touch was barely a whisper, yet he felt the impact like a blow to the gut.

He closed his fist around the words Ned had penned. In a quick, careless scrawl of ink across paper, his brother had become the man CJ feared was deep inside every Thorn. He shuddered to think what would become of Ned now that he'd given in to the dark side of his nature.

"I suppose I understand how he could give up on himself," Molly said. "But how could he give up on his own children?"

CJ heard the tears in her voice, saw the sorrow in the slump of her shoulders. He wanted to comfort her.

He took a large step back instead.

An awareness of her as a woman had been gnawing at him ever since she'd taken over Sarah and Anna's full-time care following Penelope's funeral.

Though he'd often wondered why Molly continued to serve his family, and CJ hadn't interacted with her very often, he'd been grateful for her help. The girls adored her and he didn't take that for granted. She'd been the stable force in all their lives. He realized that now.

Once, months ago, CJ had offered to pay Molly for her kindness. She'd been insulted by the mere suggestion and so he'd never brought up the subject again.

Did she understand how much his family relied on her? How much *he* relied on her? Every day, he felt her presence acutely, hovering on the edge of his life but not really part of it.

"I hadn't realized Ned's grief was this great. I thought…" Her brows pulled together in confusion. "How did I miss this?"

"We both missed it."

Ned hadn't begun drinking immediately following Penelope's death, yet it hadn't been very long afterward. When CJ had first confronted his brother, Ned had claimed he didn't have a problem. He simply missed his wife. Apparently, the loneliness hit hardest at night, and he needed help sleeping. He'd promised CJ that it was only one drink, after the girls were in bed.

CJ had wanted to believe his brother. For a while, there'd been no reason not to trust Ned's word. Still, CJ should have been more observant. He should have seen the signs that Ned was slowly spiraling out of control, in the same way their father had.

"Surely your brother will come to his senses and return in a day or two."

"Perhaps." CJ spoke without conviction. There was an unmistakable finality to Ned's actions. By leaving a note that included awarding CJ custody of the twins, his brother had made his intentions clear.

What had Ned been thinking?

CJ knew nothing about raising children, especially girls. He was a rancher, most comfortable around cows and horses. The Triple-T was barely showing a profit. He couldn't run the ranch and take care of two small children at the same time.

His life had just changed dramatically. He needed to move back into the main house. The twins couldn't sleep here alone. He'd have to learn new skills, too many to sort through at once.

"I should start breakfast before the girls wake up."

Molly's words brought CJ great comfort and reminded him that decisions didn't have to be made today. Watching her in the pale dawn light, he wondered just how much she did around the house when he was out working the ranch. "I'd be grateful."

"It's my pleasure." She turned quiet, thoughtful. "I see no reason to upset the girls just yet. We probably should tell them as little as possible and hope that Ned changes his mind."

This was one of the reasons CJ admired Molly. She always put the twins' needs first. "We're in agreement."

Her smile filled him with the sense of peace he craved, but always hovered just out of reach. He cleared his throat. "I'll head over to the bunkhouse and see if anyone spoke with Ned this morning. Maybe he told one of the men where he was going."

Or maybe Cookie knew something about Ned's departure.

Frowning, CJ reached for his hat, slapped it against his thigh. He wasn't looking forward to speaking with his ranch cook. The grizzled former army captain wouldn't be sympathetic. He'd warned CJ this day was coming.

CJ had chosen to believe matters weren't all that dire and that Ned would eventually snap out of his grief.

"We're moving the herd to the north pasture today." He paused at the door. "If Ned shows up—"

"I'll send Cookie to find you."

"Good enough." CJ opened the door, paused when Molly called out his name.

He turned back around. The hem of her lavender dress swung in soft waves around her ankles as she approached him. Her eyes, so blue, so beautiful, held the strength of her determination. In that moment, CJ felt a little less alone.

"I want you to know I'm not going anywhere." She gave him a warm, kind smile that reached inside his heart and squeezed. "We're in this together. We'll take it one day at a time."

She couldn't know how much her support meant. As he stared into her startling blue eyes, CJ fought to contain thoughts of what might have been, were he a different man. But he couldn't change who he was or where he came from.

"Thank you, Molly."

"You're welcome."

She was so good, so pure, so *beautiful*. She deserved better than a Thorn. She'd *had* better. She'd married a preacher.

CJ could never measure up to a man of God. He wouldn't even try. All he could do was work to make his ranch a success and ensure that the twins had a safe, stable home. One day at a time, as Molly said, he would provide a secure, loving home for his brother's children. Who, according to Ned's note, were now CJ's.

He jammed his hat on his head. "I'll see you later this afternoon."

"The girls and I will be right here."

For now, that was enough. He turned and walked out of the house. *One day at a time*, he told himself. With God's help, CJ would face the future one day at a time.

Chapter Two

Molly stood immobile in the doorway, unable to tear her gaze away from CJ as he strode toward the bunkhouse. She liked the way he moved, with that loose-limbed gait of a man comfortable in his own skin. He rode a horse with equal confidence.

As if sensing her eyes on him, he looked over his shoulder. Their gazes connected and, in that instant, time stopped. A silent message passed between them, something her heart understood but her head couldn't quite grasp. She'd never felt this connected to CJ before.

With a sad, lopsided grin, he gave a tug on his hat, then disappeared inside the bunkhouse. For several long seconds, Molly stayed where she was, drawing in air, willing her racing heartbeat to settle.

She and CJ had a common purpose now, and were facing a shared task that went beyond helping out a friend, or assisting a brother in need. There were two young girls relying on them to work together.

Momentarily overwhelmed by the enormity of the situation, Molly pressed a hand to her throat. She ached from the inside out for the Thorn family, and that included Ned.

She understood what he suffered. She'd experienced

her own pain after losing George. Where she'd focused on serving others to help her through her grief, Ned had concentrated solely on himself, to the detriment of his daughters.

Sarah and Anna were too young to understand why their father had taken off without saying goodbye. If Penelope were alive, she'd be devastated by her husband's selfish behavior.

A ragged sigh worked its way past Molly's lips. Ned hadn't even bothered asking CJ if he would raise the girls in his stead. He'd simply assumed.

Well, CJ wouldn't have to care for them alone. Molly would watch the girls for as long as he needed her. Eventually, he would want a more permanent solution.

Would he take a wife?

Molly's heart filled with two distinct emotions, first with a spark of hope, then with unspeakable sorrow. As much as she cared about CJ, and thought they would suit, she could never marry him.

A rancher required a large family. Her father had said as much, claiming his life would have been easier if he'd had ten children instead of a *measly five*.

Molly would love the sort of large family John Carson claimed every rancher needed, but she was incapable of bearing children. CJ deserved a woman who could give him a houseful of sons and daughters.

Taking a bracing breath, Molly stepped back inside the house and shut the door behind her. Deciding to let the girls sleep a bit longer, she entered the kitchen and went quickly to work on their breakfast. She hummed her favorite hymn, "What a Friend We Have in Jesus," as she plucked three eggs out of the basket.

She'd barely pulled a clean bowl from the cupboard

when a small, sleepy voice asked, "Is Pa going to eat breakfast with us?"

The question came from Sarah, the more outspoken of the twins. Even as she set aside the eggs, Molly couldn't help noticing that the child's first concern was for her father.

Taking a moment to think, she smiled down at the girls. Her heart gave a hard tug at the sight they made standing shoulder to shoulder in their plain white nightgowns, just inside the kitchen. Their green eyes were droopy from sleep, their baby-fine, dark brown hair pleasantly mussed.

How could Ned leave them in this house all alone, with only a hastily written note of explanation?

"It'll just be the three of us this morning." She filled her voice with what she hoped was a carefree inflection.

"What about Unca Corny? Maybe he could eat with us?"

Molly's breath clogged in her throat. The girls were sweet and adorable, especially when they called CJ "Unca Corny," their version of Uncle Cornelius. She had no idea if he liked the name, but he never corrected them, at least not in front of Molly.

"Your uncle needed to get an early start, so he's eating in the bunkhouse with the ranch hands."

"But…but…" Sarah's lower lip jutted out. "I like it when Unca Corny comes over to the big house and eats with us."

"He tells us funny stories." The more timid of the two, Anna, stood so close to her sister she was nearly on top of her. "He makes me laugh."

"Me, too." Sarah grinned. "I like Unca Corny almost as much as I like Pa."

Molly's heart gave another hard tug. The girls would

have to be told something about Ned. She was trying to decide how much to reveal when Sarah came to stand beside her. "I heard Pa leave when it was still dark outside. He stumbled over a chair and said a naughty word."

Molly tried not to show any outward reaction to this disturbing piece of information. Inwardly, she sighed. "I'm sure whatever your father said, he didn't mean it."

"Oh, he meant it." Anna drew alongside her sister. Her expression was grave and her eyes were huge in her small face. "Pa said the word before. And he got real mad when Unca Corny told him not to because it's a bad word."

Molly gave another inward sigh. Ned wasn't a terrible man. He was simply drowning in grief and clearly oblivious to the harm his behavior generated in this house.

"Miss Molly?" Sarah moved slightly in front of her sister. "When is Pa coming home?"

"Oh, sweetie." Eyes stinging, throat tight, Molly dropped to her knees and pulled both girls close. "I don't know. He didn't say."

"You think he'll be gone long?"

"Possibly." By their hurt expressions, it was obvious neither child understood their father's sudden absence. And Molly wasn't doing a very good job covering for him. She wasn't even sure she should try.

A huge crack split across her heart and she thought it might break in two. The twins were such sweet children. She loved them with the heart of a mother. How could Ned have left them without even saying goodbye?

In his note, he'd claimed that the girls reminded him too much of Penelope. There had been more in his note, hints at other reasons, but the part about his daughters resembling his wife had stuck out for Molly. It was true that the twins favored their mother, but they had a lot of Ned in them, as well.

"Your father might have left home for a while." She chose her words carefully, silently praying to the Lord for guidance. "But I know he loves you very much."

Sarah's expression turned serious. "We love him, too."

Anna nodded feverishly.

Sighing, Molly stood, reached for their hands. "Let's get you some breakfast and then we'll—"

The door swung open and in stormed an angry range cook, sputtering and mumbling incoherent words under his breath.

"Where's the note?" Cookie demanded. "I want to see it."

Releasing the girls' hands, Molly moved quickly toward the grizzled old man glaring at her from the doorway. With a full head of white hair that stuck out from every angle, and a girth as wide as he was tall, Lawrence Robbins—"Cookie" to everyone who knew him—looked as furious as he sounded.

But he was more bark than bite, and Molly wasn't intimidated in the least. She was, however, determined to keep him from saying something inappropriate in front of the twins.

"Good morning to you, too, Cookie. The girls and I were just about to sit down to breakfast." She looked pointedly at the children in an attempt to remind him to monitor his speech.

Moving deeper into the house, he parked two beefy paws on his sizable hips. "Ned's really done it this time. That good-for-nothing, worthless excuse of a—"

"*The children*," Molly growled, placing a hand on his shoulder, "are standing right here."

As if her words finally registered, Cookie's cheeks turned a bright red. "Oh, right. I, uh…" He started backing toward the door as fast as his pudgy feet could carry him. "I'll come back another time."

"I'd rather you stay a moment." She could use an ally. For all his blustering and uncensored opinion giving, Cookie was trustworthy, loyal and loved the twins with the devotion of a kindly grandfather. "The note is on the table beside the sofa."

He picked up the piece of paper and scanned the words in silence. When he looked up again, his expression was even more furious than before. But then he glanced over at the girls and his stern features melted into a look of compassion. "Poor little things."

Molly's sentiments exactly.

"I'll stick close to the house all day. You need anything, anything at all, you just ring the bell and I'll come running."

"Thank you, Cookie."

Eyes luminous with sympathy, he ruffled Sarah's hair, then Anna's, then headed for the door. By the time it shut behind him, Molly had the girls seated at the table and the eggs frying in the skillet.

She might not be able to bring either of their parents back, but she could feed Sarah and Anna a satisfying breakfast. For as long as she had the honor, she would care for the twins to the best of her ability and love them with her whole heart.

The rest she would leave up to the Lord.

CJ returned to the ranch later that afternoon bone-tired from a full day on the range. The cattle, more than five hundred of them, had been successfully moved to the north pasture, where they would fill their bellies with fresh grass. Getting them to their new grazing area had been hot, dirty work.

Ordinarily, he would be pleased with all he and his men had managed to get done in a single day. But Ned's absence had been felt. CJ was short on manpower, and he could have used his brother's help moving the herd.

Mouth set in a grim line, CJ pulled the brim of his hat low over his eyes. His three ranch hands dismounted ahead of him and guided their horses into the barn. He followed them at a slower pace, his gaze roaming over his domain.

Most days, he was proud of all he'd accomplished. With the guidance of his neighbor, Edmund McKay, CJ had learned solid ranching skills and had been able to turn his struggling spread into a modest success.

Now, he considered the cost of that single-minded focus. Perhaps if he'd tried harder to understand the extent of Ned's grief, CJ could have saved his brother.

Too late, a small voice whispered inside his head.

Frowning, CJ led Scout into the barn, removed the horse's tack, then picked up a brush off the shelf where hoof picks, files and clippers were neatly organized. He began making slow sweeps across the horse's back.

What could he have done differently with Ned?

CJ had known his brother was tipping back the bottle. Every time he tried to talk to him, Ned would promise there wasn't anything to worry about. He always stopped at one drink. The fact that Ned's drinking never interfered with his duties on the ranch had been enough for CJ to believe the claim. Until recently.

Ned's behavior had become more sporadic in the past two weeks. CJ had been worried enough to confront him. But his brother had refused to admit there was a problem.

Like father like son.

Letting out a hiss of frustration, CJ moved to the other side of the horse and resumed grooming the animal. He'd been hoping, even praying, that something would happen to make Ned realize his drinking was getting out of hand.

Ned must have finally admitted the truth to himself. His solution was to abandon his family. Of all the routes his brother could have taken, CJ had not expected that one.

Was it his fault Ned left? Had he run off his own brother?

Whatever the reason, he'd failed Ned. That was irrefutable. Despite evidence to the contrary, CJ worried that the same weak character in his father—and now his brother—lurked inside him, as well. It was one of the reasons he hadn't tried very hard to find a wife.

CJ wasn't convinced he'd make a good husband. He'd recently turned to Edmund McKay with his fears. His friend had asked him a simple question: "You ever tempted to drown your sorrows in a bottle?"

His response had been immediate. He'd never once felt the urge. Still, he was a Thorn. All Thorn men eventually broke. And CJ had never really been tested. When that day came, would he discover the same lack of character?

Anna and Sarah deserved a father who would protect them and keep them safe. What did CJ know about raising little girls?

With more force than necessary, he tossed the brush back on the shelf, then concentrated on picking pebbles and other debris from Scout's hooves. After he led the horse into his stall and gave him fresh hay, he felt calmer.

But then Cookie met him at the barn door and wasted no time with pleasantries. "I read the note Ned left."

CJ pulled in a tight breath, pounded a fist against his thigh. "I think he really means to stay gone."

"This ain't your fault, CJ." Cookie placed a hand on his shoulder in a fatherly gesture. "You did all you could."

"Did I?"

"Your brother made his choice. If he doesn't want to be here, then I say it's a good thing he left."

CJ couldn't bring himself to agree. He couldn't—wouldn't—give up on his brother. Like the prodigal son, Ned could still mend his ways and come home a changed man. For the twins' sake, CJ prayed that was exactly what occurred. Soon.

Anna and Sarah had already suffered enough. CJ would do everything in his power to provide a good life for the twins. He would give them a safe, happy home. No sacrifice would be too great. He might have failed Ned. He would *not* fail the girls.

He would rise above the Thorn legacy.

At the bunkhouse, he and Cookie parted ways. CJ washed off the trail dust before entering the main house. Little-girl squeals of delight met his arrival.

"Pa! Pa, you're home."

The children rushed to greet their father. When they realized it was CJ standing on the threshold instead of Ned, their footsteps ground to a halt.

Sarah's face scrunched into a frown. "You're not Pa."

The disappointment in her voice was mirrored in her sister's downcast expression. CJ's heart took a quick, extra thump. He'd never felt more inadequate in his life. "Your pa won't be home tonight."

"Will he be back tomorrow?"

Furious at his brother, CJ forced out a calming breath, placed his hands on his knees, leaned over and gave the girls the truth. "I don't know."

Identical lower lips trembled.

He swallowed back another wave of anger at Ned. "I was hoping I could eat supper with you two girls."

Sarah's face tightened. Anna angled her head. Then both children gave him a small, tentative smile.

"Would you like me to eat with you?"

They nodded slowly, their little minds clearly working furiously behind their clear, rounded eyes.

They looked so forlorn, so *disappointed,* CJ's heart twisted in his chest.

"Are you going to stay with us in the house tonight?" Anna asked.

"That's the plan."

Twisting the fabric of her skirt between her fingers, the child drew in a shaky breath. "Okay."

Without pause, with one single motion, he lowered himself to his knees and opened his arms. "How about a hug for your Unca Corny?"

Anna launched herself at him. He caught her against his chest, hugged her close. She smelled of flowers and everything good in this world, and he thought his heart might burst with love.

Shifting her slightly to his left, he reached for Sarah, who'd been studying him very closely. She hugged him just as fiercely as her sister. Emotion swept through him, convicting him. He would do right by these children. *Whatever it takes.*

He set them away from him and searched their precious faces for any sign of distress. It was there, of course, shimmering in their wide, sad eyes, but with the resilience of youth, they chattered over one another in an attempt to tell him about their day.

How could Ned have walked away from these sweet girls? It boggled the mind.

"...and then Miss Molly showed us how to make cornhusk dolls."

"Did she?" He looked up and found Molly watching

him with soft, watery eyes. Her expression was almost wistful.

He didn't understand that look. Yet he knew it had something to do with him. His heart pounded against his ribs. His breath clogged in his throat. His mind reeled.

Her, a whisper in his mind seemed to say. *She's the one for you.*

CJ shoved aside the thought with a hard shake of his head. There'd been a time when he thought Molly had a special affection for him. But her interest had waned right before she'd gone off and married a preacher.

"All right, girls, give your uncle a chance to catch his breath." Molly clapped her hands together. "Supper's ready."

She herded the twins toward the table, then paused when CJ didn't follow. "You are joining us, aren't you?"

"A home-cooked meal with three beautiful females? Try to keep me away."

They shared a laugh. It felt good to laugh with Molly. Despite Ned's noticeable absence, supper went smoothly. CJ credited the easy atmosphere to Molly's calming presence.

When the dishes were clean and order was restored to the kitchen, she said her goodbyes to the girls. "I'll be back in the morning. We'll spend the day making clothes for your new dolls."

"Will you read to us before you go?"

She glanced out the window, seemed to consider the question thoughtfully. "For five minutes, but no more."

That was CJ's cue. "I'll saddle your horse and bring her around to the front of the house."

"Thank you." She gave him one of her sweetest smiles.

He found himself smiling back.

He was still smiling as he made the trek to the barn.

He located his foreman and asked him to make sure Molly got home safely.

"You got it, Boss."

CJ would have preferred to escort her himself, but he couldn't leave the twins alone and felt confident sending Duke in his place. By the time he stepped back inside the house, Molly was sitting on the sofa between the girls, reading from a small, worn Bible.

The three made a cozy scene, the very essence of family. A yearning so deep shot through CJ that for a moment he couldn't seem to catch his breath.

He pulled the door shut behind him, but stayed where he was, watching, hoping, praying for something so far out of reach he couldn't make the image form in his head.

"Sadie is saddled and waiting for you outside."

Molly shut the Bible and kissed each girl on the head. The twins immediately protested her departure. After another round of hugs, and more promises to return before first light, Molly joined him at the door.

They walked outside in silence.

As he helped her into the saddle, CJ felt it again, that powerful wish for something…*more*. It was the same sensation from this morning. Once again, he pushed it away. Ignored it. Denied it. The process proved far less successful this evening.

Clearing his throat, he rolled his shoulders, shifted his stance. He couldn't seem to find his balance. His mind filled with all the tasks that lay ahead. He would have to move a few things into the main house tonight. Then he'd have to get the girls settled in bed. And—

"Relax, CJ." Molly leaned over and touched his arm. Everything in him calmed. "You aren't in this alone. I'll continue watching the girls for as long as you need me."

She'd said nearly the same words this morning. He

had no reason to doubt her sincerity, but such a promise wasn't realistic.

Ever since Penelope died, CJ had focused on ranching, while letting Ned find his own way through his grief. In the span of a single day, CJ's entire life had changed. His priorities had shifted dramatically. He must move into the future with only frank honesty between him and Molly. "One day, whether Ned returns or not, you will leave us."

She was shaking her head before he finished speaking.

He pressed on. "*One day,*" he said with emphasis, to make his point clear, "you'll marry again, and that'll be—"

"I'll *never* marry again."

CJ pulled back in surprise. He couldn't remember a time when Molly had looked this fierce, this determined or this sad.

It was the sadness that led him to say, "You're still in love with your husband."

Surely that explained her refusal to wed another man. There was tremendous honor in that kind of devotion, CJ decided, even as he felt something unpleasant twist in his gut.

"A part of me will always love George." Sorrow came and went in her eyes. "But that's not the reason I won't ever—"

She cut off her own words, glanced frantically around, then drew in a sharp breath and started again. "It's getting late. I better head home."

Her voice was even as she spoke, but the pain in her eyes made CJ regret bringing up her husband. At a loss for words, he reached for the horse's reins and handed them to her. "Good night, Molly."

"Good night, CJ."

Neither made a move to leave. They didn't smile, didn't

speak. They simply stared into each other's eyes. And then they stared some more. One moment stretched into two.

At last, Molly lowered her eyelashes and the awkward interaction was over. She gave the mare a gentle kick in the ribs and set out toward her family's ranch.

Once Duke moved in behind her, CJ closed his eyes and considered all that had happened in the span of a day. He predicted a long, sleepless night ahead, the reason as much because of the woman riding toward the painted horizon as his brother's shocking departure.

Chapter Three

The next two days passed by in a blur for Molly. Ned had not returned. In an attempt to distract the twins from missing their father, she'd kept them busy and on a relatively tight schedule. Her efforts proved successful, mostly. Apart from a few tears and a lot of questions, Anna and Sarah seemed to be taking their new situation in stride.

That said a lot about CJ and his determination to step into Ned's shoes.

Of course, it was early days yet. It was clear CJ wasn't settling into his new role as a father smoothly. Every morning, when Molly arrived at the Triple-T ranch, he would be waiting for her at the door, looking both harried and vastly relieved to see her.

His discomfort was to be expected. He was completely out of his element with the girls. However, like any Texas cowboy worthy of the name, he was tackling the challenge head-on. Oh, he was still tentative around the twins and they weren't exactly comfortable around him, either. Which begged the question, why had he given Molly the day off?

With an impatient shove, she secured the final pin in

her hair and stepped away from the mirror. Dressed and ready for Sunday service, she moved to the window and stared out across the front yard of her family's ranch. The sun had already risen, splashing golden fingers of light across the pink-tinted sky.

She should be atop Sadie's back by now, heading over to the Triple-T to help CJ with the girls. He'd insisted she spend the Sabbath with her own family. No amount of arguing had swayed him. He was one stubborn, thoughtful, kind man.

Sighing, she placed her palm against the warm glass. She wished CJ would talk to her about Ned. Molly knew he suffered. She often caught the secret pain in his eyes, when he didn't know she was looking. He clearly blamed himself.

Even without saying the words aloud, they both knew Ned's leaving could very well be permanent. Awarding CJ custody of the twins made his intentions clear. Molly had no idea if a hand-scribbled note was the same as a legal document. But Ned's actions had a feeling of finality to them.

It had been only three days, she told herself. There was still reason to hope. No matter how sad he appeared on the outside, Ned always pulled himself together enough to attend Sunday worship with his daughters. Maybe he would return today.

Ned had his faults, but even at the worst of times he'd been a committed churchgoer. Molly hated thinking any man, especially a believing Christian, could abandon his own children, but if Ned stayed gone…

Lord, please bring him home this morning.

Molly pushed away from the window and nudged her sister's shoulder.

A muffled groan was Daisy's only response.

Shaking her head, Molly poked the girl's shoulder with a bit more force.

She received yet another feminine groan, followed by a muffled, "Go away."

"Mama won't hold breakfast for you," she warned.

More mumbling.

"Fine. You're on your own." Mildly frustrated, yet still loving her sister dearly, Molly left the room with a little more noise than necessary.

The rest of her family was already seated around the breakfast table. Molly's three younger brothers alternated between passing platters of food and shoveling impressively large bites into their mouths. *Boys.*

It amazed her how much her brothers had grown in the years she'd been married to George. All three were good-looking and had the Carson blond hair. The younger two, Donny and Roy, had their father's hazel eyes, while Thomas's were deep brown.

Smiling fondly at each of them, Molly took her seat beside Roy. At twelve, he was inquisitive and seemed to be always taking things apart. Donny was the talker. Thomas was the calmest and most logical of the three. At fourteen, he was also the most mature.

As they did nearly every Sunday morning, Roy and Donny debated which one of them would ride old Walker into town and which would have to sit in the bed of the wagon.

"It's my turn." Donny's voice held more whine than reason.

Roy begged to differ, loudly, and with equal amounts of whining. The heated discussion continued another fifteen seconds before their father put an end to it.

"Thomas is the oldest," he said. "He'll ride Walker. Now eat your breakfast before it gets cold."

He pointed to their plates. Once they obeyed his command, he turned toward Molly. "I trust you slept well."

"I did, thank you." Actually, she'd tossed and turned most of the night. But there was no reason to upset her father.

Or her mother, who was eyeing her with her usual worried scowl. Keeping her own expression bland, Molly took the platter of cured ham from Roy and concentrated on eating her breakfast.

Conversation turned to the ice-cream social after service. Apparently, Mercy Green, owner of Mercy's Café, was supplying the ingredients.

Laughter soon replaced dissent among her brothers. It was a lovely, boisterous sound that represented the very heart of family. Head down, Molly took a few calming breaths.

She loved her parents and siblings, and was happy to be home, but she desperately wanted her own family. Despite what she'd said to CJ, she wanted to be a wife again and run her own household.

George had been a good husband, handsome, kind and dedicated to the Lord. During the first year of their marriage, his devotion to Molly had been above reproach. But the longer she'd gone without conceiving, the more distant he'd become.

The pressure to bear a child had taken over every part of their life together. Instead of bonding them closer, their mutual frustration had put a wedge between them. With every month that passed, and no baby on the way, Molly's life had grown a little less happy, a little less joyful.

Her eyes stung with remembered pain, from the loss of hope and the certainty that she was a failure as a wife. And as a woman.

"Molly?" Her mother's hand covered hers. "Are you unwell?"

"No." She put on a brave face and slowly lifted her head. "I was just thinking about…George."

Helen Carson's eyes softened. Molly was saved from further questioning when Daisy rushed into the room, her words tumbling out faster than her footsteps.

"I'm *not* late." She hopped to the empty chair at the table with one shoe on her foot, the other dangling in her hand. "I'm merely running a bit behind."

"*A bit behind*?" Releasing her grip on Molly, Helen Carson sat back in her chair and turned her full attention to her other daughter. "Is that what we're now calling your proclivity to oversleep?"

Daisy opened her mouth, presumably to defend herself, but wisely shut it again.

Even with Daisy's tardiness, the Carson brood set out for town with plenty of time to complete the two-mile journey before service started. Thomas did indeed receive the honor of riding Walker. The younger boys piled into the back of the wagon. Helen and John Carson took the front seat. Molly and Daisy settled on the smaller bench behind them.

Before they were even off Carson land, her parents leaned in close, their heads bent together in quiet conversation. Watching them brought Molly another wave of unexpected yearning. Even after twenty-five years of marriage, and the challenges of building one of the largest working ranches in central Texas, they were still very much in love.

It was quite lovely to witness. And utterly depressing.

Molly despaired of ever finding that kind of happiness. She'd had her chance at marriage and had failed miserably. What man would want her now? She was a barren, twenty-three-year-old widow living on her family's ranch.

From a distance, the town of Little Horn beckoned. Welcoming the distraction, Molly studied the small settlement, which had been incorporated two years ago.

As her father took the most direct route through town, Molly watched the various buildings pass by. There was the general store on her left, the grocer on her right. The shoemaker and both coopers were farther up ahead. One street over was a well-established livery and blacksmith, and a cotton gin-gristmill lay just beyond the outskirts of town.

At the end of the wide main street, Molly noticed that Mercy's Café, situated between the train depot and bank, had a brand-new sign. The pretty blue lettering really stood out against the stark white background.

The one building Little Horn lacked was a church. For now, the congregation met beneath a large, serviceable tent that had been erected for a revival last year and never taken down.

When her father pulled in beside a row of carriages, Molly gathered herself in preparation for exiting the wagon. Her brothers were much quicker. Roy and Donny scrambled out of the flatbed before the brake had even been set.

Jacob and Sam Barlow, boys from a neighboring ranch, called out to them. Her brothers quickly changed direction and met up with their friends. Thomas hitched his horse to the back of the wagon, then took off to find his own friends.

Molly, Daisy and their parents disembarked from the wagon at a much more sedate pace.

"John, dear." Molly's mother caught her husband's arm. "Would you mind keeping an eye on our younger sons? Whenever they get together with the Barlow boys, well, mischief soon follows."

"Heading over there now."

"Much appreciated. Oh, look, it's Beatrice Rampart." Helen lifted her hand in greeting. "I haven't spoken with her since last week. I'll just go over and say hello."

"I guess you're stuck with me." Daisy linked arms with Molly. "And I'm stuck with you."

She laughed at the teasing tone. "So it would seem."

Arm in arm, they stayed close to the wagon and watched the milling crowd. Daisy seemed unusually focused. Her gaze kept sweeping from one side of the tent to the other. Molly wondered what—or perhaps, *who*— her sister was searching for so diligently.

She had her answer when sixteen-year-old Calvin Barlow caught sight of them and lifted his hand in greeting, much as their mother had done moments before. Daisy returned the gesture, then let out a soft, shuddering sigh when he started in their direction.

"Promise you won't leave me alone with him," Daisy whispered.

"You have my word." Molly tried not to smile as she spoke. But, really, who was this young woman standing beside her?

She hardly recognized her sister. Daisy was outspoken and full of more than her share of opinions. She was certainly never shy. But now, with Calvin Barlow bearing down on them, Daisy's cheeks had turned a becoming shade of pink. Her eyes sparkled with an odd mix of trepidation and excitement.

Molly remembered that look. She'd seen it in her own mirror five years ago, when she'd first discovered she had tender feelings for CJ Thorn.

He'd been completely oblivious of her, which had hurt

at the time. Looking back, she realized he'd been far too consumed with running his ranch to notice her.

Now, it was too late for her to catch his eye. Even if she did, she had so little to offer him.

Calvin drew to a stop several feet away. He greeted Molly first, then put all his focus on Daisy. "Good morning, Miss Carson."

"Miss Carson? *Miss Carson?*"

Eyes wide, Calvin blinked at her for several long seconds. "That is your name."

"Of course it's my name." Sputtering in outrage, Daisy pulled her arm free of Molly's and jammed her hands on her hips. "What's with the sudden formality?"

His mouth worked but no words came out.

"Well?" Daisy demanded. "What do you have to say for yourself, Calvin Barlow?"

He frowned, clearly taken aback by her heated question. "I'm trying to show you respect, Daisy."

"No, what you've done is insult me."

"How do you figure that?"

Molly was wondering the same thing herself.

"We've known each other all our lives." Daisy said this as if it explained everything. "I should think it obvious."

"Well, it's not." Calvin blew out a frustrated hiss, moving a step closer to Daisy. "Why are you being so difficult?"

"Difficult? Me? What about you?" She leaned forward, practically touching noses with him. "If I didn't know better I'd say you were up to something devious."

Chest puffed out, eyes narrowed, Calvin launched into a lengthy defense of his actions, whereby Daisy proceeded to dismantle each and every one of them. The more they argued the happier they seemed.

Molly hid a smile behind her hand. The conversation

reminded her of several she'd witnessed early in Ned and Penelope's courtship.

They'd bickered…er, bantered much like this. It hadn't been long before they'd fallen deeply in love. Ned had been an attentive, patient, caring husband. Grief had turned him into a different man. But that didn't have to be how their love story ended. He could still return and become a father to his children, the way Penelope would have wanted.

With hope building in her heart, Molly searched the area for Ned's rangy build and shaggy brown hair. She found no sign of him. But there, beneath a tall cottonwood tree, stood the rest of the Thorn family.

CJ was larger than life, handsome and clean-shaven and so very capable. He didn't wear a hat this morning, but still looked like the quintessential rancher, strong and leanly built, yet with shoulders broad enough to carry the burdens of his loved ones.

The girls clung to his hands with utter confidence that he would keep them safe. On closer inspection, Molly realized CJ wasn't as in control as he seemed. He had that harried look again. His features were weary and a little rough around the edges. He'd had a trying morning.

He needs me.

The thought drew her several steps toward him.

"I'll be over there," she said to her sister, "with the Thorn family." She nodded toward the rancher and two little girls standing beneath the large tree.

Still in a heated discussion with Calvin, Daisy waved her away with a flick of her wrist. As Molly moved in CJ's direction, she came to the conclusion she should have never agreed to take the morning off.

He was clearly in over his head with the twins. She

couldn't begin to imagine how alone he must feel with Ned gone.

Or perhaps she could.

Hadn't she, even surrounded by her family, felt alone since returning home?

Well, she wasn't alone. And neither was CJ.

They had each other. They had solidarity in their common purpose to provide a home for the twins. Their bond wouldn't last forever, but for now, Molly and CJ were connected.

She moved quickly, suddenly in a great hurry. She'd barely made it halfway to her destination when she made the decision to sit with the Thorns during service instead of her own family.

Deep down, where she understood the pain of loss, Molly knew it was the right thing to do. Nothing could induce her to change her mind, not even the prospect of her mother's, and possibly even her father's, disapproval.

At last, CJ thought. Help was on the way.

With each step Molly took in his direction, he felt the tension draining out of him.

He let out a slow, careful breath. All morning he'd been feeling raw. Too raw. He wasn't a man who liked to accept defeat. Yet he wasn't so full of pride that he couldn't admit, at least to himself, that this morning had nearly done him in and demonstrated just how much he relied on Molly. Not only to care for the girls, but also for the day-to-day running of his household.

She was a calming influence and the stability they all needed—not just Sarah and Anna, but CJ, too.

If she ever left him…

Not the point, he told himself.

He needed to figure out how to thank her for all she'd

done for his family since Penelope's passing. Somehow he would find a way to repay her for her sacrifice.

She looked uncommonly beautiful this morning in a blue cotton dress with a white lace collar and long sleeves. The cut of the garment emphasized her tiny waist and petite frame.

He attempted to swallow past the lump in his throat, without much success. Molly took his breath away.

If he were from a different family...

"Miss Molly," Anna called out. "Miss Molly, over here! We're over here."

Sarah wasn't content with merely waving. She pulled her hand free of CJ's and raced to meet Molly across the small expanse of grass. Anna followed hard on her sister's heels.

Molly greeted both girls with a hug and a kiss on the top of their heads.

"Well, look who it is." She stepped back and smiled down at the twins. "My two favorite girls in all of Little Horn, Texas. And don't you look especially pretty this morning."

"Unca Corny picked out our dresses," Sarah told her.

"He tried to make breakfast." Anna swayed her shoulders back and forth with little-girl pride. "He didn't do so good. He burned the oatmeal and Cookie had to make more."

Molly's compassionate gaze met his. "Sounds like you had an...interesting morning."

Finding humor in the situation now that she was here to share it with him, CJ chuckled softly. "Though I wouldn't want to repeat the experience any time soon, we survived well enough."

"Is that so?" She lifted her eyebrows and simply looked at him for a single beat. The pause was small but marked.

At least she refrained from reminding him what he already knew. The exasperating morning could have been avoided if he hadn't insisted she take the day off.

"Miss Molly, look. I'm wearing my favorite pink ribbon." Sarah touched the floppy bow with reverent fingers. "I tied it all by myself."

"You did a lovely job." Under the guise of inspecting the ribbon, Molly retied the bow, then moved it around until it sat straight on the child's head. "Pink is my favorite color."

"It's Pa's favorite, too." Sarah's gaze skittered toward the crowded tent. "I wore it just for him."

The wistful note in her voice broke CJ's heart. He shared a tortured look with Molly.

Her ragged sigh told him she was thinking along the same lines as he was. His brother always made it to church, a fact the twins had reminded him of this morning.

"Pa says Sunday is the most important day of the week," Sarah had told him, while Anna had added, "And we're never supposed to miss Sunday service. Not ever."

Somewhere along the way, the two had gotten it into their heads that Ned would show up at church today. CJ wasn't anywhere near as confident. If Ned didn't make an appearance, the twins would know that their father was truly gone.

Anger at his brother burned the air in his lungs. How could Ned have done this to his children?

Service was about to begin. CJ knew this because Mrs. Hickey climbed in to the back of the wagon where an ancient piano had been carted in from the schoolhouse. Lips pursed, she positioned her sharp-boned, skinny self at the ancient keyboard and pounded out a wheezing refrain of the opening hymn.

CJ's muscles went taut. His nerves clawed and scrambled beneath his skin. He looked around, tugged on his collar. The air felt too heavy, too still. A baby's squall sounded over the din of the organ music.

Where was Ned?

Until that moment, CJ hadn't realized how much he'd allowed the girls' enthusiasm to seep through his skepticism. He'd actually been expecting his brother to make an appearance.

"Miss Molly?" Anna's small, tormented voice sounded a bit weepy, as if she were on the verge of tears. "Will… will you stay with us until Pa shows up?"

"Of course." She pasted a cheery smile on her face and reached for the child's hand. "Why don't we wait inside the tent?"

"No." Anna shoved her arms behind her back. "I want to wait for Pa here."

"Me, too," Sarah said, eyes mutinous in her thin face.

CJ closed his own eyes, gathered up his patience and stepped into the fray. "We're not going very far, just a few steps in that direction."

He pointed to the back of the tent, where they usually sat, then made the mistake of trying to steer the girls in that direction.

They dug in their heels.

"No, Unca Corny, *no.*" Sarah stomped her foot. "Pa won't be able to find us if we move from this spot. We have to stay right here."

Eyes brimming with tears, Anna joined in her sister's rebellion. "I'm not leaving until Pa comes."

Out of ideas, CJ looked desperately to Molly for help.

"Tell you what." She sank to her knees. "We'll save a seat for your father on the very last bench, the one closest to this tree. He's sure to see us there."

CJ added his own pledge. "I'll keep an eye out for your pa during the entire service. He won't make it anywhere near this tree without me seeing him. That's a promise."

"What if Pa doesn't come back?" Sarah's eyes grew wide and her voice dropped to a frightened whisper. "What if, like Mama, he *never* comes back?"

Anna burst into tears.

"Hey, hey now, it's going to be all right." Molly pulled the children into her arms. "No matter what happens here today, you will never be alone. You will always have me."

"And you'll always have me." CJ looked from one small, precious child to the other, his resolve growing with each beat of his heart.

These girls were his responsibility now. He was committed down to the bone. He would stumble along the way and surely make mistakes, but he would love Sarah and Anna until the day he died. He would protect them with his life.

Emotion ripping at his throat, he risked a glance at Molly. Their gazes locked and held. He remembered what she'd said the morning Ned left town. *We're in this together.*

Eyes never leaving his, she stood and took Sarah's hand. CJ reached for Anna's.

Together, they guided the girls into the tent.

Chapter Four

Sitting with perfect posture, in a pose of perfect serenity, Molly felt like a *perfect* fraud. It took every ounce of willpower not to fidget on the thin, wooden bench she shared with CJ and the twins. For the sake of the children, she forced herself to remain outwardly calm.

Inside, she burned.

Truly, there was nothing more trying than pretending all was well when matters were anything but. Lips pressed tightly together, Molly folded her hands in her lap and considered the heartbreak that lay ahead.

When Ned didn't show, what would Molly and CJ say to the twins? Words formed in her head, disappeared, then reformed again in a vastly different order. While she certainly agreed that "the truth shall set you free," she also knew that the truth often caused pain and sorrow. Molly didn't want that for Sarah and Anna.

Too late. The thought whispered through her mind.

Ned had made a terrible, selfish decision. How easy it would be to say something unkind about the man. But that would only upset the girls further.

Out of the corner of her eye, Molly looked down at them sitting between her and CJ. At first glance, they represented the very picture of polite, well-behaved children. Having adopted a pose similar to hers, they were uncommonly still. The hollow look in their eyes warned that the truth about their father was starting to sink in.

Molly wanted to weep for them.

CJ seemed to be fighting his own internal battle. Though his features were impassive, Molly could practically feel the tension coming off him in waves.

She nearly sighed, but the breath caught in her throat and came out sounding like a strangled sob.

Eyes full of silent understanding, CJ reached around the girls and squeezed Molly's shoulder. The gesture was so CJ, solid and yet somehow tender. For that one, brief moment, Molly let go of her anxiety and simply basked in the man's quiet strength. Everything was going to be all right. The children would survive this trauma. CJ would make sure of it.

Giving in to that sigh after all, she broke eye contact and forced her gaze straight ahead. Now that the singing had concluded, Mrs. Hickey, all-around busybody and notorious gossip, took an eternity shuffling toward her seat in the front row beside her husband.

The woman might move at the pace of turtles, but with her rust-colored hair pulled tightly against her head and her narrowed gaze sweeping over the congregation, she looked more like a rat contemplating its next meal.

Molly took the opportunity to glance at the crowd as unobtrusively as possibly. She found no sign of Ned, neither inside the tent nor out. Not that she'd expected a different outcome. But still…

Ned, where are you?

A dozen possible answers slammed through Molly's mind. But then the local preacher took his place behind the pulpit and a collective hush filled the air.

At twenty-eight, Brandon Stillwater was a big, muscular man who resembled a rancher rather than a man of God. Tall, broad through the shoulders and chest, he had piercing silver eyes, light brown hair and a surprisingly relaxed demeanor that put everyone at ease.

His identical twin, Bo, was the more reserved of the two. They owned property just south of town. Bo did most of the ranch work, while Brandon focused on serving the Lord and seeing to his flock.

He gave a wide, welcoming smile to the assembled group, then immediately launched into his sermon. "As Little Horn nears its two-year anniversary and our Founder's Day celebration approaches, I find myself thinking about journeys."

Though his smile remained in place, his tone turned serious. "Through the years, our community has enjoyed countless blessings. Yet we've also suffered our share of tragedies. We've celebrated marriages and births. We've endured drought, flash flooding, disease and the death of loved ones."

He paused, drew in a slow breath.

"The sometimes happy, sometimes tragic road we've traveled is not unlike the one the Israelites took out of Egypt." He grasped the podium and lowered his engaging voice an octave. "Why did the Lord lead His people through the wilderness instead of taking them directly to their destination? Why did a trip that should have taken a month last forty years?"

He waited while the congregation pondered the questions. Then, with a flourish, he opened his Bible.

After reading the entire thirteenth chapter of Exodus, he set the weathered book back on the podium and repeated a portion of the text from memory. "God did not lead them by way of the land of the Philistines, although that was near. For God said, 'Lest perhaps the people change their minds when they see war, and return to Egypt.'"

Securing his gaze on no one in particular, he looked out over the congregation. "What seemed like a wrong turn to the Israelites was actually a protection. The seemingly easy path would have taken them into a battle they were ill-equipped to fight."

Molly, thinking of her own journey, smiled down at Sarah and Anna. Her path had certainly not been easy, but it had been rewarding nonetheless. Ever since that first day she'd traveled to the Thorn ranch to reconnect with her best friend, Molly had been captured by the sweet innocence of Penelope's adorable daughters. In the past six months, as she'd taken over their care, Molly had grown to love them with the heart of a mother.

But they weren't her children. They weren't even her distant kin. And, she realized, with a road-to-Damascus kind of revelation, her time with the twins was drawing to a close. If Ned stayed away, CJ would have to marry.

Soon, perhaps within the next few months, some other woman would become the children's mother. That, Molly thought, would be a blessed day for the girls and one of the worst of her own life.

"… If you find yourself in a difficult season, I urge you to remember the Israelites. Perhaps God is protecting you from a threat you can't see."

Molly leaned forward at the preacher's words. Anna chose that moment to climb onto her lap. The child sighed heavily, swallowed a few times, then rested her head against Molly's shoulder.

"If you take away nothing else from my sermon today, think on this. You aren't alone in your troubles. God is with you, guiding your steps. You simply have to follow His lead."

Follow His lead.

So easy to say. So very hard to do.

Molly glanced at CJ's profile. How bleak he looked. How alone. He turned his head and something sad moved in his eyes. Yet something volatile was there, as well. He was clearly struggling with grief over his brother's actions. He must also be angry with Ned.

How well Molly knew the feeling.

"Is service almost over?" Sarah asked, loudly enough to be heard three rows over.

Chuckling softly, CJ pulled the child onto his lap. "Almost."

The low, deep timbre of his voice, and the way he wrapped his arms gently around the child, made Molly's heart behave strangely, pounding in her wrists, in her ears, in her throat.

Something shifted inside her, a strange, severe sensation that took over her entire body. An awakening, of sorts, as if she were coming out of a long, unpleasant dream.

Anna wiggled against Molly, her little chest rising and falling. The sound that came out of her tiny lips was part muffled sob, part whimper. From her position on CJ's lap, Sarah reached over and patted her sister's back. The gesture was so sweet, so grown-up and mature, Molly's breath clogged in her throat.

Ned, why did you abandon your children?

"As we prepare for our Founder's Day celebration," the preacher continued, "let us remember where we came from, but let us not dwell on the past. We must forge into the future with confidence, knowing that God is always with us. I urge you to draw close to Him, and He will draw close to you. Let us pray."

Molly bowed her head and pulled Anna closer. A sense of purpose filled her. No more dwelling on the past. She would concentrate solely on the future. She would do so one day at a time, as she'd advised CJ to do.

The preacher dismissed the congregation with a reminder about the ice-cream social. Molly and CJ set the twins on the ground as they each gained their feet.

Anna and Sarah remained unmoving, eyes wide, panic forming in their green depths. They seemed to realize that the end of service signified the end of hope for their father's return.

Five excruciating seconds of humming silence passed.

Molly reached out and closed her hand over Anna's. CJ took Sarah's. Still, no one spoke. None of them moved. They simply stood by their wooden bench, connected and silent, suspended in a wretched moment of sorrow.

People filed past them. Some smiled, a few nodded, but most didn't even look in their direction. Molly shifted slightly, turned her head. Her gaze immediately caught a pair of soulful, dark brown eyes. CJ was staring at her, unsmiling and grim-faced and seemingly caught in a moment of indecision.

That changed once the tent cleared out. Still holding Sarah's hand, he took charge and led their sad little group into the empty aisle. The four of them trooped wordlessly toward the cottonwood tree.

As they stood in the shade of the leafy branches, holding hands, waiting, waiting, *waiting*… Molly felt a bittersweet bond with each member of the Thorn family.

They can never be mine.

She could mother the girls, but she couldn't be with CJ. He deserved more than she could give him. Molly risked a glance in his direction, muffling a sigh. He had the most remarkable face, strong and handsome. The subtle weathering from long hours outdoors in the elements made him seem more approachable. Molly wanted…

She wanted…

What did it matter what she wanted?

No point in going to a place that could never be, even in the privacy of her own mind. God had provided her a temporary position with a family in need. She would focus on the time she had in their home. *One day at a time.*

People moved toward the open field south of the revival tent and joined small clusters made up of friends or family or both. Gathering around large tubs of ice cream, they laughed, shared whispered confidences and slapped each other's backs.

How could they just go about their business? Did they not realize that the lives of two little girls and their stalwart uncle were changed forever?

Molly glanced to the heavens. She wanted to pray, but no words formed in her mind. She lowered her head. Beams of light caught floating, cottony-white particles swirling from the branches of the tree overhead.

The twins remained unnaturally silent, and so very solemn. Again CJ and Molly shared a glance. But then he was no longer looking at her. His face settled into a scowl.

Following the direction of his gaze, Molly nearly groaned out loud. Mrs. Hickey, with her pinched face, tight bun and small, narrow eyes, marched straight toward them. Each step was measured and full of purpose.

Though she feared the worst, Molly forced a smile. She must be strong for the Thorn family. *Family.* The word stuck in her mind, nagging at her, reminding her they weren't really hers.

Well, she would stand with them, anyway, because today…today they *were* hers.

CJ shifted to stand directly in front of Molly and the twins. The protective move wasn't discreet and hardly subtle. He didn't much care. Constance Hickey was the town's most fearsome gossip, best known for spreading rumors based on half-truths and third hand accounts.

He knew this unpleasant fact about the woman from personal experience. Lillian had barely rejected his marriage proposal when half their community was in possession of the particulars behind her refusal. The talk had been unkind and had added an ugly blemish to the Thorn name.

CJ could weather another round of rumors and backbiting. What he couldn't—wouldn't—tolerate was talk about the twins or Molly.

He widened his stance, balanced on the balls of his feet and braced himself for the battle to come.

Mrs. Hickey drew to a stop.

"Ah, Mr. Thorn, good day to you and yours." The empty pleasantry did nothing to soften her voice. The sound and pitch were as shrill as the whistling of a stiff wind through the crack in a window.

"Good day, Mrs. Hickey." In an attempt to end the conversation before it began, he said nothing else.

A mistake. The woman filled the conversational void by making a grand show of craning her neck to the left, then the right. "I haven't seen your brother this morning." The diamond point of her chin settled back to center. "I do hope he isn't ill."

"He isn't ill." Not in the strictest sense of the word.

"Well, if that's true, I must say I'm surprised he isn't

here." She sniffed indelicately. "I've never known him to miss Sunday service."

The critical comment drew a tortured sob from one of the twins. The miserable sound ripped through the air like broken glass shattering in a million pieces.

CJ moved fast, but not fast enough. By the time he'd spun around and dropped to his knees, Anna had sucked in a big gulp of air and screwed up her face. "Anna, please. Please don't—"

She let out a piercing wail. "I want my pa."

"Me, too." Sarah's composure disintegrated slower than her sister's. It started with a wobble of her lower lip, but then her chest heaved and tears exploded from her eyes.

CJ fought for words to ease the children's misery. He'd never seen the twins this distraught. Their wretched little faces were scrunched up tight and tears tracked down their reddened cheeks.

At a complete loss, he blurted out the first thing that came to mind. "Who wants ice cream?"

The question managed to stun them for a fraction of a second, but then the crying commenced once again.

"I don't want ice cream," Anna sputtered between hiccupping sobs. "I want my pa."

Sarah's chin began to wobble and then firmed. Never a good sign. "Pa. He's got to be here. He's *got* to. I'll go find him."

She made a break for it.

CJ caught her by the sleeve. "No one's going anywhere."

"Oh, my. Oh, dear, I've upset the children." Mrs. Hickey's voice held a surprising amount of remorse. "You must understand that wasn't my intention."

Ignoring the woman, CJ hauled Sarah back to stand

next to her sister. Bottom lip trembling, she stared hard at him from her tear-ravaged face.

He had no idea what to say. What to do.

What if he made matters worse?

This wasn't his area. He was out of his element. Panic tried to take hold.

Molly's soft, calming voice cut through his rising alarm. "Mrs. Hickey, your husband is motioning for you to join him at the ice-cream tubs."

A rush of air whooshed out of the odious woman's mouth. "Why, yes. Yes, I believe you are correct."

With the welcome sound of her retreating footsteps in his ears, CJ leaned slightly forward. The gesture brought his face closer to Sarah's.

"You can't run off, not for any reason." His tone brooked no argument. "I need you to stay close, understand?"

"But I have to find Pa."

"He's not coming home. But it's going to be all right," CJ added in a rush, not sure if he was saying that for the children's benefit or his own.

"Did we do something wrong, Unca Corny?" Anna asked the question between two gasping whimpers. "Is that why Pa doesn't like us anymore?"

"Your father loves you." Of that CJ was certain. "He... that is..."

CJ lifted his hands in a helpless gesture. How did he explain something he didn't understand himself?

"This isn't your fault." He spoke with more force than necessary. Both girls flinched. Compelling himself to speak slowly, more softly, he stated, "Your father leaving home isn't your fault."

His words brought on more crying. Tears fell in rivers down the girls' cheeks. For three days, he'd managed to keep them from breaking down like this. Their misery was gut-wrenching to watch. Nothing CJ said seemed to calm them.

Cold, hard anger at Ned seeped into the very marrow of his bones. With considerable effort, he shoved the emotion aside and shot Molly a desperate look.

As if she'd been waiting for his signal, she lowered to the ground beside him. "Your uncle is absolutely correct." She smoothed her hand over each child's head. "The reason your father left home has nothing to do with you."

"Will...will Pa ever come back?"

"I don't know." Molly touched Anna's tear-stained cheek, then Sarah's. "What I do know is that your uncle isn't going anywhere."

"That's right," CJ reiterated with conviction.

"You promise?" Sarah drew in a long, shuddering breath. "You promise not to leave us, not ever?"

"I will never leave you."

The child threw her arms around his neck and clung. "I love you, Unca Corny."

"I love you, too, sweet pea." He tugged Anna into the hug. "And you, buttercup."

He placed the girls in front of him, set a hand on a shoulder of each. "How about that ice cream now?"

Sarah slowly nodded, digging her toe at an exposed root beneath her foot. "That would be okay." Sniffling, she wiped her face on her sleeve. "I guess."

Anna glanced at her sister uncertainly, then at CJ, then back at her sister. "We like ice cream."

Relieved they were feeling more agreeable, CJ rose. Molly stood, as well. The quiet support in her eyes soothed him all the way to his soul.

CJ accepted that he was in over his head with the girls. He also accepted that he couldn't keep wishing

Ned would change his mind and come home. Sarah and Anna were CJ's daughters now. They would be an integral part of his life for at least another twelve years. That was a lot of tears and sloppy hair ribbons and burned oatmeal to navigate.

The prospect of all that stood before him nearly brought him to his knees. Thankfully, things weren't as dire as they seemed on the surface. The good Lord had blessed CJ with a kind, beautiful woman willing to help him find his way.

Molly Carson Langley was a Godsend. More importantly, she'd promised to stick by him for as long as he needed her. For this one moment, that was enough.

Chapter Five

In the aftermath of the twins' emotional outburst, ripples of raw tension moved through Molly. Concern for the children continued threatening her composure. They'd been so upset, practically inconsolable. Even now, though the prospect of ice cream had cheered them considerably, the remnants of tears still glistened on their tiny black eyelashes.

Chewing on her bottom lip, Molly slipped a glance at CJ. He looked as flummoxed as she felt. Yet despite his obvious unease, he'd confronted the explosion of little-girl panic with remarkable calm. He'd called on Molly's assistance only as a last resort.

Molly hadn't thought she could admire CJ any more than she already did. But watching him with his nieces had charmed her beyond measure. If she wasn't careful her admiration could easily turn into something deeper, more lasting.

She put the thought out of her mind.

CJ asked the twins what their favorite ice cream flavor was as he steered them across the open field. Vanilla was at the top of their list. Molly agreed. Not so, CJ. "I prefer chocolate."

He said this with such conviction the girls immediately changed their minds and insisted Molly do the same.

She refused to be swayed, which earned her a wink from CJ.

There he went, charming her again. Molly focused on her surroundings instead of the way her pulse sped up.

Children of all ages and sizes ran past their subdued little group. Boys chased one another in a rowdy game of tag. Several girls played hopscotch, while others sat on blankets with dolls. Molly's brothers tossed a ball with the Barlow boys and a few others their same age.

At the end of the grassy field, a long table had been set up in front of large, wooden tubs being hand-cranked by men of the congregation, Molly's father included. Her sister and their mother had joined other smiling women and were now serving up ice cream in plain, nondescript cups.

CJ reached for two filled with the twins' new favorite flavor.

"Thank you, Unca Corny," they said in tandem as they took the cups from him. Although their faces were still red and puffy, they dug into the ice cream with enthusiasm.

CJ watched them eat. His face showed strain, yet he managed a smile for each of the twins, then another, softer one for Molly.

For the breadth of a heartbeat she held his stare.

She saw reliability when she looked into his eyes. She also saw rough honesty, conviction and the deep code of ethics that ruled him. CJ Thorn would make some woman a wonderful husband.

There was no joy in the knowledge, only an ache of longing. The sensation plowed deeper when he picked up a cup of vanilla ice cream and offered it to her. It was such a simple thing yet spoke of his attentiveness.

Unable to imagine swallowing a single bite past the walnut-sized lump lodged in her throat, she lifted her hand, palm facing him. "None for me."

"You sure?"

"Positive."

Shrugging, he set the cup back on the table, then speared his splayed fingers through his hair as he gazed at her. When he pulled his hand away, several wild strands were left sticking out.

Molly desperately wanted to reach up and smooth the black locks back in place. It was oddly distracting, this need to take care of CJ. Not as she did the twins, but as a woman took care of her man.

The thought staggered her. She deliberately glanced away, and realized her mistake when she caught her mother watching her interacting with CJ and the twins.

A familiar look of concern fell across Helen Carson's face, or was that disapproval? Dread pulled in Molly's stomach, twisting hard when the older woman made a jerking motion with her chin, as if to say she wanted a word with Molly in private.

She had a good idea what was on her mother's mind. Molly had made a bold statement when she'd chosen to sit with the Thorns during service, and then had stuck by their sides ever since.

Well, this wasn't the time for a heart-to-heart between mother and daughter. Ned's absence had been noticed and publically remarked upon by Little Horn's most voracious gossip.

No doubt Mrs. Hickey was already discussing the situation with her cronies and anyone else who cared to listen. Talk would inevitably turn to the twins, then to CJ, and ultimately to Molly's role in their family. Assumptions would be made, conclusions drawn.

A hard knot of frustration balled in Molly's stomach. No wonder her mother wanted to speak with her.

As inconspicuously as possible, Molly slipped to the other side of CJ, then made the mistake of sending another glance in her mother's direction. She was still watching her. This time, Molly definitely saw worry in the older woman's eyes.

Feeling marginally guilty, she started toward her mother, but paused midstep when a neighboring rancher moved directly into her path. He was clearly heading her way. Or rather, he was heading toward CJ.

What little Molly knew about Edmund McKay, which admittedly wasn't much, she liked. He was a hardworking, dedicated rancher and one of the most respected men in the community. Somewhere in his early thirties, he'd lived in the area for nearly thirteen years. Tall, several inches over six feet, he had a strong muscular frame, light brown hair and intense green eyes that held a hawk-like sharpness.

He was a bit rough around the edges, but he was one of CJ's closest friends, which was a large point in his favor.

Drawing to a stop at a polite distance, he took off his hat and gave Molly a kind, if somewhat tentative smile. "Good day, Mrs. Langley."

"Good day to you, Mr. McKay."

Looking slightly uncomfortable, he jammed his hat back on his head and fumbled for words. "It's…ah…" He trailed off, swallowed several times, then tried again. "It's a…beautiful day, is it not?"

Molly felt her lips twitch at the innocuous comment about the weather. Clearly, conversation wasn't the man's strong suit.

"Why, yes, it's a lovely day indeed." She brightened her smile. "I trust all is well at your ranch."

"Very well, thank you."

He broke eye contact, placed his palms on his knees and greeted the girls.

Anna grinned around her spoon. "Hi, Mr. McKay."

Sarah showed off her pink bow, which he took considerable time admiring. "It's very pretty."

"I know!" She shoved a bite of her ice cream in her mouth. "I tied it myself," she announced, after swallowing.

"Impressive." He patted her shoulder, then straightened and faced CJ.

The two men had barely shaken hands before they launched into a conversation about the unpredictable cattle prices this year due to inconsistent demand in the northern states.

Molly found the conversation fascinating. She nearly joined in the discussion, but the girls chose that moment to finish their ice cream. She took their empty cups.

As she set them on the table, a movement on her left had her looking over her shoulder. Her friend Lula May Barlow stood beneath the shade of a large oak tree. Her eight-year-old daughter, Pauline, was with her.

Though Molly's friend was also a widow that was where the similarities between them ended. Lula May had five children, ages six to seventeen. She was also beautiful and kind, with strawberry blond hair, dark blue eyes and a no-nonsense, take-charge nature Molly admired.

She waved at her friend. Lula May waved back, then beckoned to her. Molly looked in the direction of her mother, discovering she was engaged in a conversation with Beatrice Rampart.

Deciding she could use a good chat with Lula May, whose daughter looked as restless and bored as the twins had become, Molly laid a hand on CJ's arm. "If you have no objection, I thought I'd take the girls away to play with my friend's daughter."

He appeared to consider her request with a hint of indecision.

Giving his arm a reassuring squeeze, she hitched her chin toward where Lula May and Pauline waited. "We'll be right over there."

"Ah, yes." He nodded at Lula May. "That'll be fine."

Molly dropped his hand. "It was lovely to see you again, Mr. McKay."

The rancher tipped his hat. "Ma'am."

"Come on, girls." Molly placed a smile in her voice and took hold of their hands. "Let's go say hi to Mrs. Barlow and Pauline."

The twins declared this the grandest of grand ideas. They adored Pauline Barlow, as did Molly. Lula May's only daughter was a sweet girl with bright red hair, a sunny disposition and eyes the same indigo blue as her mother's.

Seeming as eager as the twins, Pauline hurried to meet them halfway across a grassy knoll, her enthusiasm propelling her forward.

"Hello, girls!" She barely stopped to take a breath before asking, "Want to play jacks with me?"

"I do." Anna all but vibrated with excitement. "I really, truly do."

Sarah frowned at her sister. "You don't even know how to play jacks."

"Neither do you."

"I can learn."

Anna stuck out her bottom lip. "Well, I can, too."

Undaunted by the girls arguing, Pauline stepped between them. "I'll teach you both how to play. I'm really good, just ask anyone."

Once she was given permission by Molly and her mother, Pauline led the girls to a flat spot on the other side of the tree, placed a wooden board on the ground and got down to the business of teaching the twins how to play jacks.

Not until the three were chattering happily away did Lula May take Molly's hand and hold on tight. "How are you? And I won't take a pat answer. I want the truth."

Something in her friend's eyes put Molly instantly on guard. "I'm…fine."

Looking far from convinced, Lula May dropped her hand, but continued holding Molly's stare. She tried not to react to the searching glance.

Her friend was known for being determined and direct. Sometimes too direct, as evidenced by her next words. "There's talk going around about Ned and—" she leaned in close and lowered her voice to a hushed whisper "—it's not very kind."

Dread swam through Molly's mind, thundered inside her ears. She shouldn't be surprised the gossip about Ned had spread so quickly. Constance Hickey enjoyed spreading rumors, the faster the better.

Molly noted ever so gratefully that the girls were deep in to learning the new game. Nevertheless, she dropped her voice to the same low tone as her friend. "What have you heard?"

Darting a worried glance at the twins, Lula May sighed. "Talk is going around that he left town without a single word of warning. And, I'm sorry to say—" she shot another quick glance at the girls "—there's speculation he isn't coming back."

Molly stared dully at her friend, dismayed at how detailed the gossip had become already. CJ and the twins had enough to worry about without having to fight off the stigma of rumors.

It was so unfair.

"I know it's been rough for Ned since Penelope died," Lula May said, not unkindly. "But I can't imagine he would up and leave his daughters without a word."

In that, at least, Molly could set the record straight. "He left a note."

"Oh. Oh, my." Lula May's hand went to her throat. "Then it's true. He's really gone."

In quick, halting terms, Molly gave her friend the bare bones about Ned's departure. She stuck to the basics and didn't mention the whiskey, or that he'd taken CJ's prize stallion.

Proving she was a mother first and foremost, instant tears sprang into Lula May's eyes. "Oh, those poor, dear little girls."

Molly nodded, her gaze automatically returning to the twins. They seemed to be having fun, but she couldn't help but notice that they were more subdued than usual. "CJ is doing his best to fill the void their father left."

"I'm sure he is." Lula May couldn't keep the obvious distress out of her voice. "It must be difficult for him, though, having to step in to the role without time to prepare."

"Ned's only been gone three days." Molly spoke the words in a near whisper. "There's still hope he'll return."

"There's always room for hope."

Yes, Molly thought, there was. With God all things were possible.

The sweet sound of giggling had Molly once again watching the girls at play. Sarah tucked her tongue between her teeth, tossed the small red ball in the air and then gathered up a handful of jacks.

Molly's smile came quickly, then faded as she thought of Penelope and all she would miss in her daughters' lives. "Death is so final," she whispered.

"Yes, it is." Lula May glanced out into the distance, seemingly lost in thought, or perhaps in memories. Molly knew she had been a mail-order bride. Yet from all accounts, and despite a rather sizable age difference, her friend's marriage to Frank Barlow had been a good one. Certainly fruitful.

Lula May had been Frank's second wife and had taken over mothering his sons, Calvin and Samuel, loving them as if they were her own. She'd given birth to three more children, two boys and a girl. Despite the death of her husband, or perhaps because of it, Molly's friend had created a large, happy family for herself and her children.

Family. There was that word again. A vague sense of wistfulness spread in Molly. *Why, Lord? Why did You punish me with a barren womb?*

Lula May took her hand again and, as if attempting to lighten the mood for them both, changed the subject to something innocuous. "Will you be attending the quilting bee this week?"

The question took Molly by surprise. "Of course I'll be there."

She never missed the quilting bee and not simply because they met at the Rolling Hills ranch. Molly liked sewing, as did all the women in her family. Years ago, Helen Carson had turned an empty room off the kitchen into a permanent quilting room. The women, eight of them counting her mother, met weekly, weather permitting. As they sewed, they shared family news, discussed recipes and addressed various community concerns.

"I assume the twins will be with you?"

"That would be correct." Molly always fetched Anna

and Sarah. It never occurred to her to do otherwise. She'd taken them into her heart, and her life, long before Ned had left town.

In truth, his departure changed very little in Molly's day-to-day existence. CJ and the twins were the ones having to make adjustments, CJ even more than the girls.

Unable to stop herself, Molly searched out his tall, lean form. He and Edmund McKay had moved away from the ice cream table and were now playing a game of horseshoes. They appeared to be in a serious conversation.

Was CJ telling his friend about Ned?

Possibly.

Probably.

Molly was glad he had someone to talk to about his situation. He surely hadn't opened up to her and that made her unspeakably sad. She wanted to be more to CJ than simply the neighbor woman who cared for his nieces while he ran the ranch. She wanted to be his friend, his companion and confidant, the woman he turned to in good times and bad.

Quite simply, she wanted what could never be.

Of course, it was early days yet. Perhaps she and CJ could be friends, at least. He simply had to learn he could trust her with more than the cooking and cleaning of his house. Perhaps he would eventually come to think of her as a friend.

What if he never did?

Molly suddenly felt very alone, though she was surrounded by nearly half the town and was conversing with a dear friend.

In the deep recesses of her mind, for what must be the hundredth time, she admitted the truth to herself. She wanted someone special in her life again. She wanted a man—*a husband*—who would listen to her darkest secrets without judgment and calm her fears, someone who would look past her failings as a woman and love her anyway. *Want* her, anyway.

Her chance for that sort of happiness had come and gone with George. She was no longer naive enough to think she had much to offer a man. Unless God intervened, or something dramatically changed, the best Molly could hope for was to spend the rest of her life caring for another woman's children.

A humbling and deeply depressing thought.

CJ's attempt at playing horseshoes was halfhearted at best. His mind refused to focus on the game. Residual stress from the twins' breakdown had his skin feeling hot and prickly, as if he were coming down with a fever. Sweat trickled a wet, uncomfortable trail between his shoulder blades.

He was fully aware people were watching him, discussing him and his family. His *brother*. CJ wasn't fool enough to misunderstand the hushed whispers and darting looks. Thanks to Mrs. Hickey's nosy interference in matters that weren't her concern, all of Little Horn, Texas, knew Ned had taken off. CJ could feel their judgment.

The pretense was officially over.

He couldn't keep living in a state of indecision tempered with hope. He had to think in terms of next steps. He was in charge of raising his nieces in his brother's stead. Drawing in a tight breath, he glanced up, thought about praying, but got distracted by puffs of silky white clouds in constant motion against the blue-blue sky above.

"You gonna take your turn or give up and forfeit the game to my superior skill?"

Rolling his shoulders at his friend's jab, CJ lowered

his head and threw the horseshoe toward a stake some fifty feet away. The clatter of metal hitting metal rang out.

"Nicely done." Edmund nudged him aside and lined up his next shot.

While he took a few practice swings, CJ found himself glancing in Molly's direction. The sun seemed to wrap its golden arms around her small, petite frame. What a picture she made in the bright midday light. CJ couldn't take his eyes off her.

Clank.

"Your turn."

Dragging his gaze free, CJ sent another horseshoe in the general vicinity of the previous one he'd thrown. This time, he missed the post by two full feet.

Edmund laughed, then slapped him on the back in commiseration. "You're distracted this afternoon. Can't say I blame you."

CJ gave his friend a sidelong glance. He'd already told Edmund about Ned's departure. He might as well share the rest. "I keep wondering if my brother will come home soon. But I fear that's nothing but wishful thinking on my part."

"You seem certain." Edmund bounced the horseshoe from hand to hand. "Is there something about Ned's leaving town you're not telling me?"

CJ reached in his pocket, pulled out Ned's note and passed it to his friend.

The other man gave the page a cursory scan. "There's not much here."

"Keep reading."

He turned the paper over, blew out a harsh, angry hiss. "He gave you custody of the twins? Is that why you think he's not coming back?"

CJ nodded, then went on to explain how he'd come to

that conclusion. "Ned hated it when our father went on benders." CJ closed his eyes, remembering those terrible days and wanting desperately to forget. "He admitted to secretly wishing that our pa would have left home when we were younger. He claimed having no father was better than having one who was a drunk."

CJ hadn't disagreed. The inconsistency that came with their father's drinking had been terrible. It was as if Felix Thorn had been two men. There was the kind one who told funny bedtime stories and the mean one who sought solace at the bottom of a whiskey bottle. They never knew which father would show up on any given day.

"Ned had to be thinking of our father when he left." CJ wiped his forehead with the back of his hand. "He probably convinced himself that he was doing the right thing by abandoning his daughters into my care."

"I don't know, CJ." Edmund fixed him with an unreadable stare. "Sounds like twisted logic to me."

CJ thought back over the past six months. He'd given his brother too much time to recover from Penelope's loss. He'd made too many excuses for Ned's drinking, hoping the experience of their father's abuse was enough to keep him from traveling down the same path.

Edmund handed back the piece of paper. "You got a plan if your brother doesn't return?"

"Not yet." CJ's gaze went to Molly again. He watched as she walked away from her friend and approached the twins. She sat between the girls and, as natural as breathing, the two scooted in close to lean against her. "I have temporary help, but I need to start thinking about a more permanent solution."

"You mean…marriage?"

It was certainly an option and made the most sense,

especially when he considered the girls. They deserved a kind, loving woman to mother them.

But who would take a chance on marrying him?

He was a Thorn, which was bad enough. Now, Ned's recent behavior added another black mark against the already tarnished family name.

"If marriage is really what you're thinking," Edmund said, "you'll want to act quickly. That temporary solution you mentioned won't stay unattached for long."

From his friend's perspective, the idea of CJ making Molly his wife probably seemed the perfect solution. Except for one small, insurmountable problem. "She deserves a good man."

"You *are* a good man." The vehemence in Edmund's voice had CJ flinching. "Don't let what happened with Lillian make you think otherwise."

"She vowed no decent woman would marry a Thorn."

Edmund brushed this aside with a hard flick of his wrist. "If that's what she said, you're better off without her."

Was he?

CJ thought about Lillian, now married to a banker and living in Waco. He waited for the familiar sense of humiliation and loss to hit him. When neither came, he cocked his head and looked back over at Molly with the twins.

"I'm telling you, CJ, Mrs. Langley is your answer. The twins adore her. You seem to like her well enough and she's already a part of your lives. Might as well make it official."

Make it official? Something about Edmund's choice of words didn't sit well. Molly wasn't a mere convenience. She was special. Good, decent, loving. She deserved the very best in life, which wasn't marriage to a Thorn.

But now that Edmund had put the idea in his mind, CJ

couldn't dislodge the hope it sparked deep in his chest. Did he dare consider asking Molly to marry him?

He certainly liked her.

She seemed to like him.

Many marriages were built on less.

Maybe, as Edmund suggested, the solution to CJ's dilemma was right in front of him. Maybe, just maybe, she was already in his life.

Chapter Six

In the days following the ice-cream social, Molly's life fell into a new, if somewhat unsettling, rhythm. Every morning, just before dawn, she would arrive at the Triple-T atop Sadie's back, loop the horse's reins over a low tree branch and pray that Ned had returned to his family a changed man.

Heart racing, mind reeling, hope building, she would climb the steps leading onto the porch. But instead of discovering a contrite Ned inside the house, Molly was greeted by a harried CJ and two little girls tremendously happy to see her.

This morning, the fourth since the ice-cream social, Molly climbed off Sadie's back as usual. She looped the horse's reins over the branch and lifted up a silent prayer for Ned's return.

She'd barely commandeered the porch steps when the front door swung open and out stepped CJ, head bent. He pulled the door shut behind him, rearranged his stance and hit Molly with the full force of his intense gaze.

She reared back in surprise.

"Oh. CJ. I didn't. Expect. That is, I…" Her words trailed off as she studied the lines of exhaustion around his eyes and mouth, etched deeper than ever before. "Another rough night?"

For several heartbeats he simply stared at her. When he finally spoke, his voice was thick with defeat. "The roughest yet."

There was no need for him to say more. Discomfort and frustration all but vibrated in the air between them. Releasing a silent groan, he broke eye contact and looked over her head, his gaze unreadable.

Molly waited patiently for whatever he had to say.

Lips pressed in a flat line, he continued staring off into the distance. He reached up a hand, gripped the back of his neck and rolled his shoulders as if shrugging off something uncomfortable.

Molly desperately wanted to make this easier for him. But without more information, she didn't know how.

"I'm not going to mess this up," he blurted out.

"No, you're not."

Her unbridled confidence seemed to surprise him. He turned to face her directly once again. Their gazes locked and held, blue against brown, and, slowly, CJ shook his head in wonderment. "You're that sure of my abilities?"

"I am."

His gaze darted to the closed door behind her. "You wouldn't say that if you knew what I did last night."

Her heart fluttered at the sound of frustration in his voice. What could he have possibly done? Surely, nothing too terrible. This was CJ, after all, a man of solid, impeccable character. "Why don't you tell me what happened."

He nodded, studied the door once again, then grimaced as if he could see right through the thick wood. "After you left, both girls got out of bed. They wanted me to tell them another bedtime story. I agreed, and once I got them settled back in their beds, I made up another tale.

But that wasn't enough. Oh no. So I made up another one and another, *and another*. This went on for a full hour."

The poor man seemed to be beside himself. Molly rushed to assure him. "That doesn't sound so terrible."

"There's more."

She waited for the rest, breathing in the familiar scents of the ranch, grass, horse and hay. "Go on, I'm listening," she said, when he remained silent. "What happened next?"

"Finally, after at least a dozen stories…"

"A dozen?"

"Maybe only five or six, I lost count. Anyway, the girls *finally* drifted off to sleep. I attempted to leave the room, but Anna woke up and begged me not to go." A corner of his mouth turned down. "I told her I'd be in the next room. At that, she started crying. And I don't mean little delicate whimpers. I'm talking about big, giant, gulping sobs. Once I had her calmed down, I headed for the door again. Then Sarah started in, wailing even louder than her sister."

Oh, boy, he really had endured a difficult night.

"The point is," he continued, rubbing a hand over his face, "I ended up sleeping in the rocking chair I'd positioned between their beds. It was the only way I could keep them calm enough to sleep."

What a good, kind, decent man. But my, he must have knots upon knots in his back and neck. "That was really sweet of you."

"*Sweet?* No, Molly, it was cowardly. I can't stand watching them cry like that. Their tears always slay me. I just wanted them to go to sleep." The desolation was there in his eyes, lurking behind the exhaustion. "I took the easy way out."

"Oh, CJ, I would have done the same thing." She put a comforting hand on his shoulder.

He gave her a tortured smile.

"It's only been a week since their father abandoned them." Molly refused to call Ned's behavior anything but what it was. "The twins are rightfully frightened. I'm sure it gets worse at night. By staying in their room, you made them feel safe."

"Did I? Or did I teach them that all they have to do is cry loud enough and long enough to get whatever they want?"

"It was one night."

He swiped a hand across his mouth. "I want to get this right, but I don't know what I'm doing." He growled the words through clenched teeth. "I seem to be making mistakes at every turn."

Molly forced a smile to hide the ache in her throat. He was trying so hard to be a good parent. How could she not admire that? How could she not admire *him*?

"Sarah and Anna have suffered a terrible trauma. Right now, what they need most is to feel secure, which is exactly what you did by staying in their room last night. Give it time. Things will get better once they're sure of you and realize you won't abandon them."

He didn't look convinced, but gave a single, brief nod as if to acknowledge her words. "I'll be riding the fence line along the southern border of my property today."

Molly made a little sound of frustration at the sudden change of topic. At least CJ had opened up to her a bit and had admitted—out loud—that he was struggling. She would consider that progress.

Watching him head down the porch steps, she felt a renewed sense of purpose on his behalf. CJ needed her, if for no other reason than to support and guide him through these first few weeks as a new parent. She waited as he took Sadie's reins and led the horse to the barn for her morning rubdown. Only once he was out of sight did she enter the house.

The girls greeted her with smiles and shrieks of pleasure. And so began another day as their substitute mother.

Later that afternoon, while Molly stirred the bean-and-bacon soup she'd prepared for supper, her mind tracked back to the days before Penelope died. Molly had started coming on a daily basis to help her friend. As an only child, Penelope had been overwhelmed with the task of caring for twins. Her fears had been very similar to the ones CJ had voiced this morning.

Anna trudged into the kitchen and rolled worried eyes to the window that overlooked the backyard. "Will Unca Corny be home soon?"

Molly set down the spoon and faced the little girl. Anna asked the same question every afternoon around this same hour. And like every other time she asked it, her panic was palpable.

Clearly, Anna expected her uncle to abandon her, along with all the other adults in her life. Granted, Penelope hadn't actually abandoned her daughters. But explaining that to a four-year-old wasn't exactly easy.

Molly leaned down and placed her hand on Anna's shoulder. "He'll be here any minute."

This sent the little girl rushing to a window on the other side of the house, which overlooked the corral and bunkhouse. "I don't see him yet."

"I'll help you look." Sarah joined her sister, all but pressing her nose to the glass. "You don't think he forgot where we live?"

The question drew a shuddering breath from Anna.

"I hope not." She pulled in another breath, then released a high-pitched squeal. "He's home!"

Molly's stomach dipped. Anna's reaction was so enthusiastic Molly wasn't sure who *he* was—CJ or... Ned?

Bouncing on her toes, Anna laughed in pure delight. "He's home! Unca Corny's home!"

Unexpected relief nearly buckled Molly's knees. For a split second, she'd thought Ned might have returned. And in that brief moment, Molly had hoped he hadn't. It was too soon for her time with CJ and the twins to end. She wanted to pretend they were a family just a little while longer.

She'd been thinking only of herself, of what it would mean if Ned actually did come home. Well, this wasn't about her. Anna and Sarah's happiness was what mattered most.

They deserved to grow up with a father who loved and adored them. They also deserved a woman who would mother them as if they were her own. A secret, rebellious part of Molly believed she and CJ were doing a fine job parenting the twins. No, their arrangement wasn't a traditional one. That didn't mean they couldn't continue on indefinitely. And...

She was thinking only of herself again.

The door swept open and CJ stepped inside the house. The girls crowded around him, asking him questions and filling him in on their day. With the measured patience that defined the man, he listened, nodded, answered when necessary. In short, he treated the girls as any loving father would.

As uncle interacted with nieces, Molly hovered on the fringes, hoping not to be noticed, and yet yearning desperately to belong.

CJ eventually lifted his head and caught her watching him. His smile came slow and easy. Molly's heart slammed against her ribs. Cornelius Jackson Thorn was one devastatingly handsome man.

She could hardly catch her breath.

It was more than his good looks that captured her. It was his inner strength, his integrity and kindness, his willingness to do the right thing for two little girls in need of a father.

They need a mother, too.

What would it be like to become a permanent part of this family, to raise the girls as her daughters and to have a man like CJ come home to her every night?

George had been a good husband and a dedicated preacher, but their marriage had been based on friendship and a shared desire to serve others.

People in need were George's first priority. Molly had respected him for that. Yet there had been too many moments when she'd felt second best. Was it wrong to want to be adored above all others by her husband?

It was a moot point, of course, and completely unfair to George, who'd been good and kind to her.

CJ moved toward her. "Hello, Molly."

"Hello."

His smile widened, becoming different, more genuine and nothing like she'd seen from him before. She was stunned by the way such a simple gesture transformed him. His face was immediately lighter, his eyes softer, his frame less tense. And she knew—*she knew*—the change in him was because of her.

She swallowed back the nerves rising in her throat. "Supper is almost ready."

He took another step. "Now that's what I like to hear."

Molly's lips lifted at the corners. One thing she'd

learned since CJ had begun eating with her and the girls. He loved food.

Well, Molly loved to cook. It did her heart good to have her efforts appreciated by someone with a hearty appetite.

Trying not to sigh, she focused her attention on the children. "Let's get you washed up and then we'll eat."

She reached for their hands, but CJ shook his head at her. "Let me help them."

And there he went, acting like a father, making Molly's heart twist. Their early morning conversation came back to her. *I want to get this right.*

Did he understand he was already getting it right?

She stepped aside and let him take charge of the girls. By the time the four of them sat at the table, Molly's racing heart had settled.

During supper, CJ amused them by telling about an incident with the cow dogs. Talk then turned to the Founder's Day celebration.

"We're going to each bake a pie for the pie-eating contest," Sarah said, with no small amount of pride.

"No kidding?"

"Miss Molly taught us how to roll out the dough."

CJ laughed, a sweet, gruff, masculine sound. "That's really...nice."

"We're going to the quilting bee at her mama's house tomorrow," Anna informed him.

Swiveling to look at the child, he took the change of subject in stride. "That should be fun."

"It always is." Anna nodded vigorously. "Miss Molly helped us make blocks to add to the quilt. Want to see?"

"Definitely."

The little girl hopped to her feet.

"*After* we finish our supper." CJ looked pointedly at her half-eaten soup.

Head down, Anna returned to her seat and gobbled down her food with large, fast bites that rivaled Molly's brothers at their hungriest. Not to be outdone, Sarah ate just as quickly.

Over their heads, CJ smiled at Molly, humor threaded in his gaze.

Moments later, their bowls empty, the girls led him to the living room, where he proceeded to admire their handiwork. The stitching was a bit crooked, but Molly had been happy to discover that Sarah and Anna had patient natures and enjoyed sewing.

Once they'd pointed out each stitch, CJ went in search of the girls' corncob dolls and a stuffed toy they'd named, rather on the nose, Furry Bear. The three settled on the couch, the twins on either side of CJ. He launched into an entertaining story that sent the dolls on a grand adventure with the stuffed bear.

Molly listened to the story as she cleared the table and then went to work washing the dishes. CJ was good at weaving a tale. His voice was rich and musical, the deep tenor comforting. No wonder the twins demanded he entertain them with bedtime stories to make them feel safe.

Thinking about the ordeal he'd gone through last night, Molly felt a wave of affection crash over her. With it came regret and a wish for what might have been. Disappointment came alive in her heart. It took every ounce of willpower not to rail at God over her empty womb.

Determined to find joy in her sorrow, Molly concentrated her efforts on cleaning the dishes. She looked out the window, noted how the sun rode dangerously low in the sky, tinting the world with a pink-hued glow. She should be heading home soon.

The thought depressed her.

No. She wouldn't let despair win. She tapped into a

tiny spark of optimism. Her time with the Thorn family was a blessing, something to be cherished.

"...and that's how Furry Bear ended up with a pink nose."

The girls giggled.

"You're silly, Unca Corny."

He pulled Sarah close and planted a kiss atop her head. "All part of my charm."

Oh, yes, Molly thought, the man was definitely charming.

Finished with the dishes, she joined the Thorns in the living room. Flanked by the twins, CJ looked relaxed. Even considering the misadventure he'd encountered last night, fatherhood suited him.

Sarah let out a loud, jaw-cracking yawn. Anna followed suit.

CJ chuckled again. "Time for all the four-year-olds in this house to go to bed."

Neither four-year-old argued, proving the emotions of the previous evening had caught up with them in the form of exhaustion.

"Will you come say prayers with us?" Sarah asked Molly.

"I wouldn't miss it." Tucking the twins into bed was one of her favorite parts of the day.

She and CJ helped the children change into their nightgowns. Molly pulled down the covers for Anna, while CJ, carefully gentle, did the same for Sarah.

Once settled, the girls adopted identical poses, their hands clasped together and their eyes squeezed shut.

Sarah said her bedtime prayers first. "Dear God, thank You for Furry Bear and my sister and Unca Corny and—"

"—Miss Molly," Anna interjected, oh so helpfully.

Opening her eyes, Sarah glared at her sister. "I was getting to Miss Molly."

"You were taking too long. Now it's my turn. Dear God—"

"I'm not finished," her twin complained.

Anna sighed heavily. "Well then, hurry up."

Bracing her hands on her forehead, Sarah added her thanks for Cookie and the other ranch hands, each one by name. She concentrated on the horses next.

"Thank You also for Betsy," the milk cow, "and all the cattle dogs, especially Roscoe—he's my favorite. And... I think that's everyone. Oh, wait." She took a quick breath. "Now that she's living with You, please tell Mama we miss her and that we know she's watching us from Heaven."

Molly flicked a gaze at CJ.

Eyes hooded, he moved to stand beside her.

"Are you through *yet*?" Anna asked with a little hum of impatience.

"Almost."

Another sigh leaked out of Anna.

"Wherever Pa is..." Sarah paused "...can You please keep him safe and let him know Anna and me miss him very, very much?"

Eyes locked with hers, CJ reached out and took Molly's hand. They shared a poignant smile.

"Amen. There," the little girl said. "*Now* I'm finished."

"Finally!" Barely taking a breath, Anna hurled herself into her prayers. "Dear God, thank You for everybody my sister said. Can You also let Pa know that Unca Corny and Miss Molly are taking real good care of us? It's almost like we have a real mama and papa, so tell him not to fret if he can't come home."

CJ squeezed Molly's hand. She squeezed back.

"Amen."

Releasing hands at the same moment, Molly and CJ moved apart and took turns kissing the girls good-night. CJ snuffed out the lantern, casting the room in the purple light of dusk.

They left the room and moved silently through the house. Outside, Molly noticed Sadie was already saddled and tethered to the porch rail. CJ must have prearranged to have one of the ranch hands fetch the horse. The man's thoughtfulness tugged at her heart.

She opened her mouth to thank him, but the words stalled in her throat at the sight he made in the darkening sky. He looked weary. And sad. So sad. And maybe a little uncomfortable.

Molly had a good idea what he was thinking. She decided to address the matter head-on. "I wouldn't take Anna's prayers to heart. She sees me as her mother and you as her father because those are the roles we're playing in her life right now."

"Although I'll admit her words took me by surprise, that's not what troubles me most."

"No?"

He lifted a shoulder, dropped it. "It's what she said about her father. Just last night she was in a state of panic over his absence, then tonight she tells God it's okay if Ned doesn't come home? I don't get it."

"Her sporadic emotions are a result of grieving for her father. The longer your brother stays away the less she'll miss him."

"Will she forget him completely?"

"Not completely. Even if she can't remember his face there will always be a place in her heart for him. Sarah's, too."

"What sort of man will they remember?"

Not knowing the answer, Molly simply shook her head sadly. For several heartbeats she and CJ stared out at the horizon, both lost in their own thoughts. A fat, round moon was already rising in the gray-tinted sky. Crickets snapped, bugs buzzed, a dog howled in the distance.

After a moment, Molly turned to look at CJ. His brown eyes were dark with private thoughts, worries and concerns.

"Have you considered your next step?"

He nodded. "I have to assume Ned won't return." His words were so final, and all the more heartbreaking because of that. "Parenting isn't one of my strengths, as evidenced by the events of last night."

"You're doing exceptionally well. Far better than you realize."

He continued as if she hadn't spoken. "The twins should have permanence in their lives and a stable home. For their sake, I need to marry. The sooner the better."

A breath whooshed out of Molly's lungs and a dozen thoughts fluttered in her mind. She'd known her days with CJ and the twins were limited. She'd thought she would have more time with them.

Not about you. "You'll make a wonderful husband."

Cocking his head, he studied her with a puzzled expression, as if she'd spoken to him in a foreign language. "I'm not so sure about that."

"Of course you will. Why would you say such a thing?"

"I'm a Thorn, Molly."

It was her turn to stare at him in confusion. His words slowly sank in and all she could think was… *Oh, CJ.* This fascinating, wonderful man thought he wasn't meant for marriage because of something as intangible as his family name.

He was wrong. So very wrong. CJ had much to offer a woman.

Molly only wished that woman could be her. But she knew how little she had to bring to a marriage. It was that knowledge that kept her blinking at him in silence, her heart beating wildly.

For better or worse, she could never be CJ's wife.

Chapter Seven

CJ waited for Molly to say something, anything. He watched her calmly, barely moving, wondering why she could no longer meet his eyes. Was it because he'd brought up the subject of marriage? Or did her uneasiness have something to do with his reminder of the sordid Thorn legacy?

Lifting her head at last, she opened her mouth, closed it, opened it again. Scowled. "You can't possibly think that your last name would prevent a woman from wanting to marry you."

Molly didn't know about his disastrous relationship with Lillian Worthington. Surely that explained the outrage in her voice. Her defense of him made CJ want to smile. But this conversation was far too serious for that. A lifetime of practice kept his thoughts hidden behind a bland expression.

Still, CJ felt a little less isolated, as if he had found an ally. Was this what it would be like to have a wife? A woman who would stand by him, always?

He thought of Lillian and the cruel words she'd flung at him the day he'd proposed. *Marry you? Why ever would I do such a thing?*

Her response had thoroughly confused him. She'd allowed him to court her for two months. Why wouldn't he assume she would consider marrying him?

When he'd voiced his bewilderment, she'd derided him. Her next words were burned in his mind forever. *You're a Thorn. The son of a drunk. And as my parents recently pointed out, you'll never be worthy of a woman like me.*

Not only had her rejection shocked CJ, but her tone had been so matter-of-fact, so cold and unfeeling.

If Lillian had hoped to break him, she'd failed. Her lack of kindness—and tact—had spurred him to prove her wrong, by turning the Triple-T into a success. Her rejection had been the final push he'd needed to buckle down and work hard to erase where he came from, *who* he came from.

CJ stood at the edge of another turning point in his life. How this conversation went would determine his next step. He needed to be sure of Molly before he ventured into the unknown.

"Around these parts my family name isn't the most respectable." He held her gaze. "With Ned's disappearance, the Thorn name has once again become the source of disgrace."

Now that CJ had explained the heart of the matter in frank terms, he expected Molly to mumble a hasty farewell, mount her horse and ride away.

She stayed rooted to the spot, her wide blue eyes lacking any sign of judgment or condemnation. The sky awash in the vibrant colors of dusk was a fitting backdrop for her beauty. He felt a burst of tenderness in his chest. It was a sensation that left him nearly as confused as Lillian's rejection had all those years ago.

In a single, fluid motion, eyes glittering with emotion,

Molly moved a step in his direction. She stood at a polite distance, but he could smell the scent of wildflowers and woman.

"Oh, CJ." She moved a fraction closer. "I realize there's considerable gossip going around town about Ned. But I refuse to believe anyone in our God-fearing community would hold his behavior against you."

Molly's words signified just how innocent she was at the deepest core of her being. She would never understand the ugliness that resided in some people's hearts. She was just that good.

"I dare you to name one person who thinks you're less of a man because your father and brother turned to alcohol when life got too tough for them."

"Constance Hickey."

"Oh, well…" A tiny line pleated the small space between Molly's eyebrows. "Name one person who matters."

He could provide several. Lillian and her parents weren't the only people in town who considered him unworthy because of his family connections.

"If there are some in this community who judge you for your father's and now your brother's behavior, well, then—" Molly squared her shoulders and lifted her chin to a haughty angle "—they don't deserve to know you."

CJ felt the corner of his mouth kick up. Molly was really quite lovely when she scowled, especially when the scowl was on his behalf.

A part of him wanted her to retain her illusions, but he needed her to know just what the good people of Little Horn thought of him and his family. "My father was lazy when he was sober, mean as a snake when he was drunk. He let the Triple-T fall into disrepair and failed to teach his own sons how to complete even the most basic tasks."

"That didn't stop Penelope from falling in love with Ned and marrying him."

Again, CJ hated to disabuse this fine woman of her innocence, but there could be a day when the Thorn reputation rubbed off on the twins. If Molly was to continue being in their lives, she needed to be fully aware of what she was getting herself into.

"Yes, Penelope took a chance on Ned. And, as I've stated before, look how that ended. Her daughters are without a father and a mother and, Molly, they carry the family name."

His speech earned him another fierce scowl.

"Well, you…you're…" Impatience showed on her face, glowed in her eyes. "The Triple-T is a success now. Despite what you seem to think, you're highly respected in the ranching community. I predict that will go a long way toward restoring your family's good name. Your actions will just as surely reflect on the twins as your brother's. You will be the one to break the cycle."

It's what he wanted most.

The twins were still so young and needed more than he could give them. They needed a woman's touch. They needed a mother, preferably one from a decent family, who would provide them with stability and love and, if he was grasping for the dream, respectability.

Was she standing right in front of him?

Molly's indignation on his behalf taught CJ to hope.

"You should be proud of all you've accomplished," she said, continuing in his defense. "I know I'm proud of you."

The look in Molly's eyes could almost be interpreted as admiration. An admiration CJ wasn't sure he deserved. "Don't romanticize what I've done with the Triple-T. I had help from local ranchers and especially from Edmund McKay."

He would never be able to repay his friend.

"Others may have given you advice and assistance through the years, but *you* did the work."

"Considering the events of the past two weeks, I can't help thinking I focused too much on the ranch, to the point of ignoring my own brother at his hour of need."

"Ned is a grown man. He made his choices."

"While I stood by and did nothing. No." CJ lifted a hand to keep Molly from interrupting. "Don't defend me in this. I should have tried harder to get through to Ned. I sensed he was heading down the same path as our father. I should have—"

"You couldn't have known how far he would spiral out of control."

"I failed my brother." CJ's tone brooked no argument. "I won't fail the girls."

He would say the words over and over until they became true.

"Of course you won't."

This wasn't the first time Molly had shown confidence in his ability to raise Anna and Sarah. He was determined to provide them with a stable home. But...

"I'm not foolish enough to think I can raise the girls on my own." The events of the previous evening had been yet another reminder of how far out of his element he really was. "I need help."

"You have help. You have me."

"I can't rely on you indefinitely."

"I've no plans of leaving you." There were no words to express how grateful he was for that.

She's already a part of your lives. Might as well make it official.

CJ couldn't ask Molly to sacrifice her future for his convenience. Yet there was no time to court someone else. In truth, he didn't want to court someone else. He liked Molly and thought they would suit.

"I know you're feeling overwhelmed, CJ. Anyone would, given the situation. There's no cause for you to rush into such an important decision as marriage because you had a couple rough nights." Her smile was wide and sincere. "You'll find your way."

"The girls and I can't continue relying on you forever. Things have to change." He closed the tiny distance between them, reached for her hand. "It's not fair to you and it's not fair to the girls."

"I…how do you mean?"

"Sarah and Anna are attached to you. The longer you stay, on a temporary basis, the harder it will be for someone else to step in if you chose to leave."

"I'm not going to leave." She tugged on her hand.

He tightened his grip ever so gently. "You could."

Releasing a heavy sigh, she nodded slowly. "You're right. The girls need a permanent mother, not a temporary nanny."

She sighed again. This time the sound was almost wistful, as if she wanted to be that mother. Or was he reading too much into her reaction?

Molly had made it clear she still loved her husband, but that didn't mean she couldn't grow to care for CJ. He would work hard to make their marriage a success. He would seek advice from others. He would grow and learn and do whatever it took to build a safe, happy home for Molly and the twins.

Perhaps, even for himself.

His course was set. He knew what he had to do.

"Molly Carson Langley." He pressed her hand against his heart. "Will you marry me?"

One. Two.
Three.
Blinking rapidly to keep tears from forming, Molly counted off each heartbeat as it pounded in her ears. Five, six, seven. CJ had just asked her to marry him. It was the most wonderful, terrible, awful moment of her life.

She couldn't seem to find her voice.

Why couldn't she find her voice?

Hand captured gently beneath his, she flexed her fingers and felt the imprint of a button against her palm.

Rendered speechless, she blinked up at him. One second turned to two. Two became three. And then Molly lost count.

CJ asked me to marry him.

It wasn't shock that sent despair rushing through her, it was hope. A marriage proposal from CJ was the fruition of so many secret hopes and dreams. The answer to wordless prayers.

No. Molly couldn't accept his offer. Not because she didn't want to marry him, but because she cared for him far too much to saddle him with a barren wife.

"I realize I'm asking a lot of you." He continued gripping her hand. "You must see the logic behind my request."

"The logic?" *The logic?*

"We are already acting like a family."

That was certainly true. She'd actually mentioned that herself barely ten minutes ago.

"You already have a routine in place. The twins are comfortable with you and you seem to care for them."

"I love them as if they were my own." Molly needed

him to know that. If nothing else, CJ must understand that watching the twins was a labor of love. "I'd do anything for them."

"As would I."

Silent understanding passed between them.

"Molly, you're good with Anna and Sarah. I can't think of another woman who would mother them better than you."

She couldn't stop her traitorous heart from filling with happiness. But then came a sensation of genuine distress. CJ's marriage proposal, while kindly worded, was all about his nieces. There'd been no mention of love. Not a word concerning the personal nature of the union between a man and woman.

"Nothing would have to change in our daily lives."

"N-nothing?"

His well-cut lips curved as he pulled her hand away from his heart and gave it a gentle squeeze before letting go. "I'd like to have more children, eventually."

"You...you want children?" Oh, please, Lord, this couldn't be happening.

"Eventually," he reiterated. "We'd want to get to know one another as friends first and then as something... more." He was being so careful with his speech, deftly skirting around the delicate nature—and true purpose—of marriage.

"You truly want more children with—" she drew in a shaky breath "—me?"

"I want a houseful of kids. And, yes, Molly." His eyes bored into hers with the expression of a man who knew exactly what he wanted. "I'd like to have them with you."

He might as well have stuck a dagger in her heart and twisted. "I always thought two was a nice number."

"Eight is even better."

Her knees nearly collapsed under her. *Tell him. Tell him you're barren.*

The words echoed in her mind, nearly tumbled off her tongue. But when she opened her mouth, only one croaking syllable came out. "Eight?" She swallowed and tried again. "You want *eight* children?"

"I'd settle for six."

"Six," she repeated, in a very small voice.

"Granted, I have a lot to learn." His smile came lightning fast. "But now that I've had a taste of fatherhood, I've come to realize I actually like children. Rather a lot."

Did he not know he was breaking her heart?

Each word he spoke brought unspeakable pain. Molly didn't know how much more she could take. She couldn't look at him directly. "I'm sorry, CJ." She spoke to his jaw, where day-old stubble had appeared. "I can't marry you."

He remained silent for five full seconds. "Can't or won't?"

"Does it matter?"

With a gentle touch, he placed a finger beneath her chin and applied pressure until she was forced to look him in the eyes. "I believe it does."

The man was entirely too perceptive for his own good. "Won't," she said on a whisper. "I won't marry you."

"Tell me, Molly." He searched her face and she could see him pulling away from her, as if he were erecting an invisible barrier between them. "Are you turning me down because you think your parents won't approve of me?"

"What? No. CJ, no!" She couldn't let him think such a hideous thing about her parents. Or of her—that she would bow to their judgment over her own. "They would never forbid me to marry you."

"Do you think we won't suit one another?"

She couldn't lie to him, not with that intense gaze boring into her, or the hint of vulnerability beneath the calm. "I think we'd suit very well. I like you, CJ. Rather a lot."

Her declaration seemed to confuse him even more. "Then why turn down my proposal?"

She owed him an explanation. She owed him the truth. She needed to tell him that she couldn't bear watching him grow to resent her as George had, once he realized she couldn't give him children. But she couldn't seem to push the words past her dry, cracked lips. How did she admit her failure as a woman to this handsome, virile man?

As she stared into CJ's beautiful eyes, a rich, mesmerizing brown fringed with dark lashes, she tried to come up with a reason that would satisfy him without humiliating herself.

Perhaps that made her prideful, or cowardly, or a combination of both. "I'm not ready to marry again."

It was the truth, if not completely accurate.

"I see."

She doubted he did. Guilt brought another rush of tears to her eyes.

"You're still grieving over your husband."

She thought of George, of the children she'd never given him, of the pain she'd caused because of her inability to satisfy her husband's greatest wish. He, too, had wanted a houseful of children. Molly couldn't stand hurting another man the same way she'd hurt George.

"I suppose I am grieving," she admitted. Grieving the loss of what might have been.

"Molly." Tenderness crept into CJ's tone, then moved into his gaze. "We don't have to marry right away. We can continue on as we have until you're ready to take the next step."

Why did he have to be so kind?

Her pulse fluttered and her head pounded. She cared for CJ. Oh, how she cared. Deeply. Too deeply to marry him.

"I won't push you to make a decision tonight. I'll give you whatever time you need." He gave her the lopsided grin she'd grown to adore. "You'll find I can be a very patient man."

CJ Thorn deserved the very best life had to offer. He deserved a woman who would give him the houseful of children he desired. That woman would not be Molly. But perhaps she could offer her assistance.

Perhaps this was the reason the Lord had brought her into CJ's life.

"In the meantime, I'll court you properly, no pressure, no expectations."

A sound of dismay slipped past her lips. She would never survive a courtship with this man.

"I have another idea," she ventured, determined to derail him from this line of thinking. She must make him see she was not and never would be the marrying kind. "I'll help you find a suitable woman to marry."

His eyes went wide. For a moment, he stared at her as if she'd lost her mind.

Perhaps she had. Molly couldn't think of anything worse than organizing CJ's wife search.

"Why would you make such an absurd offer?"

Because I care about you. "I made a promise to Penelope before she died."

"What sort of promise?"

"I told her I would keep her children safe and ensure they were well cared for. Consider this my way of keeping my word to a friend."

His lips twisted at a wry angle. "How very noble of you."

She heard his frustration, felt his confusion and experienced another spurt of guilt. She had much to atone for during her private prayer time. "I'll draw up a list of potential women for you to consider."

"Thank you, no." He took one very large, very deliberate step back from her. "I'm fully capable of finding my own wife."

She'd insulted him. That hadn't been her intention. But at least he'd deserted the idea of marrying her. Molly should be happy. She was not. CJ married to someone else? The pain that came from the thought was obscene, like sharp, burning needles to her heart.

With his expression coolly distant, he helped her swing up onto Sadie's back. The silence between them weighed thick and heavy on the air.

"CJ." Molly stopped him from turning away with a touch to his arm.

He lifted an arched eyebrow.

"I'm sorry."

For several seconds, he simply held her gaze. Then slowly, almost thoughtfully, he angled his head. "I believe you are."

He still sounded confused and maybe a little angry. How she hated turning him down. She was doing this for his own good, though she doubted he would see it that way.

She rode away with a vague sense of loss, as if she'd made a serious mistake. For three full seconds, she resisted the urge to look over her shoulder. When she did glance back, CJ was gone. In his place was his foreman, Duke Rathbone, mounting up and pulling his horse in behind hers.

Molly allowed herself a small, wan smile. CJ always made sure she arrived home safely. She knew enough about the land and respected its dangers to appreciate his concern.

How could she not care for such a decent, thoughtful man?

How could she not feel a twinge of bitterness? CJ's marriage proposal had come five years too late. Had he asked her back when they'd first met, Molly would have accepted without hesitation.

And CJ would now have an empty, joyless house, full of resentment and regret instead of children.

He was better off without her in his life.

It would be hard watching him marry another woman, but Molly would step aside so CJ could find the perfect wife for himself and a proper mother for the twins.

This time, when the tears formed in her eyes, Molly let them fall unfettered down her cheeks.

Surely the Lord had a plan for her. If Pastor Stillwater was to be believed, God had not forsaken Molly or abandoned her in this wilderness season of her life.

Then why did she feel so alone?

Chapter Eight

Back on Carson land, Molly lifted a hand in farewell to Duke. He tipped his hat, wheeled his horse around and then disappeared over the first rise. Alone at last, she led Sadie into the barn and went about bedding down the horse for the night.

With each movement, Molly's head ached. Her lungs burned. It hurt to think, to breathe. She knew she was mourning the loss of a happiness that had been within her grasp. So close, yet so far out of reach she might as well live on another continent.

What confused her most was how she could grieve something that had never been hers. The twins weren't her daughters. CJ wasn't her man.

They felt like hers. More with each passing day she spent in their home.

The situation was utterly hopeless.

Behind her eyes came the hot prick of more tears. Why did CJ have to ask her to marry him? Why couldn't he have left things the way they were? Molly now knew the exact future she wanted, a copy of their present with the added joy of wedding vows spoken to bind her to CJ, always.

It was fruitless to keep mulling over the situation. He'd asked. She'd said no. That was the end of that.

With years of practice guiding her hands, she removed Sadie's tack, brushed down her heated coat and then gave the horse a bucket of oats in reward for her hard work. The old girl was as loyal as any creature Molly had known.

Stroking the animal's muscular neck, she gave the bristly hairs beneath her hand a fond kiss, then left the horse alone to enjoy her treat.

With the sound of munching in her ears, Molly exited the barn and stepped into the night. The sky had turned a deep purple and the rising moon washed the land in pretty, silvery light. A distant coyote howl floated on the stiff wind rustling the trees overhead.

Molly should go inside and get herself settled in for the night. She hesitated, knowing her mother would be poised with yet another round of probing questions.

Helen Carson was a loving woman, but she didn't know the meaning of tact when it came to her children. As she'd done nearly every night for two weeks, she would question Molly about her devotion to a family that wasn't hers.

They would argue. Her mother would then change tactics and display a mixture of sympathy and concern. Molly would still deny anything was amiss and both of them would walk away from the confrontation frustrated.

Knowing what lay ahead, Molly wasn't up to facing her mother quite yet. Her emotions were still too raw from her encounter with CJ. She was feeling even more fragile and vulnerable than usual. No telling what she would reveal in a moment of weakness.

Taking a bracing breath, she studied her childhood home with an objective eye. The large, two-story clapboard-and-brick house was simple in design, unremarkable really. The covered porch along the front was all that gave the austere exterior personality.

Closing her eyes, Molly could hear the musical gurgle of water rushing over rock in the small creek just off the back stoop. The sound usually soothed her. Not tonight.

Stalling a bit longer, she shifted and stared out over the fields that rolled as far as the eye could see, at least in daylight. At the moment, the hills and bluffs were nothing but a collection of bumps and shadows.

She moved her gaze to the left, past the corrals, to the patch of land beyond the barn. According to her father, that particular piece of ground was excellent for producing hay. The barn itself was the largest structure on the ranch. The tall, imposing building had a slanted tin roof, a well-stocked hayloft and twenty stalls for housing horses or other livestock. The sturdy foundation was made from large stones and local river rock.

Rolling Hills was an impressive spread. The Lord had given her family many earthly treasures and none of them took that for granted. Molly loved this ranch. She treasured every minute of her childhood spent learning how to work the land.

But she wasn't a little girl anymore and the ranch was no longer her home. When she'd left with George, she'd had such hope in her young, naive heart and had planned to serve alongside her husband while also raising their large, happy family.

None of her dreams or expectations had come to pass. She'd returned with nothing to show for her time away as a married woman but a failed marriage and a husband who'd died resenting her.

So depressing were her thoughts that Molly could hardly stand her own company. She tried to pace off her melancholy. Five minutes and a lap around the barn later, she was feeling no better.

She'd stalled long enough.

Shoulders back, breath even, she entered her family's house by the back door and crept through the darkened kitchen. The deep, masculine baritone was as comforting tonight as it had been during her childhood, and she found herself listening a moment. "Cast your burdens on the Lord," her father read. "And He shall sustain you."

Excellent advice she planned to take to heart in the solitude of her bedroom.

Padding silently through the kitchen, she went straight to the back stairwell. A part of her hated this sneaking about, as if she were hiding something.

You are *hiding something.*

She ignored the thought and mounted the stairs. She would spend time with her Bible. Reading Scripture always calmed her.

Careful to avoid the third and fifth steps—they creaked—she continued her ascent. She'd nearly made it to the top when she spotted the silhouette of her mother cast in flickering shadows from a lone wall sconce in the hallway.

"I'd like a word with you, please." Her mother's motionless stance suggested a difficult conversation ahead, and possibly a long one.

Molly resisted the urge to retreat the way she'd come. *No withdrawing,* she told herself. *No fleeing.* Better to face the problem head-on. Or so she told herself.

But when she finished her climb she was finally able to discern her mother's expression in the dim light, and she nearly groaned aloud. Helen Carson wanted answers and she wasn't budging until she got them.

"You've been crying."

Molly's hand immediately went to her cheeks. Her fingertips came away wet. Some time since leaving Sadie's stall, she'd given in to tears yet again. She hadn't even known they'd leaked out of her eyes. "Only a very little."

"Won't you tell me why?"

"It's nothing that a good night's sleep won't fix." And now she was lying to her own mother, all because of pride and her inability to accept her situation with confidence that the Lord had a plan for her life.

"Something's upset you and I doubt very much a good night's sleep is all that you need."

Her mother saw too much.

"I'm tired, that's all." Molly smoothed a hand over her hair. "It's been a long, trying day."

"I can't help you if you won't talk to me. Do not attempt to put me off again, as you have every night this week. I know something is terribly wrong."

Helen Carson had only the best of intentions. Molly knew that all she had to do was admit the truth about her secret shame and the nightly interrogations would stop.

How was she supposed to tell a woman who'd given birth to five healthy children that her oldest daughter wasn't capable of conceiving even one?

Face taut with frustration, her mother took Molly's forearm and drew her forward, tugging gently until they both stood illuminated by the wall sconce. Molly tried not to flinch under the bold head-to-toe scrutiny.

"Has there been word from Ned?"

"No." Molly shook her head sadly. "It appears he's gone for good. Or at least that's how we plan to proceed."

"We?" A delicate blond eyebrow shot up. "You have become so close with CJ Thorn that you are comfortable referring to the two of you as…'we'?"

Molly pretended to misunderstand her meaning. "Of course we are close. We have a common purpose."

"You are referring to the twins."

"CJ is overwhelmed with seeing to his nieces' needs while also running the Triple-T. I'm helping him find his way."

"That's all it is?" The speculative gleam in her mother's eyes put Molly on guard. "There is nothing more between you?"

"We are friends." Or at least they had been before she'd turned down his marriage proposal. "He's made significant progress in the past week and is growing more comfortable with the girls every day. I'm really proud of him."

CJ was a remarkable man. Molly would be honored to call him husband. She wanted to tell her mother about his marriage proposal. She didn't, of course. Because then she'd have to explain why she'd turned him down.

"I'm tired, Mama." Tired to the bone. "I'd like to head off to bed now."

"I'm sure you would, but I'm not quite finished."

The woman was proving more relentless than a cow dog rooting out a stray calf from a prickle bush.

Molly crossed her arms in front of her. "Go on."

"The gossip about Ned's disappearance is all over town." She paused, seemed to consider, then gave a slight nod as if coming to a conclusion. "You must realize that it will eventually—"

"Die down," Molly finished, intentionally cutting off whatever else her mother planned to say.

"You're right, of course. The gossip surrounding Ned Thorn will dissipate with time. Talk will eventually turn to CJ and the twins. Then...oh, Molly, *then*—" her mother touched her shoulder "—the gossip will turn on you."

That was what had her mother so concerned? "I'm not afraid of a few rumors."

"You should be. You spend every day at the Triple-T, caring for two little girls who aren't your children. Your motives are pure, your father and I have no doubts about that. But others in town won't be so understanding or willing to give you the benefit of the doubt. Your reputation will be in tatters if you're not careful."

Molly thought of the twins, of their dear, sweet little faces and the love she felt for them. She also thought of CJ and his commitment to his nieces, a commitment she shared. Her favorite Bible verse from Colossians came to mind. *And whatever you do, do it heartily, as to the Lord and not to men.*

What did it matter what people thought of her or her motives, or that she spent all her days at the Triple-T ranch? She was caring for motherless children, serving the Lord in a way that filled her with joy and satisfaction. "My reputation will survive."

"You can't know that for sure."

No, but she didn't much care, either. She would never marry again. She'd already let one man down and he'd grown resentful and bitter. Her last days with George had been full of strife and accusations. Molly wouldn't put another man through that agony.

But that wasn't the point.

"You would wish me to abandon two motherless girls because of what people may or may not say about me?"

Her mother's lips turned down. "You know that's not what I meant."

"Isn't it?" Molly held up a hand to keep her from speaking. "I'm a twenty-three-year-old widow with several years of experience behind me. I am not some naive young girl venturing into the unknown. I know what I'm doing."

"I don't want to see you hurt."

Too late, a tiny voice whispered in her head.

"I'm grateful you care so much, truly I am, Mama. But the consequences of my actions are mine alone to bear."

"That doesn't make me worry any less. If anything, it makes me worry more."

"Well then, you'll be happy to know my time with the Thorns is coming to an end."

"You seem certain."

"CJ has plans to marry soon. And before you ask, no, he hasn't chosen a bride yet."

"Oh, Molly, do you think you and he could—"

"No, I do not." There was no reason to let her mother finish the thought. "When CJ does eventually marry, it won't be to me."

Her mother's sympathetic sigh and soft squeeze to her arm proved she understood the situation far better than she should. "Oh, Molly, I'm so sorry."

"As am I."

If she allowed the conversation to continue, and the topic of her marriage to George was broached, there would be no turning back. At some point, her mother would figure out the truth—that Molly's childless marriage hadn't been by choice.

She simply wasn't ready for that discussion.

Will I ever be ready?

Perhaps. One day.

But not tonight.

With nothing more to say, she bade her mother goodnight and walked away before the woman could ask the endless questions shimmering in her eyes.

The next morning, Molly left her parents' house before the sun rose. She didn't speak to her mother and she didn't leave atop Sadie's back. Since she would be returning later that morning for the quilting bee, Molly borrowed one of the ranch wagons so she could carry the twins back with her.

The closer she drew to the property line separating her parents' ranch from the Triple-T, the more agitated her breathing became. She had no idea what to expect when she arrived.

Would she receive a frosty reception from CJ? Or would she pretend nothing had changed between them?

She couldn't decide which response would be worse, and spent the remaining portion of her journey preparing for either scenario with equal parts dread.

A happy, barking dog greeted her just outside the barn.

Pulling the wagon to a halt, Molly set the brake and hopped to the ground. "Good morning, Roscoe."

The black-and-white cow dog trotted over to her and gave her a big doggy grin. His tail slapped like a whip as he danced around her. Enchanted, she ruffled the animal's fur, scratched him behind his ears. "Silly, beautiful, boy."

Roscoe rewarded her for the compliment with a lick across her knuckles.

At the sound of a high-pitched whistle from Cookie, the dog immediately forgot all about Molly—fickle creature—and ran off to eat his breakfast.

Standing just inside barn, CJ's foreman called out to her. "Good morning, Miss Molly."

"Good morning, Duke."

A man somewhere in his early fifties, with a stocky build and a bowlegged stance, he flashed her a wide, kind grin from behind his salt-and-pepper beard.

"Going to be a hot one," she remarked, breathing in

the thick Texas air. "Make sure you and the boys drink enough water while out on the range today."

He tipped his hat in a gesture that was becoming familiar. "Yes, ma'am."

With nothing more to say, she set off for the main house. Her feet were weighted with nerves, making each step seem slow and awkward. She dismissed her disquiet with a shake of her head and marched up the porch steps. Drawing in a lungful of air, she pushed open the door.

CJ met her on the threshold, his heart-stopping face registering a look of unmistakable relief. "You're here."

"Of course I'm here." Had he thought she wouldn't show up? She'd made a promise to stay on as long as she was needed. She would not go back on her word. "The girls and I have a big day planned."

"The quilting bee." His gaze slid over her face before he stepped aside to let her pass. "They've been chattering about it since they woke."

Molly paused midstep. "Anna and Sarah are already awake?"

"And dressed for the day." A look of masculine pride crossed his face, followed by stubborn determination that said far more than words.

"You didn't encounter any problems last night or this morning?" she asked.

"A few." He made a vague gesture with his hand. "Nothing I couldn't handle."

His tone was matter-of-fact, as if he was used to all the rigors of raising young girls and didn't need Molly's help as he had in the past. The past being *yesterday*. Before she'd turned down his marriage proposal.

CJ was making it perfectly clear, and not being very subtle about it, that the end of her time in his home was drawing near. Her stomach roiled and she thought she might be sick. It wouldn't be long before another woman became his wife.

How would Molly ever bear it? She would find a way. But not today. No, she wouldn't have to face her replacement today.

Still, she hated this new strain between her and CJ. In that, at least, she could attempt to form a truce.

"About last night." The words rushed out of her mouth before she could censor them. "I never thanked you properly."

"Thanked me?" His face went blank. "For what?"

"For asking me to marry you. I consider it a great honor that you think me worthy of becoming your wife."

It was the exact wrong thing to say.

Up went the invisible wall he'd erected the previous evening. They'd become strangers again and Molly had only herself to blame. But now that she'd begun…

"My refusal of your marriage proposal wasn't about you." She needed him to know that. "You are a good, decent man who will make some woman a fine husband someday."

"I appreciate you saying so." He gave her a long, silent scrutiny, then jammed his hat on his head. "The boys and I will be riding the fence line that borders the McKay place. Cookie will assist you if a concern arises today."

And with that Molly had just been summarily dismissed. "I understand."

CJ spoke without looking back. "Goodbye, Molly."

The finality of his tone made her wince. Without saying another word, he shut the door behind him with a soft, deliberate click.

In the deafening silence that followed, Molly puffed out her cheeks and whispered, "Goodbye to you, too, CJ."

* * *

Hat pulled low over his eyes, CJ stalked down the porch steps. There was a dull drumming at the base of his skull and the cause was Molly Carson Langley. The memory of their conversation from last night made his shoulders knot up. Not only had she turned down his marriage proposal, she'd offered to help him find a wife.

He didn't need help choosing a woman to marry. He'd already found her. He wanted Molly.

Unfortunately, Molly did not want him.

CJ was too much of a man, with far too much pride, to pretend her rejection didn't hurt. At least he knew where he stood with her. There was peace in that. Oh, but wait, apparently, she liked him. Rather a lot.

Just not enough.

They'd turned a corner in their relationship and couldn't go back to the way things were before he'd proposed. The humbling experience of her rejection wasn't something he wanted to revisit, ever.

Twice now he'd had his marriage proposal turned down. Lillian had refused him because of the man he was. Molly, still clearly in love with her dead husband, had rejected CJ because of the man he wasn't.

George Langley must have been a remarkable husband.

CJ could never compete with a dead man. Nor would he try.

Finding another woman to marry was the wisest course of action. The twins required stability, something that had been sorely lacking in their lives since Penelope took ill.

A stubborn part of him refused to give up yet. Molly was still the mother CJ wanted for Sarah and Anna. She'd given them a glimpse of the family they could have. Molly *was* the answer to CJ's dilemma. He knew it deep in his gut.

He also knew there was something not quite right

about her refusal to marry him. Something she wasn't telling him, something that made her sad and wistful.

Perhaps she simply needed time and distance. CJ would give her both. She would either come around. Or she wouldn't.

In the meantime, he had a ranch to run.

Once he and his men were mounted up, he led them in a south-by-southeast direction, where his property bordered Lula May's spread. The hum of conversation flowing among his ranch hands was familiar and soothing, a balm to CJ's riotous thoughts.

Atop Scout's back, he took a deep, cleansing breath and let the rest of his frustration drain out of him. He always did his best thinking on the back of a horse, even if that horse wasn't Thunder.

He felt the loss of the black stallion acutely. CJ had trained the animal from his days as a wild, unruly colt. If CJ thought too hard about why he wasn't riding Thunder, he would grow angry with Ned all over again.

That would accomplish nothing.

His brother would either come home or he wouldn't.

With a long, sweeping glance, CJ took in the land he called home. Working the range had been his redemption in the days following Lillian's harsh words of rejection.

Today, once again, the rolling hills and craggy bluffs provided a much-needed diversion from his gloomy mood after Molly's rebuff.

At the fence line, he and his men spread out, looking for weaknesses and defects in the barbed wire stretched between evenly planted posts. A few minutes into the task, a frayed wire caught his eye. CJ dismounted for a closer look.

The Texas heat punched like a fist. He pulled on his work gloves and meticulously inspected the steel fencing wire, careful to avoid the sharp, twisted points arranged at strategic intervals along the individual strands.

Though barbed wire was tricky to work with, it was inexpensive and highly effective at keeping his cattle from wandering off the Triple-T.

Twenty feet down the line, four posts in a row tilted to the left. The wire strands were uneven in tautness, as well. Some lay flat on the ground.

"Here," he called out to his men.

The ranch hands hustled over and the four of them went to work mending the section.

They were well into the process of resetting the posts and fixing the wire when a lone rider came barreling in their direction at a fast, steady gait. CJ immediately recognized his friend and neighbor. He couldn't see Edmund's face, but the way he pushed his horse indicated trouble.

Pulling the animal to a stop on his side of the fence, Edmund swung to the ground and looped the reins over a low-hanging tree branch. "Got a minute?"

"Sure." CJ finished securing a wire to the line post, then dug a bandanna from his back pocket and wiped the sweat off his face. "What do you need?"

"We've got a problem."

CJ braced himself for the bad news. "What sort of problem?"

"Cattle have gone missing from the Sorenson ranch."

"Gone missing," CJ repeated. "You mean wandered off or stolen?"

Edmund's usually mild blue eyes went hard. "Stolen."

The word was a solid blow to the gut. Cold anger began to stir inside him, outdistancing all other emotions. Cattle rustling was one of the worst crimes a man could commit in these parts. Outside of horse theft, of course.

His mind racing, CJ had a bad feeling about this turn of events. He paced a few steps, then a few more, then stopped cold. "Tell me what you know."

"Early this morning Cecil Sorenson and his foreman rode out to where his herd was grazing. The herd was decidedly smaller than the day before."

"That's not completely unusual." Cattle roamed away from the herd, often in groups of five or ten. Like the other ranchers in the area, CJ and his men spent much of May and June rounding up strays. "How much smaller was his herd?"

"Sorenson estimates he's missing somewhere between twenty-five and thirty head."

A large amount, but it still wasn't out of the realm of possibility that they'd wandered off.

As if reading his mind, Edmund added the final blow. "The wire fencing was sliced through with calculated precision, then pulled back together to hide the hole."

"And yet Sorenson found it?"

"With ease, and that's the odd part. The rewiring was a shoddy job at best, while the initial cuts in the fence line had been perfectly aligned."

"Maybe the thief was in a hurry to get away," CJ suggested. "And that's why he didn't take the same care rewiring the fence as he had cutting it."

"Maybe." Edmund shrugged. "Or maybe he was making a point and wanted Sorenson to know someone had taken his cows."

Either way, it was a deliberate act of theft.

"Sheriff Fuller thinks it's someone local, or someone who knows the area well. Maybe a disgruntled ranch hand or someone with a vendetta against Sorenson or…"

Edmund left the rest unsaid, his silence significantly hanging in the still, hot air. CJ immediately thought of his brother, of how far he'd sunk before taking off altogether. Surely Ned wouldn't resort to cattle rustling to earn a living. Their father might have been a drunk, but they'd been raised knowing the difference between right and wrong.

Thorns were known for many things, but lying, stealing and cheating weren't on the list.

Caught between disbelief and fury, CJ pinched the bridge of his nose and prayed his hunch was unfounded.

"It's too soon to start speculating. The thief could be anyone." By the look in Edmund's eyes, CJ guessed his friend's mind had gone in the same direction his had.

Edmund reached for his horse's reins. "I have to alert others in the area."

"Thanks for letting me know."

CJ watched his friend ride off. Left alone with his doubts and suspicions, his chest rose and fell in fast, hard bursts. He couldn't stop his mind from circling back to one awful thought. Any man capable of stealing his own brother's horse would be just as likely to grab a few head of cattle that didn't belong to him.

The brother that CJ had known all his life would never sink so low. But that man would never have stolen CJ's horse, or abandoned his daughters.

Plain and simple, Ned *could* be the culprit. It would be yet another strike against the Thorn name. CJ wasn't concerned about what that meant for him. But the twins... Their lives would never be the same if their father was caught rustling cattle.

A fly buzzed around his ear. CJ flicked it away with a hard sweep of his hand. He was getting ahead of himself, putting two and two together before he knew all the facts.

One day at a time, as Molly said, which translated to

facing one problem at a time, accomplishing one task at a time.

At the moment, CJ had a fence to mend.

Chapter Nine

After ensuring the twins were settled in their game of jacks with Pauline Barlow, Molly took her place at the quilting frame. Careful to avoid eye contact with her mother, she sat in the empty chair between her sister and Lula May, then scooted her legs beneath the unfinished quilt. Seven other women were already hard at work.

Picking up her needle, Molly pasted a cheery smile on her face and got down to the business of sewing. A riot of gloomy emotions churned inside her. A marriage proposal should be cause for celebration with family and friends, especially when the marriage proposal came from an honorable, upright man.

Molly only felt guilt and disappointment.

Instead of sharing happy news with women of her closest acquaintance, Molly held her tongue, tucking yet another secret deep in her heart.

A great chasm now stood between her and CJ. He'd been different this morning, cautious and distant. She could hardly measure the resulting pain his behavior caused.

Her hands started shaking and she had to pause a moment or risk creating a crooked row of stitches. As she gathered her calm, Molly proceeded to study the quilt stretched across the frame her father had made last week in anticipation.

The blanket was nearly complete. Its blue, purple and green geometric pattern was really quite lovely. The finished product would be auctioned off at the Founder's Day celebration, the proceeds going toward a new church building.

Molly forced herself to get back to work.

The sound of female voices drifted through the room, peppered every so often with the laughter of three little girls enjoying a rousing game of jacks. Discussions flitted from topic to topic with the speed of hummingbird wings.

Molly's mother sat at the head of the quilting frame. Her friend Beatrice Rampart had commandeered the chair directly opposite her. Directly across from Molly, Edmund McKay's sister-in-law, Betsy, sat between Mercy Green and Nancy Bennett. Betsy and Mercy were nearly the same age, somewhere in their early thirties. Both had pretty, ash-blond hair. But where Betsy's eyes were blue, Mercy's were a pale shade of amber.

Betsy looked tired, a common ailment for a young mother her age. Her toddler son had been up all night teething. Exhaustion had caught up with the fussy child and he was now sleeping in the next room. Molly would endure fatigue if it meant nursing a teething child through the night.

She blinked away tears.

Of the seven women in the room, Molly knew Nancy Bennett the least. She was shy and quiet. She was also kind, and very pretty with long brown hair, hazel eyes and flawless skin. Nancy had come to the area in the same manner as Lula May, a mail-order bride.

But unlike Lula May, Nancy had been in Little Horn

barely a year. Her husband, Lucas, had been around as long as Molly could remember. He was attractive, charismatic and, by all accounts, an upstanding rancher. The two made a lovely couple.

As if sensing Molly's gaze on her, Nancy looked up. They shared a tentative smile before the other woman lowered her head to concentrate on her sewing once again. Before she'd broken eye contact, something a little sad had flickered in Nancy's gaze. Or maybe it was simply loneliness Molly detected.

Maybe the woman just needed a friend.

Molly knew what it was like to be new in town. An itinerate preacher with no congregation of his own, George had kept them moving from community to community. It had been difficult making genuine connections with other women.

Determined to reach out to Nancy more often, Molly followed the other woman's lead and focused on the quilt. Her sewing skills were average at best, especially compared to her sister's. Even at sixteen, Daisy had a steady hand, an artistic eye and a penchant for detail, all of which added up to her being a very skilled seamstress.

"Helen, dear, you promised you would share your secret for fruity fritters," Beatrice Rampart reminded Molly's mother.

"So I did. It's a simple recipe," she began. "Requiring nothing more complicated than milk, eggs, butter, sugar, salt and flour. And of course, fresh fruit."

"How much of each ingredient should we use?"

At her friend's inquiry Molly's mother happily elaborated.

Since Molly had made the recipe many times for George, she concentrated on her needlework. No matter how hard she focused, she found her mind wandering back to CJ. This morning had been difficult. He was already pulling away and that hurt.

What would she do once he married?

She couldn't stay on, that was a given. Perhaps there was another family in need of her assistance. The blacksmith had recently lost his wife. Her death meant two young boys, ages nine and twelve, were now motherless. They'd grown a bit wild and simply needed a mother's touch.

There were the three Gillen boys who lived out by Kettle Creek with their chronically ill mother. Mary Gillen could use a helping hand. Why not Molly's?

"For a different flavor," Helen Carson was saying, "you can add a dash of nutmeg or cinnamon to the dry ingredients."

Once the recipe was thoroughly discussed and all questions addressed, Lula May moved the conversation in another direction.

"Now that our town has been officially incorporated for nearly two years I believe it's long past time we had a permanent church building."

The rest of the sewing circle agreed.

"This quilt is a nice start," she continued. "But it won't put a dent in the funds we'll need to break ground."

Several money-raising ideas were tossed out and discussed. During a lull, Daisy leaned forward and craned her neck around Molly to speak directly to Lula May. "What are your sons up to this morning?"

On the surface, the question was considerate and really rather sweet. It was no mystery that Lula May adored her children and loved any chance to brag about them. And although Daisy was acquainted with all five Barlow siblings, Molly knew her sister was mostly interested in one: Calvin.

"Daniel and Jacob are cleaning out the horse stalls and organizing the tack room."

Molly stifled a grin at Daisy's crestfallen expression. Lula May's response had included only two of her four boys. Calvin's name had not been mentioned.

Her cheeks slightly pinker than before, Daisy dropped her gaze to the quilt, then gave Lula May a sidelong glance. "And what are your other sons working on today?"

Technically, Calvin and Samuel weren't Lula May's sons. When she'd married Frank he'd been a widower and raising his two young boys on his own. Lula May had made an instant connection with both. The three were fiercely protective of one another now. "Calvin and Sam are mending the fence line near the creek."

Molly's brothers were doing the same with her father.

"Oh, that's nice." Daisy finished off a seam and studied the effect. With her bottom lip caught between her teeth, she ventured another quick glance at Lula May. "Be sure to tell the boys I asked after them."

Mouth twitching, Lula May winked at Molly, then schooled her expression. "I most certainly will."

Covering a grin behind a delicate cough, Molly looked directly at her mother for the first time since arriving with the twins. She was in a conversation with Mercy Green, something to do with her famous ice cream recipe.

Was Helen Carson aware that her youngest daughter had a growing fondness for Calvin Barlow? Would she approve?

Molly was reminded of her affection for CJ five years ago. At the time, her mother hadn't seemed concerned that Molly was playing chaperone for Penelope and Ned, or that her duties put her in constant contact with CJ. Not that there'd been anything to worry about. CJ had barely noticed Molly back then.

She closed her eyes for a moment. Time seemed to bend and shift in her mind, dragging her back to those carefree days when her feelings for CJ had been new and fragile.

Her tenderness toward him hadn't diminished with time. On the contrary, her feelings were deeper now, based on the man he'd become and the father he was trying to be for his nieces. She opened her eyes and watched the twins playing with Pauline Barlow.

The three had tired of jacks and were pawing through a bag of sample material, chattering about what pieces would go best in a new quilting block. Molly swallowed the emotion that had ascended into her throat. Her wayward thoughts, however, were not so easily dismissed.

I wish Anna and Sarah were mine.

The thought came so quickly, and with such impact, she had to set her needle aside to catch her breath. *Breathe, Molly, just breathe.*

Caught up in reclaiming her composure, she didn't notice that the conversation had shifted yet again. Mrs. Rampart's voice came at her as if from a great distance. "Molly, dear, I understand a certain widowed father is still missing."

The words were carefully spoken and no names were mentioned, yet Molly experienced a powerful urge to glare at the woman.

"This isn't the time for that discussion, Mrs. Rampart. I'm sure you understand." She hitched her chin toward the children to emphasize the need for caution.

The older woman shifted uneasily in her chair. "They can't possibly know who I mean."

Of course they could. The twins were four and far smarter than the woman apparently realized. At least she'd been circumspect enough to avoid using Ned's name. But still… Sarah and Anna were barely five feet from the quilting frame.

Molly cleared her throat. "Lula May—" she turned a pleading look on her friend "—I'd love to know your secret for chicken and dumplings."

"It's a friend's recipe from back home and—"

"Molly, dear." Mrs. Rampart spoke right over Lula May. "Has there been any word, a letter perhaps?"

All eyes settled on Molly, with varying degrees of interest and sympathy. She dragged in a tight breath. "I don't see how that's relevant to today's sewing."

"Oh, but surely you wouldn't mind keeping us informed of the situation. We do worry about the family."

"Beatrice." Molly's mother gave her friend a warning look. "I have a new recipe for fry bread. I added sugar to my last batch and my boys tell me it's a wonderful addition."

It was a valiant effort to change the subject, but now that the topic of Ned had been broached others in the room had their own questions. "It must be hard for all of you," Mercy said. "Not knowing when—or if—he'll return."

"We manage." Molly's voice echoed through the room. "And that's all I'm going to say on the subject."

"I've overstepped." Mercy had the good grace to look embarrassed. "Forgive me."

"Of course." She glanced at the girls, who were admiring a pretty pink polka-dot gingham. "No harm done."

Praise God.

"I think it's quite wonderful what you're doing, Molly." Betsy McKay smiled at her from across the quilting frame. "You are a fine example of Christian duty."

Christian duty? The term gave Molly too much credit

and made the Thorns sound like a charity case. Neither was true.

In an attempt to find a comfortable position, she rearranged her legs beneath the quilt. Her agitation remained, heightened by the silence that had fallen over the room.

Giving Molly's hand a squeeze, Lula May spoke into the conversational void. "Helen, I believe you were about to reveal your new fry bread recipe. How much sugar did you say we should add?"

Molly couldn't hear her mother's response over the buzzing in her ears. She wasn't caring for the twins out of duty. Penelope's children were precious to her. Her motivation was love. Love for her dead friend. Love for Sarah and Anna.

Though she knew it was best to let the matter drop, Molly refused to allow Betsy, or anyone else in the room, to misunderstand her motives. "I'm not serving out of Christian duty."

"No?" A glimmer of intrigue in her eyes, Mrs. Rampart leaned over the quilt. "Then why, dear?"

Realizing all eyes were on her once again, Molly considered her answer carefully. She'd started this. Now she had to finish it.

She glanced over at the girls again. Anna was still sorting through the samples with Pauline. Sarah, however, had risen and taken several steps toward the quilting frame. She was watching Molly with rounded eyes, lower lip caught between her teeth.

Molly felt a twinge of guilt. She'd allowed her emotions to get away from her and had said too much, enough to gain Sarah's attention. And her worry.

She held the child's gaze and spoke from her heart. "It

is a joy and an honor to care for Sarah and Anna Thorn. I love them dearly."

At the sound of her name, Anna stopped what she was doing and angled her head in confusion.

Sarah shuffled closer, stopping once she was standing between Molly and Lula May. "You really love me and my sister?"

"With all that I am." She pulled the girl tightly to her. "And I always will."

Sarah buried her face in Molly's shoulder. "I love you, too."

The muffled words shot through Molly like a ray of sunshine splitting through a seam in a dark, menacing cloud. Out of the corner of her eye, she caught her mother's sympathetic smile, tempered with a speculative light. Only then did she remember her words from the previous evening.

CJ has plans to marry soon.

Anna pressed in on the other side of Molly. "Is it time to add our blocks to the quilt?"

"Almost." She ran her fingertips along one of the child's braids. "Once we're finished with this section we'll add yours to the next."

"Can we stay here and watch until then?"

"Of course." Both children kept their eyes on Molly's hands as she made stitches in the quilt, while pulling the fabric taut to keep it from puckering.

It wasn't long before the two grew bored and began fidgeting.

"Girls, why don't you lie down on the floor beneath the quilt and watch us work from there?" Molly suggested.

"Okay."

Pauline crawled under the quilt, as well.

Molly smiled, remembering the days when she would sit beneath the quilting frame and watch the individual needles poke through the fabric. It was always a wondrous moment when the stitches became fully formed shapes.

Molly could hear Pauline quizzing the twins. "What does that one look like?"

"A circle," shouted Anna.

Sarah was more fanciful than her sister. "I think it looks like Cookie's round belly."

The women around the quilting frame laughed. Molly did, as well. For a dangerous moment she found herself fighting off a deep blast of yearning. Then came the guilt. She'd declared her love for the twins in a very public manner. A small matter with huge consequences. When her time with the Thorns was over someone was going to end up hurt.

Molly prayed it wasn't the twins.

At the end of the long day, CJ left the job of getting the horses bedded down for the night to his hands and went in search of Cookie. The older man needed to know about the cattle rustlers in the area.

He found the grizzled cook in the bunkhouse, working in the makeshift kitchen, which was nothing more than a nook in the back corner that included a small fireplace, a potbelly stove and an assortment of pots and pans hanging from hooks on the wall.

Stirring a large, black kettle full of what could only be beans, a Triple-T staple, Cookie whistled a slightly off-key version of "Clementine."

As he made his way past the bunks with blankets tucked tightly over pristine sheets, CJ took a look around. He appreciated the way Cookie kept the bunkhouse spotless, a remnant from his years as an officer in the army.

Removing his hat, CJ ducked beneath a low beam and called out to the older man.

Cookie glanced over his shoulder and frowned. "Boy, you look like you've lost your best friend."

"Maybe I have." There'd been a time when he and Ned had been as close as any two brothers could be.

Eyebrows cocked, Cookie stepped away from the pot-belly stove. "You gonna explain that comment?"

He told the cook about the missing cattle and his misgivings about Ned's possible involvement.

"You really think your brother has something do with this?"

"He stole my horse," CJ said bluntly. He attempted to swallow back the anger that surged. It came anyway, searching for release like fingers seeking a nagging itch. "Cattle rustling isn't a logical next step, but if Ned fell in with a bad crowd it's a strong possibility."

Cookie didn't argue the point, nor did he offer any sympathy. At least the older man didn't remind CJ that he'd warned him this day was coming. "You share your suspicions with anyone else?"

"No. But Edmund McKay seemed to come to a similar conclusion. It's only a matter of time before others in the area will, as well."

Not for the first time, CJ wanted to go hunt down Ned and drag him home. But his brother had made his decision and CJ had too many other responsibilities pressing in on him, including raising Ned's abandoned daughters.

Suddenly weary, he said, "I need you to be on the lookout for anything suspicious in the next few days."

"Goes without saying."

"Still needed to be said." CJ left for the main house, heavyhearted.

With each step, he felt conflict growing inside him, torn as he was between hoping he was wrong to suspect his brother of thievery and convinced Ned was behind the missing cattle.

In the months since Penelope's death, Ned had made one bad decision after another, culminating in the abandonment of his own flesh and blood.

CJ's mind went back to the day of Penelope's accident. After putting the girls down for their afternoon nap, she'd gone outside to help Ned fix a busted wagon wheel. She'd become distracted and had let the cinch slip. The wheel had fallen on her leg. She'd hidden the severity of her injury for nearly a month. The wound had become infected. She'd contracted gangrene and died weeks later.

Weighed down with grief, CJ pumped water from the well and washed off the day's trail dust. As he rubbed away the dirt, he couldn't help thinking Ned's downfall was partially his fault. CJ had been so consumed proving he wasn't their father that he'd failed to help his brother in his hour of need.

He would find a way to atone for his behavior, if not with Ned, then somewhere else. Filled with resolve, he rinsed out the now dirty rag and hung it over the edge of the well to dry.

Feeling no better, CJ headed for the main house. His feet ground to a halt at the sound of a throaty female laugh mixed with little-girl giggles. A series of high-pitched barks followed.

The sounds of happiness, CJ thought, of family. Of home. Momentary peace emerged. He let the sensation wash over him like a fresh spring rain. He would give the girls the life Ned couldn't. He would give them stability and, God willing, a houseful of siblings.

He suddenly wanted—needed—to be inside the house, with the twins, Molly and one high-spirited cow dog.

Seconds later, CJ stood there, hat in hand, heart stuck

in his throat. Molly and the girls hadn't noticed him yet. He took the opportunity to watch them at play.

They sat on the floor, taking turns playing tug-of-war with Roscoe and what looked like a knotted piece of chewed-up rope.

Low, guttural, good-natured growls accompanied each yank on the dog's end of the makeshift toy.

Joy, happiness, renewed hope—in that moment CJ felt all three. As he watched Molly and the twins, he knew— *he knew*—exactly the life he wanted. A large, cheerful family with at least seven children, a rowdy dog or two and, of course, a beautiful wife to share every chaotic moment with, a woman he would love until the day he died.

Dare he reach for the dream? Dare he risk another humiliating rejection for a chance at such happiness?

Did he even deserve such a blessing from the good Lord?

CJ swallowed hard. He'd reached for the prize twice now, and had been spurned both times. But where Lillian's refusal had been final, CJ didn't believe Molly's was. *I like you, CJ. Rather a lot.*

He had no cause to doubt her sincerity. Which meant something else was holding her back from marrying him, something that didn't have to do with him. If he could uncover the cause of her reluctance, maybe he could change her mind.

Molly was worth taking a chance on, that much CJ knew. But if he went for the dream with her, and failed, he could very well forfeit far more than his pride.

His very heart was at stake.

Spotting him, Roscoe let go of the rag and spun around to face him. The swift release sent the twins tumbling backward, straight into Molly's lap. The three rolled on the floor in a tangle of skirts and laughter.

Distracted once again, Roscoe changed direction. Barking wildly, the animal danced around the laughing trio.

Molly's eyes shone with pure happiness. Feeling her pull, CJ stepped deeper into the room, his gaze never leaving her face. Had he not been peering so closely he might have missed the look of distress that came and went in her eyes.

The emotion had been there for no more than a second, maybe two, but CJ had felt the impact of her sadness all the way to the depths of his soul.

Molly was harboring some hidden pain, something that caused her great anxiety.

"Unca Corny!" Anna shouted between laughs. "Did you see what Roscoe did?"

"I sure did." He stroked the dog's head, lowered his voice to a teasing note. "Bad dog."

The black-and-white animal went into a full body wag.

The girls jumped to their feet and proceeded to talk over one another as they told CJ all about the quilting bee.

From her spot on the floor, Molly smiled fondly at the twins. CJ saw "the look" again before she shifted her gaze to him.

Oh, yes, Molly Carson Langley definitely had a secret.

Whatever it was, CJ suspected it was the reason she'd turned down his marriage proposal.

The realization gave him confidence. He was going to find out what Molly hid deep in her heart. And then he was going to erase every single doubt and fear. He wouldn't relent until she agreed to become his wife.

Chapter Ten

CJ was not the man for her. That's what Molly told herself as she watched him lower himself to the floor and drag the twins onto his lap.

CJ was *not* the man for her.

Unfortunately, she was having a hard time remembering why.

There was no denying he was a good person, full of Christian integrity and strong character. Loving, loyal, hardworking. No matter how or why Ned had left home, CJ hadn't hesitated to take over the twins' care in his brother's absence. In spite of a few missteps and shaky moments, he was already acting less like an uncle and more like a father.

Reality beat at Molly with an angry fist. CJ becoming comfortable in the role of father…

Right. Of course. *That* was why he wasn't the man for her. Or, more to the point, why Molly wasn't the woman for him. He wanted a houseful of children and was ready to move toward that goal as soon as possible.

His increasing ease with the girls, especially after such a short amount of time, foretold how he would be with them for the next fifteen years. Sarah and Anna couldn't ask for a better substitute father.

Roscoe performed several fast spins, then attempted to wedge himself onto CJ's lap with the twins. When the poor animal realized there was no room for him, he released a pitiful whimper. When that didn't work, either, he dropped to the floor and rested his chin on CJ's knee. Complete adoration showed in the animal's gaze.

Molly figured her own face had a similar expression.

Chuckling, CJ gave the dog a pat on the head. The twins took turns mimicking the move. Then Sarah added a noisy kiss to Roscoe's nose.

Molly felt hopelessness reach up and nearly choke her. The Thorns were so…very…wonderful.

She turned away and focused on putting supper on the table. She'd made a simple meal of beef stew and johnny-cakes, the children's favorite.

CJ scrubbed Roscoe's face between his hands. "All right, old boy, it's time to take you outside and make sure you get fed with the other animals." Pausing at the door, he caught Molly's eye. "I'll be back shortly."

Not quite meeting his gaze, she nodded.

Man and dog trooped out the front door.

Sarah dominated the conversation throughout supper, regaling CJ with repeated stories from their busy day.

Clearly tired of her sister hogging their uncle's attention, Anna tapped CJ's arm. "Unca Corny." Tap, tap, tap. "Unca Corny!"

He swiveled his head. "Yes, Anna?"

"We got to sew our blocks on the quilt all by ourselves."

"Did you now?" He lifted a brow in Molly's direction. She could practically hear his silent question. *Aren't the twins a bit young to be wielding needles?*

"Lula May and I guided their hands," she assured him.

"We did mostly all the work," the child countered.

Smiling that lopsided grin Molly was growing to love, he tugged on the little girl's braid. "Impressive."

Anna agreed with a wide grin. "I hope the quilt sells for lots and lots of money so we can buy a church building real soon."

The comment reminded Molly just how closely the girls had been listening to the women's conversation. Had they understood Mrs. Rampart's thinly veiled questions about their father?

Neither child had mentioned Ned since they'd returned from the Rolling Hills ranch, which was a strong indication that they hadn't heard or at least hadn't understood the adults' talk about their father.

Shoving aside her worry, Molly explained to CJ how the women in her mother's sewing circle planned to auction off the finished quilt at the Founder's Day celebration.

"What a clever idea."

"There's to be a picnic sale, too," Sarah announced.

"A picnic sale?" CJ sent Molly a confused look.

"She means a picnic basket auction."

"That is…?"

Molly smiled at the way his brows pulled together. "Unmarried women in the community make a picnic lunch and place it in a pretty straw basket. Unattached men bid on their favorite and the winner gets to eat lunch with the woman who put together the meal."

CJ stared at her a moment, his mind clearly working through this information. "Will you be preparing a picnic basket?" he asked.

"I…" Molly struggled with holding CJ's gaze. "Yes."

"Good." Satisfaction flared in his eyes. "That's real good to know."

What, Molly wondered, was *that* look about?

"There's one important point I forgot to mention about the auction," she said in a rush. "The identity of the basket owner is kept secret until after the bidding is complete."

CJ frowned at this. "Why?"

"To make things more interesting, of course. It's more fun with a bit of intrigue."

He muttered something unintelligible under his breath.

"Unca Corny. Unca Corny." Anna tapped him on the arm again. "Miss Molly said that me and my sister get to eat with her and whoever buys her basket. And I get to decorate the handle with one of my favorite ribbons."

Warmth returned to his eyes. "I like that idea."

"Me, too."

Supper ended on a pleasant note, with the twins and CJ making suggestions for what Molly should put in her basket. All the items happened to be CJ's favorite foods.

As had become their custom, Molly washed the dishes and put the kitchen back in order while CJ helped the girls prepare for bed.

They were acting like a family again and Molly was more relieved than worried. She decided to enjoy the evening for what it was, time spent with people she enjoyed.

She arrived in the girls' bedroom just as CJ finished telling one of his stories. The twins were already tucked in bed, their eyes drooping, but their faces were scrunched in identical looks of fervor.

"You have to buy Miss Molly's basket," Anna said in earnest. "We don't want to eat with anyone but you."

"I can't make that promise."

"Why not?" Sarah demanded.

"Because I won't know for sure which basket belongs to her."

"But, Unca Corny, that's not a problem," Sarah said in her most helpful tone. "Anna and I will tell you which one is hers."

"No, you won't. That's cheating." CJ straightened his shoulders as if taking on a heavy weight. "We don't cheat in this family."

His voice was adamant.

Anna's bottom lip quivered. "Don't you want to eat with us and Miss Molly?"

His expression became a mixture of thoughtful reflection and something else Molly couldn't quite discern. "I'd like nothing better."

"Then it's settled."

"Not quite." He scooped his hand through his hair, his lips quirked at a determined angle. "I need you to promise there will be no cheating."

"But, Unca Corny, can I at least put a pink ribbon on the handle?"

"That would still be cheating."

"Not if I don't tell you it's mine."

"Now, girls, that's enough." Molly moved into the room. "Stop pestering your uncle. The picnic basket auction will work out however it's supposed to unfold."

Neither child looked happy by this, but they didn't continue arguing.

"Thank you," CJ mouthed to Molly, punctuating his gratitude with a smile that reached inside her heart and tugged.

Not the man for you, she reminded herself.

Molly could feel the twins watching them, but she couldn't seem to move, to breathe. She was too riveted by CJ, all six feet of handsome cowboy that he was.

He seemed equally mesmerized with her. She couldn't think why, especially after she'd turned down his marriage proposal. The awkward moment was interrupted by a knock at the front door.

Shaking herself free of CJ's gaze, Molly said with no small amount of relief, "I'll find out who it is."

"I'll go. You stay and say good-night to the girls."

"All right."

He touched her hand before exiting the room. It was a brief, barely-there connection and yet her blood charged through her veins and roared in her ears.

Molly took her time telling the girls good-night. They could hardly keep their eyes open and drifted off to sleep quickly, a testament to their full, busy day. Molly kissed them each on the forehead, then headed out of the room.

As she made her way to the front of the house, she heard Cookie and CJ speaking in low, hushed tones that prevented her from deciphering what they actually said. Their rapid-fire interchange and rigid body language suggested an argument was brewing.

"Why didn't you tell her what happened?" The concern in Cookie's voice was echoed in his fierce scowl.

After a few seconds of eloquent silence, CJ answered, "I didn't want to worry her. Besides, there hasn't been time."

"Make time."

Sensing matters were coming to a head, Molly cleared her throat and finished her trek through the house. "The girls are asleep."

An uncomfortable silence fell over the men, pulsing with all kinds of nebulous meaning. Molly sighed. "Have you received word from Ned?"

"No." CJ drew in a tight breath. "At least, nothing substantive."

Molly had no idea what that meant. She eyed the two men closely, taking in two sets of bunched shoulders and scowls. "Then what were you and Cookie arguing about just now?"

"Cookie and I weren't arguing."

The man in question made a strangled sound deep in his throat.

CJ shot him a sharp look.

Cookie returned the favor before shifting his attention to Molly. "Your wagon is parked by the porch steps and ready to take you home."

Dividing a look between the two glowering men, Molly tried not to let her imagination run away with her. "Thank you, Cookie."

Grunting again, the grizzled range cook swiped the back of his hand across his mouth. "You be careful on your ride home."

"I always am."

Seemingly dissatisfied with her answer, Cookie turned to glare at CJ. "You should see Molly home tonight. I'll stay with the girls until you return."

"That won't be necessary," she said.

The older man turned his scowl on her. "With night comes a host of dangers, Miss Molly. Not to frighten you or anything, but snakes, coyotes, even wild hogs can appear without warning. Outlaws, too."

If that was his way of *not* frightening her, she remained thoroughly unimpressed. "I'm sure Duke will follow me home, as he does every night."

Stubbornness flared in the older man's rheumy eyes and he barked out his next words as he would to a regiment of subordinates. "CJ will escort you home tonight."

Molly shot a glance at CJ. He'd been surprisingly quiet

and continued holding his silence as she studied his closed expression.

Oh, joy. He'd erected that invisible wall between them once again, though she couldn't think what could have changed in the time she'd spent saying good-night to the girls.

She spun back to Cookie. "Why should CJ escort me home?"

"Because he has something he needs to tell you." To punctuate his words, the range cook gave the younger man a nudge with his shoulder.

Finally. CJ broke his silence. "I'll saddle a horse and meet you out front in a few minutes."

The moment the door shut behind him, Molly turned on Cookie. "You want to tell me what that was about?"

He lifted his hands, palms out. "It ain't my place."

"Of course not." Aware that her voice sounded more than a little impatient, she attempted to wheedle information out of him. Cookie turned surprisingly tight-lipped.

Giving up, Molly walked out of the house without a single glance back.

She found CJ waiting by her wagon as promised. Silhouetted in the shadows of dusk, he looked like the quintessential cowboy. The rugged Texas landscape was a perfect backdrop and added dimension to the already attractive image.

"Are *you* going to tell me what's going on with you and Cookie?"

"Nothing to concern yourself over."

For the first time in their acquaintance, Molly sensed CJ wasn't being completely honest with her. She didn't know how to respond.

He helped her into the wagon, then mounted Scout and pulled up beside her.

"CJ, clearly there's been some sort of falling out between you. Won't you tell me what happened?"

"Cookie and I are fine."

"Then why the hushed whispers and angry scowls?"

"Something happened on the range."

She waited for him to expand. When he didn't, Molly got a firsthand glimpse of her mother's frustration with her own unwillingness to share information.

Proving she was, indeed, Helen Carson's daughter, Molly pressed CJ from a different angle. "How do you expect me to keep the girls safe if I don't know what I'm up against?"

Her question was met with continued silence. But she could see CJ's mind working, as if he was trying to figure out how much to tell her and how much to keep to himself.

Giving him a moment to gather his thoughts, Molly looked out across the land she loved. The sun was minutes away from dipping below the horizon, painting the rolling countryside and low-hanging clouds a brilliant array of oranges, pinks and purples. The thick evening air filled with the buzz of various night creatures crawling out of their holes.

"I hadn't planned on telling you this," he began. "But you make a compelling argument."

He paused.

She waited.

"Cattle have gone missing from Cecil Sorenson's ranch."

At CJ's hard tone, a shiver navigated along Molly's spine. "You mean—" she swallowed "—stolen?"

He nodded, then shared in cold, unemotional terms all he knew about the incident. He ended with the number of cattle that had been taken.

"Twenty-five to thirty?" she repeated. That was far too many to be explained away as a simple wandering off. No wonder CJ seemed certain it was theft.

"Sheriff Fuller has been alerted."

More bad news. If the county sheriff was involved, then the situation was serious. As soon as the thought emerged, a terrible suspicion took hold. "You don't think… Oh, CJ, you don't think Ned is the thief?"

She whispered the question in such a low tone she wondered if CJ heard her.

"It occurred to me." He shifted in his saddle. "Sadly, the more I contemplate the situation the more I fear it's a real possibility."

Molly's heart tightened and began to throb. CJ's tormented expression had her wanting to soothe away his worries with a few kind words. But he'd erected that wall between them once again and she couldn't think of a subtle way to shove past the invisible barrier.

"I hope our suspicions are proved wrong," she said with all sincerity.

"As do I."

They rode to her parents' ranch in silence, each lost in their own troubling thoughts.

Just as they crossed onto Carson land, Molly slid a glance at CJ from beneath her lowered lashes. Although he always looked good atop a horse, any horse, there was something not quite right seeing him riding the bay-colored gelding instead of the tall black stallion. Thunder and CJ were a magnificent pair that should never have been separated.

If Ned was bold enough to steal his own brother's horse, it stood to reason that cattle rustling was but one step away.

Oh, Lord, let me be wrong.

Because if it was true, if Ned had become a cattle rustler, Molly feared CJ would take the blame for his brother's behavior.

He had enough to worry about without carrying that additional burden.

Now that he'd shared his worry concerning Ned's involvement with the stolen cattle, CJ's first instinct was to defend his brother. Or at least make excuses for Ned's poor decisions.

After all, he could be innocent of the crime. There was no proof that Ned was still in the area, and there was certainly nothing concrete pointing to him as the thief.

Thief. The word reverberated wasplike in CJ's mind, buzzing and stinging with accusation.

He glanced over at Molly. Her fingers curled around the wagon reins with a white-knuckled grip. She was clearly upset about the missing cattle.

There was also outrage in her eyes. CJ realized, with an alarming jolt of insight, just how well he could read Molly's moods. One glance and he could tell whether she was sad or happy, amused or worried. He could also tell whether she was being completely open with him or hiding some secret hurt.

He'd felt a connection with her ever since their first meeting. Their bond had grown stronger since Ned's departure. Despite her turning down his proposal, CJ knew she was the best woman to mother the twins. He knew it all the way to his marrow.

She claimed she would never marry again. But there was something in her eyes that warned CJ there was more to the story than devotion to her dead husband.

Somehow he sensed if he walked away from her now, he would be letting her down. He didn't know how or why, or even if he had the right of it. But there it was, growing inside him, driving him to continue pursuing the issue of marriage despite her initial refusal.

I like you, CJ. Rather a lot.

Words to live by, at least a little while longer.

"Molly, hold up a minute." He gave his horse a gentle kick in the ribs, enough to get the animal moving. "Let me help you down."

She'd already pulled the wagon to a stop outside the large barn and was in the process of setting the brake.

CJ dismounted and strode toward her. She placed her hands atop his shoulders. His own palms secured at her waist, his eyes never leaving hers, he lifted her from the wagon and set her gently on the ground.

Unwilling to release her just yet, he kept his hands pressed lightly to her sides.

She remained equally motionless.

They stood there, staring at each other in the soft, moody light of dusk. The world seemed to pause, take a breath and wait.

There was so much CJ wanted, needed, to say to this woman, but his breath stalled in his chest and words eluded him. It was as if he'd been waiting for this moment all his life.

A breeze rustled through the trees overhead, whispering secrets to the fast approaching night.

Slowly, Molly blinked her dreamy blue eyes, giving CJ the courage to pull her a step closer.

"Molly."

He wasn't sure what he meant to say or do next, only that he wanted her near. He could smell the scent of her, lilacs and freshly milled soap and crisp night air.

A wisp of a sigh glided past her lips. "Thank you, CJ. I appreciate you telling me about the missing cattle."

Her words came out husky, slicing through the fabric of his restlessness and reminding him why he'd asked her to marry him in the first place. She brought peace to his chaotic world, and comfort, and things he wasn't sure how to articulate.

"You needed to know." He tugged her a hair closer. "As you pointed out, you spend a lot of solitary time with the twins."

An echo of a smile trembled across her lips. "You're worried about the girls."

"And you, Molly. I worry about you, as well."

Framed by long, thick lashes, her eyes turned a warm cornflower blue, a beacon in the gray light of dusk.

CJ never tired of gazing at Molly. Tonight she looked so sweet, so innocent. So kissable. He breathed in a sliver of hot summer air and pulled her the rest of the way into his arms.

She said nothing, simply stared up at him. Several strands of hair had escaped her braid. He reached up and tucked them behind her ear.

The warm June air wafted between them and still she remained silent, blinking up at him as though attempting to decipher a difficult puzzle. "You're a good man, CJ Thorn."

He gave a small, humorless laugh. "That's debatable."

"It's the truth."

CJ had no illusions about who he was. He'd been raised by a hard man. He didn't know how to treat a woman like Molly. She deserved romance, flowers and whatever sort of female things women enjoyed during a proper courtship. His lack of knowledge was a perfect example of what Lillian had meant when she'd said no decent woman would have him.

CJ needed a decent woman to see past his sullied last

name and rough upbringing. Not for himself, but for the twins.

Molly didn't hold his legacy against him. She saw him with the goodness of her heart instead of the reality of his name.

Smiling down at her, he raised her hand tenderly to his lips and pressed a soft kiss to her knuckles, before cradling it against his chest. She released a shuddering sigh.

His heart beat a rapid tattoo against his ribs. Resolve took hold and he lowered his head toward hers. Closer, closer, until their lips met with a whisper of a touch.

Seconds later, he lifted his head and stepped back.

The woman staring up at him looked a little shocked, and certainly confused. She did *not* look outraged. After the day he'd had, CJ decided to take that as a very good sign.

Chapter Eleven

CJ crossed onto Triple-T land with an odd sensation in his heart, part confusion, part conviction. He drew in a breath, smelled the familiar scents of Texas dirt, saddle leather and horse. A fat moon, white as bone, illuminated the darkened sky and splashed its pale glow over the rough terrain.

Feeling less overwhelmed than he had in weeks, CJ actually allowed himself a small, tentative smile. He had no idea what the future held for him and the twins, or even if he would have the honor of raising them to adulthood. There were too many extenuating circumstances dependent on what his brother did next.

Renewed fury spiked, abrupt and almost violent.

At least the twins had Molly. For now. He had no idea if he could convince her to become a permanent part of their lives. Her reaction to his spontaneous kiss gave him hope.

Dismounting, he took care of bedding down Scout with quick, sure hands. Though he doubted he had an endless supply of days to change Molly's mind about marriage, she wasn't going anywhere.

CJ wasn't going anywhere. Time was on his side.

Whistling filled his ears, a lighthearted tune he hadn't heard since his youth. It took him several seconds to realize the happy sound was coming from him. Warmth poured through his remaining doubts. One brief kiss, nothing more than a momentary meeting of lips, and CJ's whole world had become less gloomy.

Was this Molly's doing? Was it a preview of what marriage to her could be like?

CJ wouldn't know. He had no real memory of his parents' life together before his mother had taken ill. He'd been a boy when she'd first gotten sick, and though she hadn't died until years later, he couldn't remember his parents ever having a close relationship. His childhood home had been safe. His and Ned's basic needs had been met, but there hadn't been much love. And certainly no joy.

That left CJ with no model for marriage, other than what he could glean from observing other couples. Ned and Penelope had seemed happy, but CJ had given them a wide berth and a lot privacy to find their way. He didn't know much of what had really occurred in their marriage, leaving another hole in his knowledge. When CJ did finally marry, he would have to trust his instincts and rely on the Lord's guidance.

But first he had to convince a certain stubborn woman to marry him. No small feat. She'd already turned him down once. To step back into the fray could prove devastating. But Molly had tugged at him from their first meeting. There was something between them that wouldn't let go.

Anticipation stirred inside him, outdistancing all other emotion. Everything was going to work out. Ned was gone, but his daughters would still have a good life. They would never be alone. They had CJ. Soon, God willing, they would have a mother, as well.

Hope for the future filled him to near bursting, until he stepped onto the porch stairs and heard little-girl sobs and pitiful whimpers.

Had one of the twins been hurt?

Heart in his throat, CJ raced into the house and came to a dead stop. Stunned speechless, he could only blink in shocked silence. The main living area was as tidy as the average pigsty.

The twins' toy box had exploded, sending dolls, stuffed animals and who knew what else to the farthest corners of the room. Blankets were strewn everywhere. One even hung from the ceiling, all but defying the laws of gravity.

And there, in the middle of the mess, stood Cookie. Wringing his hands and looking as if he was under attack by an entire regiment of enemy soldiers, when he was really facing down two small four-year-olds. Granted, they were very upset, very red-faced four-year-olds, who seemed to be crying, whimpering and quarreling all at once.

CJ could actually feel the poor man's torment. He felt oddly validated that the seasoned army cook was finding no more success at playing nursemaid than CJ.

Tunneling his fingers through his hair, he sorted through the mess and blubbering with the speed of a hawk swooping on its prey. No blood—always a good sign. No broken bones—more good news.

That left a bona fide mystery as to what had upset the girls to such a level.

"I want my Unca Corny," Anna whimpered, looking pitiful and exhausted and as pale as the moon on a clear night.

"Like I told you before," Cookie groused, "he's coming back soon."

Sarah marched up to the man, slapped her hands on her hips and stomped her foot. "My sister doesn't feel good." She stomped her foot again. "And you don't care."

"Oh, I care."

Their stares locked, collided. "Her tummy hurts."

"You said her head hurt not one minute ago." Pulling a face, Cookie peered at the whimpering child. "Which is it, her stomach or head?"

"Both." Anna's shoulders slumped. "My eyes feel sticky, too."

Cookie stabbed a hand through his bristly hair. "That's because you've been crying for going on near twenty minutes."

"I want Unca Corny."

"Me, too," Sarah echoed, dry-eyed and clearly furious on her sister's behalf. "He promised he'd never go away. But he did. And now he's never coming back."

"I told you he didn't leave you." Cookie's voice held a great deal of panic. "You gotta believe me."

CJ had heard enough.

"Here I am." Not knowing what else to do, he scooped up Anna.

Big mistake.

She twisted frantically against the cage of his arms, which only managed to get her all worked up again.

"Hush now, sweet pea. Shh, calm down. I'm right here."

"I feel sick." Her face went dead white, then turned a sickening shade of green. No kidding, it actually turned *green*!

CJ recognized the curling in his gut as dread. He knew what was coming next, but he moved a second too late.

The little girl threw up all over them both.

This was disconcerting for a couple reasons: one, Cookie hightailed it out of the house as fast as his stubby legs could take him, abandoning CJ; and two, no one had warned him that a child as tiny and cute as Anna Thorn could hold that much in her stomach.

For several beats, he simply stared at his niece in a frozen state of shock. All CJ could think was *poor kid*. She looked as miserable as he'd ever seen her.

"I'm sorry, Unca Corny." She did that choking thing she did whenever she was trying to keep from crying. "I didn't mean to get sick on you."

"These things happen."

Her bottom lip trembled and then she gave up the battle and started crying again. "You hate me."

"No, I don't." Not even close. He loved her with a fierceness he hadn't known himself capable of feeling.

She tried to wiggle free. He tightened his hold on her.

"You hate me and you want to leave me," she moaned. "Just like Pa."

The kid was breaking his heart.

"Ah, Anna, my sweet girl." He avoided bringing up her father and focused on the other, more immediate problem. "We all get sick sometimes."

"Even you?"

"Even me. What do you say I get us both cleaned up?"

"You…" she did that shaky inhalation thing again "…you're not mad at me?"

"Not even a little bit." He actually felt terrible for the girl. She looked pale and not quite herself, and a jolt of terror slammed through him. What if Anna's illness was serious?

Didn't some children die when they got sick?

Heat crawled under his skin, turning to ice in the pit

of his stomach. What if he missed some important sign that would save her life?

The ice in his gut moved to his throat. Why had he thought he could do this? He wasn't cut out to be a father.

Past overlaid the present and he was transported back to the day Penelope took ill. She'd never recovered. Would her daughter die under his care?

One day at a time, he reminded himself. One problem at a time. One task at a time. It was the only way he would survive this latest nightmare. "Let's get you cleaned up."

Sarah came up beside him and pulled on his sleeve.

"You can use this to clean up the mess my sister made." Eyes glittering, she offered him her favorite blanket, the one she slept with every night.

CJ's heart took an extra hard tumble. Sarah had to be one of the two sweetest little girls he'd ever met. The other was, of course, her twin sister. Who had just been violently ill and was still looking far too pale for CJ's peace of mind.

One problem at a time.

Careful not to jostle the sick child in his arms, he moved Anna to his hip and smiled down at Sarah. "That's a nice offer, buttercup. Hold on to that a bit longer. We may need it for later. Right now, I'm going to take Anna outside and clean her up with soap and water."

"Oh, but..." Sarah's bottom lip jutted out and she looked to be on the verge of crying. "I want to help make my sister feel better."

Appreciating Sarah's intentions, and not wanting to suffer through another round of tears, he gave her head a gentle pat. "How about you go rustle up another night-gown for her to wear?"

The child's face instantly lit up. "I can do that."

As she raced for the bedroom, CJ headed out the front door.

He might not be angry, but the foul smell was starting to get to him. Eyes watering, he picked up his pace and made a beeline for the pump. Halfway there, Cookie met him with a bucket of water, a bar of soap and a handful of rags.

CJ gave the other man a cold-eyed stare. "I thought you deserted me."

The heavyset man ducked his head sheepishly. "Crossed my mind."

"You're here now, that's what counts."

Ten minutes later, CJ and Cookie had Anna cleaned up and dressed in a fresh nightgown. Color had returned to her cheeks and her crying had become an occasional sniffle. Relief threatened to buckle CJ's knees.

Against every instinct, he left Cookie in charge of the twins while he went back outside to take care of his own soiled clothing. A tick twitched in his jaw as he considered all the things that could go wrong in his absence.

Not much else he could do. He needed to get cleaned up before he could assess just how ill Anna really was. *Lord, please, let it be nothing serious.*

With another bout of panic nipping at him like little rat teeth, he made quick work of washing up and changing his clothes. He returned to the house, carrying a bucket of clean well water.

Cookie was alone in the main living area, righting the mess with the speed of a cyclone. Clearly, he couldn't wait to get gone. He'd already put away the toys and was now folding blankets with focused precision.

CJ took the bucket to the kitchen and ladled water into a small tin cup. "Where are the girls?" he asked over his shoulder.

Head down, Cookie paid an unnatural amount of attention to the blanket he was folding. "In their bedroom."

"All right, Cookie." CJ moved back into the room and studied the bent head. "Out with it."

The other man's hands paused midfold. "I didn't say anything."

"You're thinking so hard my ears are ringing."

"All right, fine." He looked up, hooked his gaze on a spot just over CJ's right shoulder. "I didn't believe the girl when she said she didn't feel well. I thought she was making it up to get out of bed."

Concealing his annoyance, CJ gave the other man the benefit of the doubt. They were all trying to find their way, after all, Cookie included. "When I walked out of this house an hour ago," he said, grasping for his nonexistent patience, "Anna and Sarah were tucked safely in their beds. What happened between then and now?"

"They got up."

Never let it be said Cookie was a man prone to rambling. "I'm going to need more explanation than that."

Sighing, the cook rubbed two fingers across his temple. "Sarah came out first, under the guise of being thirsty. Anna was two steps behind her with the same request. When they discovered you weren't here they wanted to know where you were and when you were coming back. Nothing I said made a difference."

"They were probably afraid I took off like Ned."

"That was my guess." Now that Cookie had begun, the story spilled out in a rush. "I assured them you were coming back, and put them in bed. I stayed in the doorway until they fell asleep. Two minutes later, they came out and wanted to know if you were home yet. I got them tucked in, *again*, and read a few pages from a book of nursery rhymes, and back to sleep they went. You can guess what happened next."

"They got out of bed a third time."

"That was when I pulled out the toy box and gave them dolls to sleep with. But the ones I picked out weren't good enough, and so round and round we went."

The frustration on the older man's face was almost comical, but CJ wasn't finding any of this amusing. "When did Anna get sick?"

"She started complaining that her head hurt sometime after my third attempt to get them asleep. Then her sister got involved, whereby I gave the little meddler a stern lecture about minding her own business, which she promptly ignored, and then took *me* to task, and then—" he blew out a tortured breath "—you came home."

After sorting through the jumbled tale, CJ had a moment of clarity. Fear that he'd abandoned her had been the cause of Anna's sickness. But just to be sure...

"You think Anna's stomachache was brought on because she was afraid I'd left like Ned?"

"The longer you were gone the more worked up she got."

CJ contained the relief that threatened to take him to his knees. He was inclined to remind Cookie he'd brought this on himself, but thought better of it. Having been through similar evenings with the girls, CJ knew what sort of strain his friend was under.

"I don't know how things got so out of hand." Collapsing in a chair, the grizzled old man leaned his head in his hands. "I kept telling myself, you can do this, Cookie. You can get two pint-size mites to stay in bed. How hard can it be?" He lifted his head, rubbed the back of his neck. "Near impossible, that's how hard."

"Thanks, Cookie." Feeling generous, even though the

old man had brought this on himself, CJ added, "I owe you one."

"Don't think I won't come collecting."

After showing the other man to the door, CJ took the cup of water into the girls' bedroom. Anna was tucked under the covers, looking bleary-eyed and exhausted, clinging to Sarah's favorite blanket.

Sarah sat on her sister's bed with an open book in her lap. She was only pretending to read, flipping the pages at random while she told the story from memory. It was such a sweet scene that CJ felt a little unsteady on his feet. He struggled to subdue the burst of love shooting through him. Parenting was not for the faint of heart.

His hand began to shake and some of the water in the cup sloshed over the rim. "How are my girls?"

Two sleepy-eyed children looked up at him.

"Better now that you're home," Sarah said, with mild accusation in her tone.

"How about you?" he asked Anna, moving to stand beside her. "How's your tummy feeling?"

"Okay, I guess."

"Let's see if you can drink some of this." He brought the cup to her lips.

She took a small sip, swallowed, then went for a longer one before leaning back against her pillow.

After several moments of anxiously waiting to see what would happen next, CJ let out his own sigh of relief. It seemed Anna's stomach was going to accept the liquid offering.

He tucked Sarah beneath the covers and, deciding they'd been through enough drama for one evening, sat in the rocking chair positioned between their beds. He picked up the book Sarah had left open and began reading.

Halfway through the first page the girls drifted off

to sleep. Seconds later, CJ managed to sneak out of the room without them waking. The moment he stepped into the next room he started thinking about the fear the girls must have experienced when they'd learned he wasn't on the ranch. It had been enough to make Anna physically ill.

Guilt warred with his own exhaustion. Guilt won.

He returned to the rocking chair in the twins' room. Unable to find a comfortable position, he retrieved a recently folded blanket and spread it out on the floor.

He woke up hours later to find Molly standing over him, looking as though she wasn't quite sure what to make of his sleeping arrangements. "Another difficult night?"

"Nah." Pushing himself to a sitting position, he rolled his shoulders, winced at the pain that shot down his spine. "Just testing out the floorboards for any structural flaws."

Molly had to press her lips tightly together to keep from laughing. Whatever had happened during the evening, CJ seemed to be taking the events in stride. He'd clearly camped out in the girls' room to keep them from being frightened. It was really quite sweet.

But, oh my, he looked decidedly worse for wear. "Come to any conclusions as a result of your overnight examination?"

"A decided lack of spring." He shook his head as if clearing out the last traces of sleep. "But otherwise quite sound."

She made a grand show of inspecting the floorboards. "Doesn't look very comfortable."

"You are not wrong."

He rose to his feet, turned to study the twins.

Molly drew alongside him. The girls slept soundly.

Whatever drama the Thorn family had endured, it had worn them out. "I say we let them sleep in this morning."

"Probably a good idea."

In silent agreement, they congregated in the kitchen for the rest of their conversation.

In the weak predawn light, CJ looked rumpled and tired, his eyes sleepy and a little dazed. His square jaw was dusted with fine black stubble and a lock of dark hair tumbled over his left eye.

Molly's heart switched places with her stomach. She wanted to stand there and simply look at him. Had she accepted his marriage proposal, this was the man she would meet every morning upon waking. They would share a kiss to start off the day, a kiss similar to the one he'd given her last night, light and tender and—

Bad place for her mind to travel.

She blinked, then blinked again, trying to bring her mind into focus. With considerable effort, she managed to draw herself a few inches away from him. "I'll make coffee."

"Best offer I've had all morning." He punctuated the statement with a dazzling smile.

Oh, my. Molly didn't know what to do with this softer, gentler, sleep-rumpled CJ. The kiss had changed things.

With a shaky exhalation, she murmured some sort of response and then busied her hands with the task of making coffee. The process felt entirely too domestic, made even more so when he engaged her in light conversation while she worked.

As they waited for the liquid to brew, she leaned against the counter and asked, "Want to tell me what happened?"

The story of Cookie's misadventures spilled out. With each new portion of the tale, CJ's eyes filled with amusement, the same expression Molly assumed was in her own. But then the story took on a new, more serious spin and she gasped.

"Oh, CJ, Anna actually threw up on you?"

"Her aim was quite impressive," he said with a rueful twist of his lips. "My clothing will probably have to be destroyed."

Molly tried to picture the scéne in her mind. "That had to have been…" She lifted her hands in a helpless gesture. There were simply no words.

The coffee finished brewing. Molly hurriedly poured him a cup and handed it over. "You definitely earned this."

For several seconds, he stared into the dark liquid, his brows furrowed. "I thought I was prepared to be a father. But now, when I think about all the stomachaches and tears that lie ahead, I have to wonder. Are the girls worse off with me?"

"You're doing a fine job." Molly glanced at the closed bedroom door. "The twins are in excellent hands."

She watched as he smiled, a small lift of his lips all the more powerful for its subtlety. Just as quickly as it came, the smile disappeared. "I'm not too proud to admit I feel overwhelmed most days. It's not as if I had parents who taught me how to guide a child into adulthood."

If only Molly could offer CJ some solace. He worked hard and did most everything right, and yet was not at peace with who he was at the core.

"I know a bit about your father," she said, treading carefully. "But I know very little of your mother. Will you tell me about her?"

He lowered his gaze. When he remained silent, Molly assumed he wouldn't answer her question. But then he lifted his head and said, "My mother became ill when I was ten years old. The sickness ate at her mind as much as her body."

Molly could see the sadness the memory caused him.

"I loved her desperately. We'd shared a special bond. She taught me how to read and to see the value in gaining knowledge from every source at my disposal, conventional or otherwise. She was an amazing, bright, intelligent woman. But then her mind went and she became a different person."

"I'm sorry."

He acknowledged the words with a sad tilt of his head. "Though she didn't die until years later, I lost my mother long before the day we buried her."

Molly couldn't imagine it. "That had to have been difficult."

"Devastating. I lost my father around the same time she became ill."

"I'm not following."

"That was when he took to drink. There I was, more boy than man, overwhelmed and lost. I was forced to grow up ahead of my time, not for myself, but for Ned." CJ shook his head. "Childhood departs quickly with that kind of responsibility."

"Oh, CJ." He deserved every ounce of happiness that came his way. "You are such a good man."

"How can you say that, after I just told you how badly I failed Ned?"

CJ's logic was off. Molly couldn't let him go another day thinking he was somehow less because of his tragic childhood.

"My father says it's not what we say or feel that shows our character. It's what we do." Molly moved to CJ, took his face in her hands. "Your actions tell me the kind of man you are."

He held her gaze. "And what kind is that?"

"The very definition of integrity."

Chapter Twelve

The morning of the Founder's Day celebration dawned bright and uncomfortably warm, promising a scorching day ahead. CJ had insisted Molly ride into town with her family. She'd reminded him what happened the last time he'd attempted to feed and dress the twins on his own. He'd held firm, but had agreed to meet her at the cottonwood tree closest to the revival tent.

Since their discussion about his mother there'd been no attempts at another kiss. And no more talk of his childhood challenges. Yet Molly felt a new closeness to CJ that went deeper than before. His life had not been easy, certainly nothing like her happy childhood. She couldn't help but feel sympathy for him, as well as a desire to give him the family he'd never had.

Looking forward to spending the day with him and the girls, regardless of the heartache that eventually lay ahead for her, Molly rode into town with her family as planned.

She took her usual seat next to Daisy. They'd finished preparing their picnic baskets for the auction earlier this morning and had ensured that neither the contents nor the decorations were too similar. Daisy had tossed in leftovers from the supper table. Molly had been more particular, including CJ's favorite foods.

All three of her brothers sat in the flatbed. They were looking forward to the various events, especially the baseball game that Pastor Stillwell had promised to organize later that afternoon. He'd first seen the game played in Austin during a church revival and had begun teaching the local children the rules.

Molly wasn't sure she understood all the nuances of the game, but she enjoyed watching. The crack of the bat was always an exciting sound.

Her father steered their wagon across land the color of pine and crumbling rock, then down Main Street. The town pulsed with the hum of laughter and voices in different octaves coming from all ages and genders. The sun drenched Little Horn in a dazzling burst of heat and light.

"I'm going to win the gunnysack race this year," Donny declared, his chest puffed out in little-boy confidence.

Roy scoffed at this with a loud snort. "Not if you have to compete against me, you won't."

"We'll see about that," Donny countered.

"You will lose." Roy seemed certain. "I plan to show no mercy."

"Now, boys." Helen Carson twisted in the seat to give each a look. "It doesn't matter who wins or loses as long as you have fun playing the games."

Molly's brothers stared at their mother, mouths agape, one of them saying, "But winning *is* fun."

"Yeah," her father agreed. "Winning is the best part of any competition."

And so began a rousing argument about how it felt to be the best of the best, which Donny had never experienced and Roy made sure to remind him of several times.

Sighing heavily, Molly's mother returned her attention to the front of the wagon and muttered, "I have raised heathens with no small amount of help from my husband."

Chuckling, John Carson pulled the wagon into an empty spot alongside the others, set the brake, then reached over and patted her hand in sympathy. "No, my dear, you've raised boys."

His wife's shoulders shook with laughter. "Well, that certainly needed clearing up."

Still amused, she pressed her forehead against her husband's and whispered something only he could hear. They exited the wagon laughing.

A gnawing ache twisted in Molly's stomach. Would she ever know that closeness with a man again?

Her brothers scrambled out of the wagon and rushed over to where their friends were already congregating in small clumps. Molly and Daisy set out to deliver their picnic baskets to Floyd Farmington, the man in charge of the auction. Per his stern instructions, they'd draped blankets over their baskets in order to keep their identities anonymous.

Calvin Barlow fell into step beside Daisy.

"That looks heavy." He reached for the covered basket in her arms. "Let me carry it for you."

"Go away, Calvin." She shoved him back with her shoulder.

He made another attempt. "I really don't mind helping."

"I'm perfectly capable of carrying a picnic basket all by myself."

Dodging around her, he attempted to lift the edge of the blanket.

She shifted the basket out of his reach. "No peeking."

"You're killing me, Daisy."

"You'll survive."

"How am I supposed know what basket to bid on if you don't give me a quick look?"

"You…" Daisy's steps faltered and her cheeks colored. "You truly plan to bid on mine?"

"That's what I just said."

Molly and the arguing teenagers arrived at the table where a stack of boxes, straw baskets and miniature hampers already took up most of the space.

"Give me a little peek," Calvin urged, eyes pleading. "Just one."

Showing no mercy, Daisy lifted her chin to a haughty angle. "You'll just have to figure it out on your own."

"Come on, Daisy," the boy wheedled. "I thought we were friends."

"Of course we're friends. What an odd thing to say."

"If you were really my friend you would give me a hint." He fiddled with the edge of the blanket. "Just one harmless, tiny little peek."

With her bottom lip caught between her teeth, Daisy looked over at Molly. Molly set down her basket, then glanced away, giving her sister a moment with her… *friend*.

The rustle of cotton sliding across straw was followed by Daisy's soft huff. "There. Satisfied?"

"You better believe it."

Molly turned back around to find Calvin grinning at Daisy as she set her basket, now uncovered, on the table.

He took Daisy's hand. "Let's go find out where they'll be running the three-legged race. My little brothers have been practicing all week and I don't mind saying they're terrible. I predict they'll cross the finish line last."

Daisy laughed. "*That* I've got to see."

The two wandered off, heads bent close, whispering and making plans for the rest of the morning.

Molly smiled after them, thinking how lovely they looked together, Daisy's blond locks contrasting with Calvin's dark hair, her frame so petite compared to his taller, leanly muscled build.

Wondering where their young affection would lead, and praying it was a good place, Molly went in search of CJ and the twins. She found them right where he'd said they would be. Unlike that Sunday morning a few weeks ago, he looked decidedly less anxious. Actually, he seemed quite relaxed, happy even, as if he were settling into his new role as their father.

Her heart lifted and she sighed.

Did CJ know how decent he was, down to the core? Did he know how worthy he was of admiration?

He caught sight of her before the girls did. A slow grin spread across his face, reminding Molly of the time he'd pressed those full lips to hers. He'd been so tender, issuing a silent promise meant only for her.

Hands shaking slightly, she closed the distance and greeted him first, the girls next.

"You look very pretty, Sarah," she said, eyeing the blue ribbon in the child's hair. Fully aware of the significance of the color change, Molly touched the bow. "Did you tie this all by yourself?"

Sarah shook her head. "Unca Corny helped, but I picked it out all by myself because blue is his favorite color."

"How lovely." Molly looked up at CJ and found him watching his niece, a look of love and gratification in his eyes.

Brandon Stillwater called everyone into the tent normally used for Sunday church services and gave a short speech to launch the day's festivities. "Two years ago Little Horn officially incorporated and today we come together in celebration."

He continued, expanding on the history of their small community and the value of sticking together through good times and bad.

"We have a fun day planned. There will be games, booths selling all sorts of goodies and wares, a pie-eating contest and a picnic basket auction. We'll finish the day with a baseball game and square dancing, called by our very own Mr. Harold Hickey. Before we get started, let us pray.

"Bless us, O Lord," he began. "And keep Your hand upon us. Thank You for the joy of coming together and celebrating the founding of our town. As we go forward into the future, we ask that You teach us to love one another as You first loved us. May we always serve You with cheerful hearts. We ask these things in Your Son's name. Amen."

He lifted his head, smiled and then dismissed the townsfolk. "Have a wonderful day."

The people scattered.

"What are we going to do first?" Sarah asked before her sister could.

With everyone in agreement, Molly, CJ and the twins made their way to the large open field where the games were to be played.

The gunnysack races were already under way. Because of the large number of participants the organizers had to run several smaller races first. The winners of each would then compete for the ultimate prize, a big blue ribbon and a cake made by Mercy Green.

Ropes had been strung along each side of the field in an effort to keep the spectators from disrupting the action. Molly and the Thorn family found a spot on the west side and waited for the next race to begin.

"They look silly." Anna pointed to the starting line, where participants were stepping into large burlap sacks and pulling them up. Due to their varying heights some were able to tug the bag up past their waist, others barely to midthigh.

"My brother Thomas is in this race," Molly said, pointing to the line of competitors. "He's in the blue shirt."

The race began.

Cheers rose up from the crowd. Anna and Sarah shouted Thomas's name. "Go, Thomas. Go, go, go!"

And they cheered when he won.

The four of them watched three more races. Then, losing interest, the girls began playfully grabbing and poking at each other. Molly shared a look with CJ.

"Maybe it's time for another activity," she suggested.

"How about a snack? I hear Mercy Green is selling cookies, cake and ice cream."

The twins thought this a wonderful idea. At the booth, CJ treated them each to a dish of ice cream. Molly chose an oatmeal cookie.

They watched the three-legged races next. Ate more ice cream. Then, to Molly's amusement, the girls talked CJ into entering the pie-eating contest.

Taking note of his uneasy expression as he sat at the long, wide table, she asked, "Are you sure you want to do this?"

"Why wouldn't I? It's a pie-eating contest."

Knowing the girls had practically begged him to take part, Molly raised a disbelieving eyebrow.

"Cherry." He pointed to the pie at his elbow. "My favorite."

"Oh. Well, then." She raised her hands in surrender. "Eat to your heart's content."

He gave it a grand effort. Molly and the twins laughed and cheered and clapped in encouragement. He managed to consume four entire pies before time was called. The judges reviewed the empty pie tins and CJ was declared the winner by half a pie.

The twins cheered even louder.

His face white as a sheet, eyes slightly bulging, CJ shoved away from the table and got shakily to his feet. Breathing through clenched teeth, he graciously accepted congratulatory backslaps from his fellow contestants.

When he joined Molly and the girls, he presented his reward with a grimace. "A cherry pie." He handed the prize to a passing kid.

"Gee, thanks, mister."

CJ waved off the excited boy.

"You did good, Unca Corny." The girls bounced around him, giggling and tugging on his arms.

If possible, his face turned even whiter.

Although it took considerable effort to contain her amusement, Molly felt a glimmer of sympathy for the poor man. "That was a lot of pie you just ate."

Pure misery played across his face. "Now that's an understatement if I ever heard one."

Several more people came over and congratulated CJ, including Pastor Stillwell, who'd come in second place. He had a pale green tint to his skin similar to CJ's sickly pallor.

"Congratulations, CJ. The best man won."

"Thanks." He grimaced. "I think."

The two men shook hands and shared a moment of commiseration. CJ's color had yet to be restored. He looked as if he could use time away from the festivities.

"Girls, what do you say we take a look at our quilt? It's on display over by the booth selling hair ribbons and bows." She took their hands, glanced over at CJ. "We'll leave you to let your pie settle."

"That might not be a bad idea." He patted his stomach, let out a soft whoosh of air.

Molly swallowed the laughter bubbling inside and, because the poor man looked genuinely unwell, directed the twins toward the row of temporary booths.

Only after they were out of CJ's hearing did she give in to the amusement.

"What's so funny, Miss Molly?"

"I'm just happy," she told Anna. "So very, very happy."

For the rest of the day, she promised herself, nothing would be allowed to ruin her good mood.

Still feeling slightly nauseous, CJ tried not to moan. He could go an entire week without eating and would still feel full. Yet even in his miserable state, he found himself debating the possibility of bidding on Molly's picnic basket.

Aside from his complete disinterest in food right now, there were countless other reasons he shouldn't. Most notably, she'd turned down his marriage proposal. A wise man would take her at her word and cut his losses.

A smart man would turn his sights toward another woman. The sooner CJ created a stable, loving home for the girls the better. It all started with a wife. Today was the perfect day to begin his search.

Problem was, he didn't want to find another woman. He wanted Molly and he wasn't ready to give up without a fight. His jaw tightened every time he thought of her and the twins sharing the afternoon with another man.

They were *his* family.

Needing to work off the pie, he roamed around the general area and paused at the one-room schoolhouse. The building had its beginnings in 1893, mere days after Little Horn was incorporated. Bo Stillwater, the pastor's brother and a highly successful rancher and landowner, leased the plot of land to the town for a pittance.

In a few years, the twins would be students at this school, an important milestone in their lives that Ned would miss if he didn't come home. Completing his pass around the building, CJ noticed Molly fifty yards away, speaking with Lula May Barlow. The twins sat on a blanket nearby, playing some sort of game with Lula May's daughter.

Molly looked fresh and lovely in a soft green dress that highlighted her blond hair and fair coloring.

Their gazes met across the schoolyard. Even from this distance, and not actually being able to see her eyes, he knew they'd turned a warm blue under his quiet scrutiny. He lifted his hand.

She did the same.

The moment was so unaffected and honest it brought forth a surge of joy. CJ had never felt this connected to anyone before Molly had come into his life. He'd missed out the first time around. He'd been given a second chance. A blessing he would not squander.

Lula May said something that gained Molly's attention. No longer ensnared, CJ exhaled slowly. Needing to clear his head, he scanned the horizon, where the distant hills met the sky. The day was clear and he could see all the way to the rooftop of Lucas Bennett's ranch house in the east.

To the north lay the main outbuildings of the Carson ranch. There weren't many white barns in this part of Texas, but the Carsons had one.

Someone jostled him from behind and the contents of CJ's stomach threatened to make an appearance. Out of self-preservation, he moved away from the main traffic areas and propped his shoulder against a tree.

Edmund McKay and Hank Snowden sauntered over, both grinning over his discomfort. They sported the Texas ranchers' unofficial uniform of button-down shirt, denim pants and scuffed boots.

Hank was the foreman on Lucas Bennett's ranch, the Windy Diamond, and was one of CJ's few friends besides Edmund. CJ and Hank were nearly the same height and build. They both had dark hair, but where CJ's eyes were brown, Hank's were a startling blue.

From what little CJ gleaned, Hank was an indispensable member of Lucas Bennett's cattle operation.

Laughing softly, Edmund whistled low and with meaning. "You, my friend, are clearly paying the price for winning that pie-eating contest."

CJ turned his head, a quelling comment at the ready, but the simple movement caused his stomach to roil in protest. He swallowed, managed a halfhearted grimace, which earned him another chuckle.

"You bidding on a basket?" Edmund asked him.

"Still debating." He drew in a slow, steady breath. "Not much interested in food right now. What about you?"

"Gotta eat, don't I?"

"Got any particular woman in mind you want to do that eating with?" CJ asked.

His friend lifted a nonchalant shoulder, dropped it. "Doesn't much matter. Long as she can cook."

"I hear Lula May Barlow made a basket." Hank offered up this information oh so innocently.

CJ tried not to laugh at the horror-stricken expression on Edmund's face. Just picturing him and Lula May picnicking together was beyond amusing. The two had a prickly relationship on a good day, adversarial all the others.

If Edmund won Lula May's basket, they would probably argue their way through the entire lunch and both end up sick to their stomachs.

"After Mercy Green, I hear Frank Barlow's widow is the best cook in the area." Hank added this piece of information with an elbow jab to Edmund's ribs. "And there's no denying she's a pretty woman."

"That may be true," he agreed reluctantly, stuffing his hands in his pockets and rocking back on his heels. "But she's also the bossiest. In a word, no thank you."

"That's three words," Hank pointed out.

"You get my meaning."

His only response was a smirk.

Nancy Bennett, the wife of Hank's boss, moved in their direction and called out softly to Hank.

The cowboy responded with a lift of his chin.

CJ didn't know the young woman very well. She'd been in the area only a year. She smiled tentatively as she wove her way through the tangle of humanity.

"Good afternoon, gentlemen." Her demeanor was perfectly polite, but on closer inspection CJ could tell she was slightly uncomfortable. She didn't quite make eye contact with any of them. Most notably Hank, which made little sense. She must know him pretty well, since he worked on her husband's ranch.

"Good day, Mrs. Bennett," Hank said, before CJ or Edmund could speak. "What can we do for you?"

Her jaw went taut. After a long hesitation, and an encouraging smile from Hank, she seemed to relax. "I'm selling chances to win a quilt my friends and I recently made."

CJ's ears perked up. "Are you part of Molly's quilting bee?"

"That's right." She spoke in a soft, almost musical lilt. "We worked hard to finish in time. It's a very lovely blanket, quite decorative in fact."

"What would I want with a decorative blanket?" Edmund asked, his face showing genuine bafflement.

Nancy blushed furiously. "Oh, well, I do see your point. It's just..." She hesitated. "The proceeds will be donated to the fund for a new church building and—"

"I'll take three," Hank said, cutting off the rest of her stilted speech.

"Oh, why, thank you, Mr. Snowden." Head down, she wrote his name on three slips of paper, then handed them to him. "You'll want to put these in the box next to the quilt. The drawing will be held later this afternoon."

CJ felt obliged to buy three chances, as well, though he was inclined to agree with Edmund. He had no use for a decorative quilt. Although now that he thought about it, he remembered that the twins had done a portion of the sewing. "I'll take three more."

Nancy Bennett's face lit from within. "Oh, lovely."

"I'll take another six," Hank offered, giving Edmund's foot a hard nudge with the toe of his boot.

"Fine. I'll buy three chances."

Hank nudged his foot again.

"All right, all right, I'll take six."

Hank seemed determined to help Mrs. Bennett with her sales. CJ supposed that made sense. The woman's husband had taken a chance, hiring him when no one else in the community trusted the drifter. It had turned out well for both men. Hank had a good job and Lucas had a competent foreman who practically ran his ranch for him.

Speaking of Lucas, where was he? CJ hadn't seen the other rancher all morning.

Before he could ask Mrs. Bennett about her husband, she completed yet another transaction with Hank and then wandered off to the next group. Left in her wake, CJ and Edmund were each in the possession of six chances to win a quilt neither needed, and Hank was the proud owner of fifteen.

With the foreman leading the way, they sauntered over to the booth where the quilt was hanging on display. The three men studied the colorful geometric pattern.

"What are you gonna do if you win this *decorative* quilt, Snowden?" Edmund angled his head toward the item in question. "You live in a bunkhouse."

It was Hank's turn to lift a nonchalant shoulder. "I'll figure something out."

As Edmund continued to rib him, a pack of local boys ran past. CJ counted five, their ages ranging somewhere between nine and fifteen. Two belonged to James Forester, the widowed blacksmith. Forester's wife had died eight months ago in childbirth along with the baby.

CJ remembered the funeral as a somber, dour affair. James had been stone-faced and silent. The boys had bravely tried not to cry. Before his wife died, the big, burly man had been full of humor and the first to crack a smile at any gathering. These days, he never laughed, and worked every waking hour in the smithy.

James was a good man, and his sons, Brody and Butch, were decent kids. But with their mother dead and their father buried in work, they'd become a bit wild, more so now that they were running with the Gillen brothers.

Those three had no father and a mother who'd given up on life the day her husband ran off, years ago. *Just like Ned.* Mary Gillen hadn't endured the abandonment well.

She looked decades older than her thirty-some years. She had a wrinkled, weather-beaten face and a thin, rickety build much like the bridge that led to her shack down by Kettle Creek.

No one seemed to be supervising the pack of boys. Sean Gillen was the oldest and likely the leader. His brothers were only a few years younger. With their filthy clothes, matted hair and half-tamed natures they were walking, talking trouble. In the past three months, CJ had broken up more than one fight the Gillen brothers had instigated.

It looked as if he would be doing so again this morning, when Sean shoved the smaller Forester boy a bit too hard. His older brother raised his clenched fists.

"Edmund, Hank, we've got trouble."

Chapter Thirteen

Moving at a clipped pace, CJ took off in the direction of the fight. Edmund and Hank followed hard on his heels.

"Leave this to me," CJ said over his shoulder. "The Gillen boys tend to fight dirty."

Edmund gained on him, coming up on his left. "I've broken up a few of their brawls myself. With the two of us stepping in, we have a better chance of avoiding bloodshed."

"If that's the case," Hank said, pulling up on CJ's other side, "then three hands are better than two."

They were almost at their target when Sheriff Jeb Fuller fell into step beside Edmund. "Someone needs to take those boys in hand," he grumbled.

CJ agreed. A long-term plan was needed, one that would keep the boys out of trouble and maybe even provide some direction. But now wasn't the time to work out a strategy. Sean said something low and menacing to Butch Forester, and then, as was usually the case, threw the first punch.

CJ broke into a run.

One of Sean's brothers knocked Butch to the ground. The other sent Brody down with him. The three Gillen boys got in a few good kicks. Then, seemingly unsatisfied with the results, they jumped on top to issue a series of punches.

Closing the distance at last, CJ grabbed the nearest Gillen by the waistband and yanked him free of the pile of tangled arms and legs. Jeb and Hank took hold of the other two and did the same.

Edmund took control of the small crowd that had begun to gather. "Move along," he told them, arms outstretched as if to create a physical barrier between them and the fight. "Nothing to see here."

People pressed in closer.

Only when the sheriff issued the same order did the crowd slowly dissipate.

Sean attempted to break free of CJ's hold. Having none of it, he spun the kid around to face him. "What were you thinking, starting a brawl in the middle of a family event?"

He got nothing but closed-lip, stony silence in response.

"Fighting is no way to solve a problem," he added.

"There weren't no problem, we were just having fun."

"You've got an unusual definition of fun."

"We were bored." Sean lowered his head, scuffed his shoe on the ground. "There's nothing to do in this stupid town."

The other boys agreed vehemently, including the two Forester brothers, who were getting slowly to their feet.

Edmund and CJ exchanged a look. "We have potato sack races and three-legged races and—"

"Those games are for babies." Sean spat out the last word as if tasting something foul.

"Yeah, babies," his brothers echoed.

Jeb entered the discussion, looking every bit the sheriff

of their town. "You don't want to engage in the organized activities? That's up to you." His tone was hard and unbending, a bold reminder that he represented the law in Little Horn. "We'll take you back to your folks and you can sit out the festivities at home."

Sean's expression turned horrified. "There's even less to do there."

"Then I'd suggest you behave yourselves and stay out of trouble. This is your one and only warning." Jeb nodded to CJ and Hank, a silent signal to release the boys. "If I hear of another brawl, or even get a whiff of another fight, you'll spend the rest of the day cleaning out my jail cells."

The threat seemed to hit home, because all five boys snapped their mouths shut and threw their shoulders back.

They started to leave, but Jeb wasn't through with them. "Now shake hands and say you're sorry."

They did as they were told, then scurried off once Jeb issued the go-ahead. As Jeb sauntered away to find his new mail-order bride and her little brother, CJ watched the boys run away, thinking of his own childhood, the fears and insecurities that came from an unstable home life.

He might not have gone around the community engaging in fistfights, but he felt a connection with the troubled youth. All five were at a precarious age, poised on the threshold of manhood, where decisions mattered. A few missteps could be forgiven. If they made too many mistakes, they could be lost forever. Surely something could be done to steer them in the right direction.

Erasing their boredom was the key. Giving them something to do, something important that would teach them lifelong skills, would be the best route of all. CJ had an idea, a program that would benefit the boys and the local ranchers, but he wanted to ponder the scheme before presenting it to the others.

Out of the corner of his eye he noticed that Molly and the girls were heading back in his direction. They were all smiles and sunshine, giving him something far more pleasant to think about than what to do with a pack of town ruffians.

For the second time that morning, Brandon Stillwater took to the stage beneath the tent and called everyone over. The main festivities began in earnest. A couple girls recited bad poetry. A family of seven sang a song.

At last, Floyd Farmington took his place beside the preacher and the picnic basket auction began.

An assortment of straw hampers and pretty boxes were set on a table next to the stage. No identifying markers or labels were apparent.

CJ felt a tiny tap, tap, tap on his arm. He looked down into Anna's wide eyes. She crooked her little finger, indicating he bend closer, then cupped her hand around his ear. "I put a ribbon on Miss Molly's basket just like she said I could."

"Remember," he said in a soft tone, "no cheating. You promised."

Registering the scold, she lifted her little chin in defiance. "I didn't tell you what color the ribbon was."

CJ considered the child's cheeky argument just as Floyd Farmington picked up a basket from the table and took the stage.

"Who wants to start the bidding?" Floyd raised the item in his hand. Since there was a large red bow tied around the handle, CJ knew it didn't belong to Molly. Anna and Sarah owned only pink, purple and blue ribbons.

So much for no cheating.

"We've got us some tasty looking cold chicken—" Floyd rummaged around in the basket "—an apple, johnnycakes and half a dozen cookies." He closed the lid. "Let's get down to business."

A hand shot up from the back of the crowd. "Two pennies."

"I have two pennies, do I hear three?"

"Three," came the response from somewhere on CJ's left.

Floyd, clearly in his element, enticed the crowd to continue bidding. "Now, you already know this basket is filled with tasty goodies. I also happen to know this lunch was prepared by the prettiest lady in all of Little Horn, Texas."

"One nickel." The bid came from Clyde Parker, a crusty rancher in his forties long set in his ways. He was short and stocky, overly gruff, but also kind when it suited him. It was no secret he wanted a wife.

"Sold," Floyd declared when no other bids were forthcoming. "To Mr. Parker for a nickel."

The crowd applauded when Mercy Green claimed ownership of the basket.

The process continued similarly for three more baskets. There was a memorable moment when Calvin Barlow got into a minor bidding war with Harvey Tucker. Calvin eventually won. He let out a hoot, rushed over to Daisy Carson, picked her up off the ground and spun her in dizzying circles.

"Well," Floyd said, blinking at the boy's exuberance. "I see I won't have to reveal the owner of this particular basket."

That got a laugh from the crowd.

When Floyd picked up the next basket, Anna poked CJ in the arm. "There's my ribbon," she said in a whisper loud enough to be heard three counties over. "Right there on Miss Molly's basket."

Sure enough, CJ recognized the child's favorite pink hair bow. He was going to have to explain the definition of "no cheating" later that night.

Even if Anna hadn't given the secret away, Floyd's description of the contents would have been enough of a clue. Molly had included all of CJ's favorite foods.

He glanced over at her, but she didn't return his look. She was too busy studying the toes of her shoes.

The bidding began at two pennies, from Pastor Stillwater, who glanced over at Molly and smiled. Apparently, he'd heard Anna. Bo Stillwater, doubled his twin's bid. He, too, smiled at Molly.

CJ ground his teeth together. The Stillwater brothers were good men, but neither was worthy of Molly.

No one was worthy of her.

The bidding went back and forth, each offer punctuated with rousing cheers and encouragement from the crowd. The more the two brothers fought for the honor of eating a picnic with Molly, the more unsettled CJ became. He could hardly stand the idea of either man winning the chance to eat lunch with her and the twins.

"Ten cents from our illustrious pastor, going once, going twice…"

Bo raised his hand. "Three nickels."

Trying to figure out Bo's angle, CJ blinked at the other man. Was he interested in courting Molly?

"Three nickels," Floyd repeated. "We have a bid for fifteen cents. Going once…" He paused, stared at Brandon. "Going twice." A longer pause. "Going three times…"

CJ opened his mouth. "Sixte—"

"*Sold*," Floyd yelled out, "to Mr. Bo Stillwater for three nickels."

Blood roared in CJ's ears. He'd missed his chance. He'd waited too long to step into the bidding war.

Anna glared at him. Sarah shook her head in disappointment. He couldn't blame either of their reactions. He, too, was disgusted with himself.

Two more baskets were auctioned off and all CJ could think was that he'd made his move a fraction of a second too late. Now he would have to watch Molly share her food—and her pretty smiles—with Bo Stillwater.

CJ's stomach rolled inside itself, a sickening sensation not unlike what he'd experienced after the pie-eating contest.

The auction ended. The drawing for the quilt came next. It was no surprise that Hank won. Other prizes were awarded, including a certificate for lunch from Mercy's Café, a bag of oats from the Feed Mill, a free one-day rental from the livery and a block of cattle salt from the mercantile.

And then it was time for lunch.

One by one, the picnic basket winners went in search of an empty spot somewhere to enjoy their spoils. Molly hung back, glancing nervously at CJ. The twins stared up at him, too.

CJ liked Bo well enough, but he didn't want his girls— all *three* of them—to have lunch with the man. The very thought burned a hole in his gut.

"Unca Corny? Are you okay?"

He cleared his expression and smiled down at Sarah. "Sure am."

"You don't look so good," she countered.

"Still full from the pie-eating contest." He patted his stomach. "Think I'll find a quiet spot and rest my eyes a bit."

Molly moved into his line of vision. "CJ, if you're not feeling well we can—"

"I'm good. Go enjoy your picnic."

Bo appeared at Molly's side, ending the discussion.

"Mrs. Langley." The rancher swept off his hat and gave her a ridiculously formal bow. CJ was pretty sure the man had practiced the move. "I'm looking forward to our lunch together. I hear your chocolate cake is the best in town."

"The best?" She laughed this off, her cheeks turning bright red. "I don't know about that."

The girls swarmed around Bo. He gave them his full attention, which seemed to make the two very happy, but only managed to increase the rolling in CJ's stomach.

Sarah, evidently deciding she liked Bo—*a lot*—told him, "Miss Molly said my sister and me can eat with you."

"Did she now?" Bo tugged on the little girl's pigtail. "Can't think of anything I'd like better."

The rancher sounded sincere. CJ tucked his hands in his pockets, attempting a casual stance. He'd made a huge mistake not bidding on Molly's basket. Now, he couldn't do a thing about his blunder except stand back and watch *his family* enjoy another man's company.

"I'll run get the basket," Molly offered, showing one of her prettiest smiles. "Then we can find a nice shady spot to enjoy our lunch."

"We'll come with you," Sarah announced, grabbing her sister's hand and skipping after Molly.

Maintaining his relaxed pose, CJ scowled after the trio.

"The twins are sweet," Bo said.

"They are." There was nothing more to say.

Molly picked up her basket. She said something to Anna, then Sarah, and all three laughed. They looked

right together, comfortable, as if they were a family. CJ
scowled. They could be a family, *his* family, if a certain
stubborn woman would have accepted his marriage proposal.

"You okay with this, CJ?"

No. "Of course."

He had no claim on Molly. Yet.

"You sure about that?" Bo angled his head, considered
Molly with a touch too much masculine appreciation for
CJ's liking. "She's a beautiful woman."

Enough.

"Don't get any ideas, Bo." CJ's shoulders shifted and
flexed. "Molly's still in love with her deceased husband."

"That a fact? And you know this because…?"

"She told me."

"That must have been an uncomfortable conversation
for both of you."

"You have no idea," CJ muttered.

Molly and the girls moved back within earshot, spar-
ing him from further conversation.

"You ready, Mr. Stillwater?"

"Indeed, I am." He grinned at CJ, said, "Good talk,"
then reached out and took the basket from Molly.

The girls bounced around the tall rancher, asking him
all sorts of questions. CJ had to give the man credit. He
answered each one, no matter how personal, with patience and entirely too much charm. CJ hadn't realized
how slick Bo Stillwater was until today.

The four left the cover of the tent, looking entirely too
much like a family. CJ ground his teeth together so hard
it was a wonder his back molars didn't disintegrate into
dust. That nagging thought came back to gnaw at him.

Should have bid on Molly's basket.

* * *

Feeling surlier by the minute, CJ leaned up against the tree at his back. Did Molly and the girls have to look quite so happy in Bo's company?

CJ observed the scene for several long, painful minutes, his heart heavy in his chest. He wasn't usually prone to brooding. Yet here he stood, propping up the tree with his shoulder and *brooding*.

Edmund, having failed as well to bid on a basket, adopted a similar pose. "You're frowning, my friend."

No doubt he was.

"Want to tell me what has you upset?"

"No."

"Didn't think so." Edmund laughed, then changed the subject. "More cattle have gone missing."

CJ tensed. "What ranch was hit this time?"

"Clyde Parker's. He left town as soon as he heard."

Still contemplating this new turn of events, and thinking the problem wasn't going to go away simply by mending weaknesses in fence lines, CJ stared at his friend. "We're going to have to come up with an actual plan to catch the rustlers."

"My thoughts exactly." Edmund shifted his stance. "Jeb Fuller is only one man. He can't hunt them down on his own."

"He'll need help," CJ agreed. The question was what sort of help, and how much organization would it require?

Running the dilemma around in his mind, CJ scanned the area immediately to the left of the revival tent. His gaze landed on various couples picnicking. Unable to stop himself, he glanced at Molly with Bo and the girls.

A growl started low in his throat.

"If you wanted to spend time with the woman," Edmund commented, his voice amused, "you should have bid on her basket."

"Tell me something I don't know."

"Have you noticed how Mrs. Langley keeps looking over at you every other minute?"

Actually, he had noticed. "Your point?"

"She likes you."

"Fat lot of good it does me," CJ muttered.

Edmund cupped a hand behind his ear. "What's that?"

"Didn't say anything."

"Right." He laughed. "My mistake."

They stood in silence for several minutes.

"It's been a good day." Edmund pushed his hat back and scrutinized the crowd. "I declare Little Horn's second Founder's Day celebration a success."

CJ bobbed his head. There was a lot of laughter. A lot of eating. Some good old-fashioned courting going on, as well, and, glimpsing Molly laughing with Bo, CJ found his mood plummeting. There was a little too much courting going on for his liking.

He moved his gaze to the north. Sunlight danced off the granite and rolling hills. The sky was a hard, crisp blue unmarred by a single cloud. Except…

There, in the distance, one black smudge spiraled up into the brilliant, cloudless sky, a shocking stain on the otherwise pristine blue. At first glance, CJ thought the unusual looking plume was a thundercloud, and he nearly said, "Rain's coming." But there was something not quite right about the coiling black funnel.

His heart began to thud and every muscle in his body jerked. He shoved himself away from the tree, took an involuntary step forward.

The cloud spiraled upward, dense and black. Not a tornado, but something else, something just as menacing.

"You see that?" he asked, pointing to the northern horizon.

Shock jumped in Edmund's eyes. "*Smoke*."

From a large fire, CJ judged, given the size and height of the black cloud. His heart clutched in his chest as he battled for control.

Little Horn didn't have a fire department. They'd recently purchased a fire engine, which was housed at the livery. Only a handful of men knew how to work it, CJ one of them. Edmund another.

"I can't pinpoint the source." Edmund narrowed his eyes.

"It's coming from the Carson ranch."

"I'll alert John." Edmund was already on the move. "Then take care of getting the fire engine out to his place."

"I'll gather as many men as I can and meet you out there." After he asked Molly to keep an eye on the twins.

The friends separated, moving quickly across the open field.

Keeping his voice calm, CJ asked Bo for a quick moment of his time. As though sensing trouble, the other man hopped to his feet and moved away from the blanket.

"What's happened?" He'd lowered his voice to keep his words from drifting back to Molly and the girls.

With cold precision, CJ told the rancher to look to the north. Bo's stance went instantly rigid.

"Fire," the man snarled. "Looks like it's coming from—" he squinted "—the Carson ranch."

"Edmund is alerting John Carson as we speak."

"What do you need from me?" Bo asked.

"Gather every willing and able-bodied man you can muster, then meet at the edge of town."

"You got it." Bo muttered a hasty goodbye to Molly and the girls, then left without another word.

Eyes wide, Molly gathered the girls in close and stared up at CJ in silence. A dozen questions swam in her gaze. She voiced none of them. Appreciating her calm, he asked her to watch the girls for the rest of the afternoon.

She sucked in a tight breath, glanced down at the twins, then back up at CJ. "Is everything all right?"

Since it was her family's home under siege, she deserved the truth. "There's a problem on your parents' ranch."

Her head reflexively whipped to the north. Her gaze fastened on the spiraling smoke. "Oh, no."

Her voice held considerable alarm. To her credit, she contained her terror. The only sign of her fear showed in her pinched expression. But then she lifted her chin and promised to keep the girls with her.

Word of the fire spread. Chaos would have ensued had Bo Stillwater not taken charge. He organized people into groups, dispatching half of them to gather buckets and various other supplies they would need to fight the fire, then sent others to find ways to transport the items out to the Rolling Hills ranch.

Confident the rancher, a natural leader, had the situation in hand, CJ headed out to the Carson ranch with well over a dozen sturdy, capable men. Even though they pushed their horses hard, it took them another ten minutes to make the trip from Little Horn.

The noise hit him first, an earsplitting sound that sent a thick blanket of tension over the riders.

Dread immediately pounced, digging deeper when CJ saw the source of the deafening noise. The far right corner of the big white barn was on fire. Thick, menacing flames stabbed toward the sky in vicious red-and-gold columns.

Some of the larger flames curled backward, licking at the wooden structure with greedy tongues.

Smoke rolled, pluming upward, rising, rising. It stung CJ's lungs, the stench seared his nose, and the whirling dance of flames burned his eyes. Ash floated in the sky like dingy snowflakes.

The fire was burning too hot, too fast.

John Carson and his sons rode up on the fire engine with the blacksmith and livery owner. Edmund and the sheriff followed on their horses. John Carson's expression was filled with bewilderment. And fury.

CJ pulled his horse to a halt and reached for a calm he didn't feel. The heat already touched his face and hands. He could hear the screams of frightened horses from the main corral.

"Get those animals out of the pens or they'll kick one another to death," John Carson told his sons.

The boys, with the help of several others, went to release the animals.

CJ strode to the fire engine and Molly's father, and shouted over the roaring flames, "What's inside the barn?"

"Hay, oats, cereals, tack. And—" Carson's face went deadly white "—horses."

A wild, high-pitched animal scream followed the grim comment.

Jaws tight, the two men took off toward the barn, their footsteps pelting the ground. The heat was oppressive, intensified by the mid-June sun beating down from the sky.

CJ sucked rancid air into his lungs and reached for the barn doors with his gloved hands. "We'll rescue as many as possible."

Heads down, they got to work saving the animals.

Chapter Fourteen

Molly arrived at her parents' ranch to the roar of fire, the screams of panicked animals and the shouting of men. Her father and CJ seemed to be in charge, issuing orders, organizing manpower and working side by side. Their calm in the midst of chaos created a well-oiled firefighting machine.

Edmund McKay was in control of the animals. He and Hank Snowden, along with Molly's brothers and the Carson ranch hands, led wild-eyed, panicky horses away from the fire toward an open field. As each animal ran off, screaming in terror, Molly wondered how many would return and how many would never come home again.

The barn was under siege, nearly half of it engulfed in flames. Tears and smoke burned her eyes. Oddly drawn to the blistering sight, she stepped forward.

Her mother caught her wrist. "We have to stay together," she murmured, hooking an arm around Molly's waist, "and try to keep out of the way."

Daisy and Lula May stood nearby, each holding one of the twins' hands. Anna and Sarah were silent, their eyes wide and frightened.

No longer willing to be held by the other women, the girls moved closer to Molly. Wanting to ease their fear, she slipped away from her mother and reached out to them. They immediately came to her and clutched their tiny fingers around hers.

"Make it stop," Sarah whispered. "Please, Miss Molly, make it stop."

She sighed, pulled the child against her. "The men are doing everything they can."

She shouldn't have brought the girls to the ranch; she knew that now. At the time, she hadn't realized the fire would be so out of control.

None of them had known.

With a shaky hand pressed to her heart, Helen Carson blinked tear-filled eyes. "This is terrible."

Cast in the light of the fire, her mother's face was red and splotchy. Lines that hadn't been there this morning were now etched around her eyes and mouth.

Molly gave her a sympathetic grimace.

The barn was already half consumed in flames and smoke. Molly wanted to weep right along with her mother. Something built by her family, something that had been standing her entire life, was crumbling right before her eyes.

The majority of the flames had yet to be extinguished. If the wind shifted it could carry sparks to the main house. The thought horrified Molly. The idea of her childhood home burning was far worse than the fire itself.

From a safe distance, she focused on the men fighting to save her home—CJ, her father, Edmund McKay, Hank Snowden and so many others. Each of them tall, well-built and muscular, so capable that her fears lessened. A bit.

CJ was in the midst of it all, barking orders, manning the pump on the fire engine. Something squeezed in

Molly's heart when she noted the backdrop of the smoke and flames behind him. He could be hurt.

She stuffed down her panic with a hard swallow and lifted up a prayer for all the men's safety. So many had come to fight the fire on her family's behalf, working together to save the Carson home.

Women had come, too. Lula May took charge of them, putting most to work in the kitchen. She even attempted to coax Molly's mother to join the efforts inside the house.

"The men will need to be fed," Lula May reasoned.

Helen Carson balked at this, agreeing only after Daisy, Molly and the twins promised to go inside with her.

As they made their way toward the house, CJ called out to Molly and trotted over. His face was blackened with soot. His eyes were already bloodshot, made worse by his constant blinking.

"We're going to be at this a long time," he said, rubbing his dirty hands over his equally dirty face. "Probably all night."

Molly touched his filthy sleeve. "What can I do to help?"

"Take the children home. I've asked Hank Snowden to escort you."

"No, Unca Corny." Sarah wrapped her arms around his waist and clung. "Don't send us away."

"I need you to go home. Where it's safe." He pried the child's hands away, then crouched until his red-rimmed eyes were level with hers. "It's already been a long day and—"

Both girls started crying.

CJ gave Molly a helpless look. She was torn. She wanted the girls far away from the danger, but she couldn't bear not being at the ranch. What if she left and something terrible happened in her absence? What if her father was injured, or her brothers, or...or CJ?

As if experiencing a similar fear, both girls catapulted themselves at him. "Please don't send us away," Anna whispered.

Frustration showed on his face as he pried them gently away from him. He attempted to use reason, with no success.

"I'll get them inside the house and keep them out of harm's way," Molly offered. "If the danger gets too much I'll take them to the Triple-T."

He rose, turned to pace and, splaying tense fingers through his hair, gave a short nod. "That'll be fine." He leaned over the twins. "Go inside the house with Miss Molly, quickly now."

"We don't have to go home?"

He shook his head. "Not yet. But it's dangerous out here. Promise me you won't come out unless I say it's all right to do so."

"We promise."

He pressed a kiss to each of their foreheads, gave Molly a grateful, weary smile, then went back to helping squelch the fire.

People who weren't a part of the fight eventually left for their own homes, with the promise to assist in any way they could in the coming days.

Helen Carson thanked each of them personally. Her gratitude was sincere. Yet Molly wondered if her mother would take her friends up on their offers. Accepting help wasn't the Carson way, mainly because they'd never been in a situation that required charity. They'd always been the ones providing the assistance.

What would they do now that they were in need?

The Bible taught that giving was better than receiving.

But sometimes bad things happened. Surely, accepting a helping hand, and doing so with graciousness, was as virtuous as giving.

Under the circumstances, it was time the Carson family learned how to receive.

The fire continued to burn. It was loud and hot, and CJ could see sparks flying in every direction. He felt the oppressive heat on his face and arms, like sitting on the sun.

The flames were winning.

Frustrated, impatient and aware of the growing danger to the other buildings if they didn't get the flames doused soon, he shouted for the men now working the fire engine to pump faster.

The battle was far from over. CJ opened his mouth to issue an order to work quicker, faster, with more efficiency. He never got the words out. Something hit his back, hard.

Instinctively, he spun away from the impact.

The pain didn't register at first, then...

He felt a searing sensation rip through his shoulders and down his spine. He barely had time to register that he'd been hit by a burning piece of word before John Carson threw a blanket over him and tackled him to the ground.

CJ landed hard, gaining a mouthful of dirt.

Spitting, nearly gagging, he braced against the pain shooting through him. He couldn't actual feel his skin burning. Was that a good thing?

After a series of hard pats, Molly's father pulled away, taking the blanket with him.

"You're good." Relief tinged John Carson's voice as he helped CJ to his feet, giving his shoulder a fatherly squeeze. After a thorough study, he added, "Your clothing is a bit singed, but the flames didn't reach to your skin."

CJ rolled his shoulders, winced. He might not have been burned, but pain sliced through him. He predicted considerable bruising in the coming days.

"Those quick reflexes saved you, son."

Son. It had been a long time since CJ had heard that word directed at him, even longer since he'd been on the receiving end of genuine fatherly concern. He'd become the adult in his home at such a young age he could hardly remember what it felt like to be cared for as a *son.*

The backs of his eyes stung. He blamed the uncomfortable sensation on the smoke.

John Carson eyed him thoughtfully, then gave him another pat on the shoulder. "If you're done lazing about," he said gruffly, "let's get back to work."

CJ bit back a smile, liking Molly's father even more. "Right behind you."

They were halfway to the fire engine when CJ heard his name being shouted in a frantic female voice. He looked over his shoulder and saw Molly rushing toward him.

"CJ!" she yelled again, louder and with more fervor. She nearly stumbled, but righted herself midstride and kept coming toward him. Toward the fire.

"Molly. Stay back." He shot out a restraining hand, uncaring that his voice held a note of censure. No time for gentleness.

Proving she had a stubborn streak, she continued forward, eyes glued to him, seemingly uncaring of the danger. He usually admired her determination. Not so today. *Today,* it terrified him.

By the stormy look on her face he figured she'd witnessed the accident. Knowing her penchant for taking care of others, she wouldn't leave the area until she was satisfied he'd escaped injury.

He took her gently by the arm and led her back the way she'd come, away from the blaze. He wasn't sure where he was taking her, just knew he had to put distance between her and the dangerous flames and flying debris.

Setting a fast, steady pace, he hustled her in the direction of the house.

"Molly. I appreciate your concern. But you can't be out here right now." Conflicting emotions moved through him. He didn't know if he was angry or scared or some combination of both. "I need you to get back in the house."

"You certainly enjoy giving orders."

"Here's another one. Don't come outside again until I say it's safe."

The stubborn woman held firm. "*You're* out here."

"Inside, Molly. Now." Out of patience, he directed her to the back door. "I'm not playing around."

"Neither am I." Making a face at him, she broke free of his hold and started walking quickly. Away from the house, but also—praise God—away from the fire.

Where was she going?

CJ found himself following her against his better judgment. She stopped at a spot along the side of the house, away from prying eyes.

What was the woman up to now?

She spun around and glared at him. "I was so afraid for you."

The truth of her words was there in her glittering, angry eyes, and in her carefully modulated voice. She was worried. For him. Any other time he would be pleased with this discovery.

Right now, he felt only a rush of impatience. He had

one goal: get the stubborn woman inside the house. "I'm fine, Molly."

"Fine? *Fine?*" Her gaze drifted over him. "You were on fire."

"Only a little."

"Why do you have to be such a...a *man*?"

For the span of a heartbeat he absorbed the joy of the moment. Molly cared about him, really cared. His safety mattered to her. As he stared into her beautiful face, he felt his pulse roar to life.

Standing here, just the two of them, he felt happy, exposed and utterly defenseless. He didn't know what to do with the sensations running through him. He wanted to smile. To shout with glee.

To pull her into his arms and kiss her senseless.

Dropping his head, he pressed his lips together and tried to think pure thoughts. He needed to get back to the fire, not wrap Molly in his embrace.

His feet refused to cooperate. His breathing quickened.

This sudden, vivid awareness of her concerned him. There was a growing tenderness in his heart he'd never felt before, a willingness to give of himself, to sacrifice all, for this woman.

Molly whispered his name.

He dragged in a hard breath.

"CJ," she said again. "Are you truly unharmed?"

"Yes."

"Then why won't you look at me?"

The woman was killing him. Slowly, deliberately, he lifted his head and locked his eyes with hers.

Caught in CJ's stare, Molly felt the impact of his intensity like a fist to the stomach. There was something far too serious about him at this moment. The bond between them seemed to be growing stronger every day.

Remembering what she'd seen from the kitchen window, her lungs burned with fresh terror. The piece of debris engulfed in flames breaking away from the barn and flying toward him, hitting him in the back, his shirt igniting. Her father tackling him to the ground.

"Are you sure you aren't hurt?"

"I'm sure."

"You aren't just saying that to get me to go back inside the house?"

"No."

CJ never spoke more words than necessary, and right now, more than ever, his penchant for brevity drove her mad.

Unwilling to take him at his word, she circled him slowly, studying every inch of his clothing, from collar to boots, front to back. His pants were black, his shirt singed, but the fire hadn't burned through to the skin.

Sighing in relief, she lifted her hand, ran her fingertips across the charred material stretched across his back. Her touch was feather-light, but CJ's muscles bunched. She sighed again, dropped her head to gather her composure.

The man confounded her. Breath rattling in her throat, she finished her inspection, then returned to face him head-on.

He raked a hand across his mouth, not one wasted motion in the gesture.

A third sigh leaked past her lips. When had she become the sighing sort? She wanted to know so much about CJ, wanted to know what he was thinking when his brows scrunched together as they were now. Wanted to know what was going on behind those beautiful, chocolate-brown eyes that held her rooted to the spot.

Molly was attracted to the man. Even knowing all the reasons for keeping her distance, she didn't want to fight her feelings anymore. Not at this precise moment. Maybe tomorrow.

But today? She wanted no more barriers. The past few hours had been harrowing and full of too many emotions, one trial on her nerves after another.

Molly wasn't by nature impulsive or reckless. She certainly wasn't irresponsible. Letting down her guard around this man would require all three.

And yet...

What would it hurt—just this once—to give in to her feelings for CJ? He could have been killed had the flaming board hit his head. She could have lost him forever.

Just this once, she told herself.

After that they could go back to being...whatever it was they were.

"CJ." She moved a step closer, placed a hand on his arm. "I want to thank you for your efforts on my family's behalf."

CJ, being CJ, didn't brush off her gratitude or pretend to misunderstand what she meant. He simply said, "You're welcome."

Something that felt like a promise passed between them. They'd been in this place before, on more than one occasion. They'd even kissed. This moment felt different. It felt like...more. Permanent and life-altering.

She'd been so scared, watching him go to the ground. Her feet hadn't been quick enough, nor her screams of warning loud enough.

All those pent-up emotions boiled beneath her skin and she thought she might explode. No more thinking.

She gripped his shoulders, rose slightly on her toes and pressed her lips to his. The kiss started out slowly, a brief meeting of one mouth with another. But then CJ wrapped his arms around her and pulled her close.

She was the one to start this kiss. She must be the one to end it. With considerable effort she lowered her heels, the move sufficiently breaking the connection of their mouths. CJ loosened his grip but didn't let her go completely.

For several long seconds they stared at one another, their breathing taking on a similar sporadic cadence.

The sweet tenderness in CJ's eyes stirred something in Molly, something that had died with George. Something that felt like hope. Hope for the future.

CJ's lips curved at the edges. "Well, that was…"

He appeared at a loss for words. Molly wasn't feeling especially verbose herself. Kissing CJ had only added dimensions to an already complicated situation.

She let out a shuddering breath.

He touched her lips once more with his, then smiled down at her. "Go back inside."

This time, she did as he requested.

Hours after kissing CJ, with the sun skimming the horizon, the fire was nearly contained. Nearly, but not quite. Molly was weary from worrying and fidgeting. Her back was one giant knot.

Most of the neighboring ranchers and men from the community had left. Only CJ, Edmund McKay and Hank Snowden remained working beside Molly's father, brothers and their ranch hands. Their diligence had saved the main house and outbuildings.

The barn, however, was a total loss, nothing more than a pile of glowing ashes. According to Molly's father, the danger was not yet over. At any moment, one of the smoking embers could ignite into something more serious.

Making food for the men had proved to be the perfect distraction for Molly's mother. Food was always something they could do. Lula May was proving a master at organizing the spattering of volunteers left in the house. She'd sent her sons home, but she and her daughter remained.

Helen Carson put Daisy in charge of entertaining the twins and Pauline.

After making yet another urn of coffee, Molly went to check on the twins. They were sprawled across Daisy and all three had fallen asleep on the large, overstuffed sofa in the living room. They looked comfortable, which defied logic, considering their awkward position. Nevertheless, Molly decided to leave them sleeping a bit longer.

She returned to the kitchen just as her mother picked up a tray of food. Molly reached for another and followed her outside, making the short trek to the wooden picnic table set up near the back porch.

There was a bitter stench in the air and pockets of smoke hung over the general area. Drifting ash had settled over everything like a blanket of dingy snow. It would take weeks for her family to clean away the debris.

Suddenly overwhelmed, Molly set down the tray and studied the barn, now a black skeleton. A river of wet soot and dirty water dripped from the few pieces of wood still standing. The grass, once green and thick, lay trampled.

Her mother called out to let the men know more food had arrived. Her brothers ran over and inhaled their sandwiches faster than most people breathed air. They seemed not to care that their faces and hands were black with soot. A few of the ranch hands joined them, digging in as gustily as the boys.

His expression cheerless, his eyes bleak, Molly's father walked over to her mother. As a single unit, they faced the carcass of the once white barn, their hands locked together, their heads leaning toward one another.

CJ strode over to speak with them. The three conversed for what seemed a long time. At one point her father shook his head, but CJ continued to talk quickly, gesturing to the barn.

As Molly eyed his tall, muscular build, so similar to her father's, she realized CJ hadn't taken a break since the accident. That had been hours ago. He finished whatever he had to say and walked toward the remains of the barn.

Still hand in hand, her parents bent their heads again and spoke softly. Occasionally, they would look up and watch CJ moving through the debris. Then they would huddle together and begin conversing softly once more.

Molly grabbed a clean plate, filled it with cold chicken, mashed potatoes and three buttermilk biscuits. She paused beside her parents. "CJ hasn't eaten."

"Hasn't he?" Helen Carson eyed her with a shocked expression. "I hadn't noticed."

"You've had a lot on your mind." She gave her a soft smile and started toward the barn.

"Molly, stop." Her father's voice held an authoritative note. "The fire isn't completely out. The hem of your dress could run across a hot ember and ignite."

She'd known this, of course, but she'd been so caught up in making sure CJ ate that she hadn't thought of the dangers to herself.

Sighing, she handed the plate to her father. "Will you see that CJ gets this?"

"I'll take care of it right now." He kissed his wife, then set out across the crushed grass.

Not wanting to go back inside, Molly stepped next to her mother and linked their arms.

Helen looked from CJ to Molly, then back again. "He's a good man."

"Yes, he is. The very best I know."

"He's very..." her mother paused, seeming to search for the right word "...capable. The other men naturally look to him for guidance, as do your brothers. I've decided to like him."

Molly laughed softly. "Me, too."

Her father said something to CJ, who looked over his shoulder and settled his gaze on her. Heart pounding, she lifted a hand.

He started toward her, paused to set the plate on a nearby table, and then resumed his approach.

Untangling their arms, her mother stepped aside. "I think I'll check on Daisy and the girls."

Molly could tell her they were fine, but emotion clogged in her throat and all she could manage was a nod.

She swung back around, and kept her eyes on CJ as he continued striding toward her. He was filthy, clearly exhausted, but she couldn't take her eyes off him.

"Your father insisted I take a break." His smile flashed white in his soot-covered face. "There was no arguing with him."

"We Carsons are a stubborn lot."

"This is true."

"Come with me." Giving him no chance to argue, she took his hand and drew him to the table recently vacated by her brothers and the ranch hands.

He sat, then, lifting up a hip, pulled out a bandanna from his back pocket and wiped his face. The gesture only managed to smear the soot around. Despite that, Molly had never been more attracted to him than she was at this moment.

Fighting for calm, she lowered herself to the bench directly across the table from him. "Were you able to save anything inside the barn?"

"We freed all the horses. But everything else was destroyed." He glanced over at the ruins. "The hay and cereals went up fast, faster than they should have. It was as if…"

He fell silent, his expression thoughtful as he absently took a bite of chicken.

"It was as if…?" she urged.

"Nothing." He concentrated on his plate. "I shouldn't have said anything."

"Please, CJ." She placed her hand on his forearm, waited for him to look at her. "Finish your thought."

"The barn burned so quickly I have to wonder if some sort of ignition fluid or kindling was involved."

"Oh, CJ." Her hand flew to her throat. "You don't think someone started the fire deliberately?"

"I didn't say that."

"You didn't have to." It was written all over his face.

He set down his fork, turned his head toward hers. What she saw in his gaze frightened her. "Let's not get ahead of ourselves. It could have been something already in the barn that set off the fire."

"You don't think it was an accident."

"No," he admitted after a long pause. "It's the timing. Cattle keep going missing, and now this. A barn is the most important structure on a ranch."

And losing theirs was a terrible blow to her family.

"I can't help thinking someone is deliberately hitting our community with hardships."

As she pondered the possibility, Molly's senses seemed unnaturally heightened. Who would do something so intentional, so vicious? "To what end?"

"I don't know." He shifted on the bench, studied the dying embers. "But I plan to share my concerns with Sheriff Fuller."

He started to rise, as if he meant to hunt down the lawman immediately.

"Not so fast." Molly slapped a hand on the table. "You're not going anywhere before you finish eating your supper."

"Why, Mrs. Langley. Are you issuing me orders?"

"I learned from the best." She gave him a pointed look. "Sit. Eat. I'm not going to relent until you do."

An echo of a smile passed across his lips. "If I didn't know better I'd say you were worried about me."

"I am." She snatched a quick pull of air. "I care about you, CJ. You must know that."

"Then marry me."

"I..." *No fair.* The man was playing dirty, striking when she was vulnerable and willing to do anything to lighten his load.

Regrettably, marrying him would only add to his burdens. "I can't."

"Molly, whatever is keeping you from—" He was cut off by the bright flash of flames shooting out of a pile of ashes. "Hold that thought."

He was on his feet a half second later. He took a step, paused, then leaned over the table. "We'll continue this discussion later."

His expression was full of fierce resolve.

Giving him even a moment of hope wasn't fair to him, or the twins, or even to herself. Molly knew it was time to pull back. "There's no need to continue this discussion."

"Yes, there is. But not now." He motioned to Edmund,

some sort of silent gesture that the other man understood, because he headed in the direction of the small fire.

Without another word to Molly, CJ trotted over to where his friend fought the latest batch of flames.

Chapter Fifteen

Although the fire had been extinguished, the smoking embers required watching through the night. CJ took the first shift. He'd sent Duke to the Triple-T hours ago, knowing he could count on his foreman to manage the ranch in his temporary absence.

With John Carson and his sons inside the house grabbing some much-needed rest, CJ waded through the wet, sooty debris that had once been the largest barn in the community. In the stingy, early morning light, he kicked over a charred board, checked to make sure there were no hidden flames beneath.

Finding none, he moved on to the next pile of rubble.

The chore required his full concentration and helped keep his mind off Molly. This was not the time to be mulling over how her lips had felt pressed to his in a kiss she'd initiated, or how perfectly she'd fit in his arms.

Prior to those precious few moments with her, CJ hadn't known, hadn't understood, that his heart had been much like the charred remains beneath his boot. Seared, splintered, a heap of smoldering ashes waiting for the right spark to set it aflame.

Molly, with her good heart and generous spirit, had

provided that spark. She'd changed how CJ saw the legacy of his past, and gave him hope for the future. Her confidence in him had restored his faith in himself.

A certain Bible verse flashed in his mind. He couldn't remember the Scripture exactly, something about beauty from ashes, joy instead of mourning and a garment of praise instead of despair. Yes, that described perfectly how CJ felt this morning. Standing in the rubble it was as if he teetered on the brink of a new beginning, a new life.

He was determined to court Molly properly. He would approach her father once the shock of the fire had settled. He would declare his intentions in plain terms and ask for John Carson's permission to court his daughter.

Eyes gritty, limbs weighed down with fatigue, CJ blinked away his exhaustion and contemplated the space where the big white barn had once been. His suspicions about the cause of the fire had only grown more pronounced through the night. Something about the way the structure had burned didn't sit right.

The flames had been concentrated inside at first, the hayloft specifically, indicating the first spark had come from there. That meant weather hadn't caused the fire.

Then what?

Not sure what he was looking for, CJ paced around the other outbuildings. Due to the combined efforts of the entire town, the other structures on the Rolling Hills ranch had been untouched. That spoke well of their community and how they pulled together in times of need.

So what had started the fire? CJ's mind kept circling back to that question.

The timing struck him as odd, or rather oddly convenient. Nearly every man, woman and child had been gathered in Little Horn for the Founder's Day celebration. Since the Carson ranch was one of the closest to town, someone could have easily slipped away from the crowd, made the short journey across the hills and then returned to the celebration with no one the wiser. Surely, that ruled out Ned.

Or did it?

CJ just didn't know. He continued studying the rubble, working the details of the past week through his mind. First the stolen cattle and now this fire, the evidence suggesting foul play in all cases.

The sun could have created the spark to start the fire in the barn. But according to John Carson, the doors and shutters had been closed against the heat of the day.

CJ's gut instinct told him someone had deliberately started the blaze.

Riders appeared in the distance, coming in fast and hard. CJ kept his eyes on the men, recognizing Edmund and Jeb Fuller as they rode closer.

The moment they pulled their horses to a stop and dismounted, CJ tilted his head toward the heap of ashes.

The two men, grim-faced and silent, followed him there.

Standing near the charred carcass, CJ broke down his concerns about the fire.

Frowning, Edmund yanked off his hat and slapped it against his thigh. "Everything you've laid out has also occurred to me. What I can't figure out is why this barn?"

CJ pondered the various theories that had come to him. "My logical guess is that the Rolling Hills is the largest ranch in the area. If someone wanted to put fear in our community, this was the one to strike."

Jeb's eyebrows arched nearly to his hairline. "You think the fire was set on purpose?"

"It's a possibility."

"Although I too have wrestled with a similar thought,

jumping to conclusions without hard evidence is always a mistake."

"Not to mention, I see one, very large problem with your theory, CJ." Edmund turned over a piece of smoking rubble with his toe. "John Carson doesn't have any enemies."

"A valid point, I'll admit, but not necessarily a reason to rule out foul play." CJ rubbed his thigh, working out the particulars as he kneaded a sore muscle. "Maybe the fire was only meant to get our attention, but it got out of control and burned too fast."

"Could be," Jeb allowed. "I can't help thinking this incident is connected with the missing cattle."

The three men fell silent. Then, slowly, each turned to study the distant landscape, as if the answer was somewhere just over the first rise.

Jeb drew in a tight breath and restated CJ's earlier conclusions. "The Founder's Day celebration would have afforded the means and opportunity to start a fire without being noticed. And the Carson ranch *is* the closest to town."

"Cattle rustlers, arsonists, it boggles the mind." Edmund ground the toe of his boot on a seared board, splintering the wood.

"I'm only one man," Jeb pointed out unnecessarily. "I'm going to need help catching the culprit."

"You think it's only one individual?"

Jeb lifted a shoulder, let it fall. "Does it matter? One person, ten, twenty—whatever the number, in order to make an arrest I'll have to be in the right place at the right time to foil the next attack."

The words hung thick in the air, as putrid and menacing as the smoke-laden haze swirling around them.

"What if you had help?"

Even before the words left Edmund's mouth, the sheriff was shaking his head. "The town can hardly afford me. A deputy is out of the question."

"I was thinking of something considerably less costly."

"What did you have in mind?"

"Ranchers in other communities like ours have addressed these types of concerns by organizing into formal groups."

As one, CJ and Jeb leaned in. "Go on," the sheriff urged.

"Take Graham, for instance. Ever since the local ranchers created an association, theft has dropped significantly in their county. Don't see why we can't do the same." He studied the blackened rubble at his feet. "Look how well the community worked together to fight this fire. Imagine what we could do if we banded together in an official capacity."

CJ mulled over the idea. They had a cattle rustler and an arsonist, who may or may not be the same person, and a barn that needed rebuilding. Pulling together in an organized fashion made sense. But it wouldn't be easy. "The ranchers will need convincing, some more than others."

Clyde Parker came to mind. The man had always been a loner. Lucas Bennett also preferred doing things his own way. Then there was Lula May Barlow. By definition, she was a rancher. But she mostly raised horses and not everyone in the area would take kindly to a woman joining an association of cattle*men*.

"We'll need to act fast," Jeb said. Looking directly at Edmund, he added, "Can I count on you to lead the effort?"

The question seemed to stun the rancher. "Why me?"

"It was your idea."

"I'm not a man of fancy words."

Jeb claimed the same malady. Both men looked to CJ. He raised his hands, palms outward. "My name isn't the most respected in the area."

"The men deferred to your leadership yesterday," Jeb pointed out.

Was that true?

CJ thought back over the fight to contain the fire. John Carson had been in charge. CJ had merely worked alongside him.

After more discussion, it was agreed that CJ and Edmund would approach the other ranchers together. "Let's start first thing tomorrow," Edmund suggested. "I'll meet you at the edge of town at daybreak."

"Why not start this morning?"

"I want to do some more research on cattlemen associations so we can go into this fully armed."

That made sense. It also couldn't hurt their cause to have one of the most influential ranchers in the area on their side. "I'll run this by Mr. Carson later this morning."

"Good thinking."

The other two men mounted up and rode off, Jeb toward town, Edmund toward his ranch.

A half hour later, cleaned up, yet still looking exhausted, John Carson exited his house. CJ met him at the edge of the trampled grass. "Mr. Carson, I—"

"CJ, after all we've been through, you can dispense with the formalities and call me John."

There was genuine warmth in the other man's voice that took CJ a moment to process. He thought of Lillian's father and the way he'd addressed CJ, as if he were one level below human.

"John," CJ began again. "Have you considered your next step?"

The other man looked out over the ruins of the once

grand structure, circled his gaze to the outbuildings and then clamped his attention on the distant horizon. Suppressed anger flashed in his gaze, then was gone.

"Rounding up the horses is the logical first step. Then we'll see what tack can be salvaged." He glanced down at his feet. "This debris will have to be cleared before we can rebuild the barn. There's also the matter of replenishing the lost hay and cereals and—"

He broke off. A silence fell, awkward and full of meaning. Then the older man stood tall, as if shouldering a large burden came naturally. "We'll get it done."

"You won't have to do any of that alone."

CJ told him about Edmund's idea for forming a cattlemen's association. "Our first order of business would be to organize a barn raising. With the proper preparation and everyone pitching in like they did yesterday, we could raise the building in ten, maybe twelve hours."

Clearly uncomfortable with the idea, John shifted from one foot to another. "Carsons don't accept charity."

"It's not charity. It's neighbors helping neighbors, no different than our combined effort to fight the fire."

John's throat seemed to stick on a swallow.

"I'd like to take the lead on this project," CJ said.

Eyes guarded, the other man searched his face in the morning light. "This is all in the name of one neighbor helping another?"

"That's right."

"You sure that's the only reason you're offering your assistance to me and my family?"

There was an easy way to respond. A simple yes would do. And it would be truthful, if not the complete truth. Because John's question was issued so simply, so easily, CJ gave a more honest answer. "No," he admitted. "It's not."

"You're doing this for my daughter."

Now that he'd started down this road, he must continue. "Molly has been a Godsend to me and my family. It is only right that I give back to hers."

He paused, thinking to stop there. But something in the other man's eyes, a level of respect and admiration that he'd never known in his own father, had CJ continuing, "Penelope leaned heavily on Molly. After her death, Ned did the same. Once Ned was gone, it was my turn. I'm grateful for all she's done. I don't know what I would do without her. I pray I don't ever have to find out."

"That was quite a speech."

CJ wasn't through. "I owe Molly more than I can put into words. Let me do this for her. Let me organize the barn raising as a small repayment for her generosity."

"You care that much for my daughter?"

For three full seconds, CJ held the other man's gaze. He would have preferred to wait to have this conversation at a more appropriate time, but it seemed now was it. "I do. Very much."

"If Molly stopped taking care of your nieces, would you still offer your help?"

"Yes." CJ answered without hesitation. "We're part of a community. There may come a time in the future when you'll return the favor for me or another rancher in the area."

John Carson stayed silent a moment longer than was comfortable. There was the look of a father in his eyes. But CJ didn't see an ounce of judgment staring back at him, only respect and admiration.

He'd never experienced this kind of unconditional acceptance. His own father had been a hard, rigid man, even before he'd turned to drink.

"...We're happy to have her home, but her mother and I still worry she's not embracing life as fully as she could."

CJ shook his head, realizing the other man had continued talking about Molly. About something that made him and his wife not only uncomfortable, but also concerned for her welfare. The conversation had turned in an unexpected direction. CJ forced himself to concentrate.

"Caring for your nieces has given her purpose. However, I have to wonder if it's the best use of her talents."

CJ's heart kicked in his chest. "You don't approve of her caring for the twins?"

"That's not what I said." John clasped his hands behind his back. "Nor what I meant."

It certainly sounded that way to CJ, who hastened to assure him, "I would never use your daughter for my own convenience."

He'd made that clear to Molly on several occasions and needed to make it clear to her father, as well.

"I know that, son."

Son. There was that word again. CJ was a grown man, yet he couldn't stop the desire to rely on John Carson as a son would rely on his father.

"What I'm trying to say is that I fear Molly is hiding some secret pain in her heart." John's face became a landscape of angles and lines, a look that aged him right before CJ's eyes. "Her mother and I worry that her choice to watch your nieces is her way of avoiding whatever is troubling her."

CJ prayed the other man was wrong. He didn't deny that Molly's devotion to the twins was real, but he would be wise to keep her father's concerns in mind.

"When she came home after her husband's death she was different. Not herself. Sadder."

Except for nodding his head, CJ remained perfectly still. "She was grieving the loss of the man she loved."

"True, but I've seen grief. Molly's suffering was more

than that. She was unnaturally despondent and was no longer the daughter I'd always known."

Time reversed itself and CJ thought back to the days he'd known Molly before she'd married George Langley. Her father was right in his assessment. The woman who'd returned to Little Horn was more subdued than the vibrant young girl of the past.

Not for the first time, CJ wondered about the secret sadness he often witnessed in Molly. Something had happened in her marriage to take away the shine and sparkle that had been an integral part of her younger self.

Evidently her father's thoughts had gone in a similar direction. He let out a breath of air, stuffed his hands in his back pockets. "Molly's mother and I have always taught our children that when life gets hard, or seems hopeless, serving others is the best way to gain perspective."

"That's good advice."

"Assisting Penelope with your nieces helped Molly through her grief. It wasn't long before my daughter became less sad." John glanced over his shoulder, back to the house, to an upstairs window. "She's not fully herself, but she's happier now and, praise the Lord, she smiles more."

"It's the twins' influence. It's hard not to feel happy in their presence."

With a very deliberate motion, Molly's father swiveled his gaze to meet CJ's. "I believe you're also a large part of the reason for my daughter's transformation."

Was he? She'd certainly made a difference in CJ's life. He couldn't imagine going through the next day, week or fifty years without her by his side.

This was it, the moment of truth, the perfect opportunity to declare his intentions to her father. "She's transformed me, as well. Your daughter is a remarkable woman."

"That she is."

"Sir." CJ cleared his throat. "Mr. Carson, I…"

"John. You agreed to call me John."

"John." CJ's heart knocked against his ribs, but he held the man's stare. "I'd like to ask permission to court Molly."

A smile spread across the rancher's weary face, reaching all the way to his eyes. "You have it."

The quick response took CJ a moment to process. "That's it? You don't need time to think about your answer? Talk it over with your wife?"

"Helen and I have already discussed the matter." The rancher clasped CJ's shoulder, squeezed. "Molly's mother and I would be honored to give our permission to court her. God willing, one day soon we'll be able to call you son."

CJ's responding smile came fast. "The barn raising?" he asked, pushing his advantage. "Will you allow me to take the lead on that?"

The other man's agreement came slower this time. "Yes."

"I won't let you down."

He wouldn't let Molly down, either. With patience, persistence and prayer, CJ would get past every barrier she erected between them. He would woo her until she agreed to marry him, and would continue courting her long after they said their vows. He wouldn't rest until every remnant of her sadness disappeared.

They would be good together, and happy, and raise a houseful of kids.

Molly was in the process of cleaning up the breakfast dishes when her father and an exhausted-looking CJ entered the kitchen through the back door. She shook her head in wonder at the way the two men were getting along. They seemed more like father and son than neighbors.

CJ smiled slowly, giving her a long, steady once-over. "Good morning, Molly."

That smile. That face. That voice. He was looking at her with the eyes of a man who cared deeply for a woman. It was a lovely, scary, heart-pounding thought. Words failed her. Coherent thought disappeared.

"I hope you slept well."

Pulse pounding, her breathing coming fast, she watched him exchange a glance with her father. The man was up to something.

If only she knew what.

"I...yes. I slept very well." For two entire hours.

"That's good." He added a bit of charm to his smile.

Her knees nearly gave out from under her. "I..." *Get hold of yourself, Molly.* "There's fresh coffee."

She was pleased to discover that none of her confusion sounded in her voice.

"Thank you, dear." Her father kissed her cheek on his way to the stove. "CJ?" he asked over his shoulder. "Want some?"

CJ continued holding Molly's gaze. "More than air."

John Carson chuckled.

Still meeting Molly's eyes, CJ cocked his head. "Where are the twins?"

Frozen by his gaze, her throat suddenly dry, she forced words past her tight lips. "They're upstairs with my mother and Daisy, digging through a trunk of old clothes from when Daisy was their age. They've found quite a few treasures."

When his smile widened, Molly nearly forgot to

breathe. A deep inhalation restarted her lungs. "There's oatmeal if you're hungry."

"I could eat."

Her father called him over to the stove, a mug of coffee in his outstretched hand.

Taking the offered brew, CJ dragged in a long, slow sip.

Her insides shaking slightly, Molly filled a bowl with oatmeal and set it in front of him at the table. Her father took the seat across from him, clearly of a mind to continue whatever conversation they'd been having outside.

Molly had watched them from the window.

As she cleaned the breakfast dishes, the two men fell into a deep, serious discussion. From the snippets she caught over the clanging of pots and sloshing of water, her father seemed to be yielding to CJ's expertise on how to go about rebuilding the barn.

"We'll want to remove the debris first," he said in answer to CJ's question. "It'll take substantial manpower, something I don't have a large supply of right now, not with the need for rounding up the horses and the regular business of ranching."

Turning thoughtful, CJ took a sip of coffee. "I have an idea to help with the cleanup."

"I'm listening."

"There are a handful of boys in town who need guidance and a firm hand."

"You mean the Gillen boys, living down by Kettle Creek."

"I was thinking of James Forester's sons, too. Butch and Brody aren't bad kids. I'm not sure what to make of the Gillens. I'd like to believe they're more bored than mean-spirited."

"Putting them to work would be a perfect way to address their boredom," her father said. "It would also give them something to do with their time and help them learn to feel pride in a job well done."

"We could eventually start a Young Ranchers program and actually teach the boys skills that will serve them in the future."

"Would we pay them?"

"I'd like to think the work itself would be its own reward." CJ filled his spoon with a large helping of oatmeal, then turned thoughtful. "But I know that's naive. Paying the boys a small stipend might be a good incentive to get them interested in helping, initially. Once they experience the joy that comes from a job well done, they may be open to the idea of a more formal program."

"You've certainly thought this through."

CJ set down his spoon. The morning sunlight streaming in the window played off the planes of his face, turning his features into something that reminded her of a work of art sculpted by a master.

"It wasn't all that long ago I was a struggling young rancher. A little guidance from men such as yourself and Edmund McKay made a big difference in my life. I want to do the same for others."

"So it's a simple matter of giving back?"

"Something like that."

Molly could stay silent no longer. "I think it's a wonderful idea."

CJ turned his head toward her. The look in his eyes was so tender her breath stalled in her lungs yet again. She stared at him a moment, his name a whisper in her mind. He broke eye contact first and, sighing, Molly deposited another dirty dish in the soapy water.

As he and her father discussed the ins and outs of getting local ruffians off the streets and into more productive pursuits, Molly's heart took a dive toward her stomach. CJ clearly wanted to be a role model to a pack of wild boys in desperate need of masculine guidance.

He was born to be a father, a startling reminder that any hope she had of marrying him was doomed. Somehow Molly would get them both to accept that sad truth.

Then she would spend the rest of her life getting over losing him.

Chapter Sixteen

It took CJ and Edmund several days to meet with all the ranchers in the area. More than a few had been openly skeptical, claiming they weren't altogether sure their community needed a formal association for cattlemen. Nevertheless, every last one of them had agreed to attend the first meeting, if only as a show of good faith.

As Edmund had predicted, Clyde Parker and Lucas Bennett were the toughest to convince. Clyde hadn't been keen on the idea for no other reason than because he didn't especially like people—his actual words.

After a gentle reminder from CJ about the Carson fire, and how they were able to save the majority of the ranch because of the combined effort of the entire community, Clyde had reluctantly conceded.

"That's a valid point. When disaster strikes we need to pull together," he'd grumbled in his gravelly voice.

As CJ and Edmund rode away from Clyde's place, CJ had a good idea why, at forty years old, the rancher was still unmarried.

They came up against a slightly different problem at the Windy Diamond ranch. Lucas Bennett claimed he didn't have time to meet regularly. The cattleman's problem was easily solved when his foreman offered to attend the meetings in his boss's place. Since he preferred Hank's company to Lucas's, CJ was satisfied with the compromise.

He and Edmund set the date of the first meeting for Sunday afternoon. The ranchers would meet in the most central location possible, beneath the revival tent in Little Horn immediately following church service.

With Sunday being several days away, CJ took the opportunity to travel to Kettle Creek early one morning. It seemed the perfect time to speak with Mary Gillen about his idea for a Young Ranchers program.

Mary didn't much care about the plan, thought it was a waste of her boys' time, but she wasn't completely against the notion, either. Understandably, her biggest concern was money. "Will it cost me anything?"

CJ assured her it wouldn't.

She still hesitated, until he mentioned the small stipend. "Fine, they can go with you."

Giving the woman no opportunity to change her mind, CJ piled her three surprisingly eager boys in his wagon and headed into Little Horn to speak with the town's overworked blacksmith.

Cast in the light from the raging fire of the smithy furnace, James's hard features took on a relieved expression. He offered his gratitude with a sincere word of thanks, then asked, "When would you be starting the program?"

"No time like the present," CJ replied.

He gestured for Butch and Brody to climb in the flatbed with the two younger Gillens. Sean took the seat next to CJ on the bench and off they went. The trip to the Rolling Hills ranch was filled with the boys' endless questions about the Young Ranchers program.

Sean asked the most, including the main one that

seemed to be on all their minds. "Will we get to herd cows?"

"Eventually, but not today."

"Tomorrow?"

CJ couldn't find fault with the lad's enthusiasm. "Not tomorrow, either."

"When?"

"Not for several days." He raised his hand to keep the boy from interrupting again. "We're going to focus on raising the Carsons' barn first."

"No kidding?" Butch leaned over the bench, his eyes lit from within. "We're going to help build a barn?"

"There's a lot of preparation that goes into building a barn." CJ steered the wagon onto the dirt road leading out of town. "That's where you boys come in. You're going to assist the Carson brothers with clearing away the debris left by the fire."

"Doesn't sound very fun," Sean grumbled.

One of his brothers agreed. "Definitely not as fun as herding cattle."

"You boys prove yourselves today, show me that you're hardworking and reliable, then we'll discuss getting you out on the range."

They made the rest of the journey to the Rolling Hills ranch with the boys asking more questions and CJ answering. Finally, his mouth dry and his patience slightly frayed, he and the five founding members of the Young Ranchers program stood beside the huge pile of ashes.

Cleanup was hard, physically challenging labor. With so many hands working together under CJ's efficient guidance, however, the task progressed.

Throughout the slow-going process, CJ found himself thinking often of Molly. Her father had given him permission to court her. CJ even had a strategy for winning her heart. He would take his time, gain her trust, let her get to know him as a friend first, then something more.

Unfortunately, there'd been little time to put his plan into motion. There'd been too many other tasks vying for his attention, especially drawing up a plan for the barn raising he would present the ranchers at their meeting Sunday afternoon.

In the sweltering heat, CJ took a swig of water from the canteen strapped at his waist. He shut his eyes a moment. The image of Molly's stunning face played in his mind, around and around, like an echo in a deep canyon. His head full of the woman, he forced his eyes open and went back to work.

By noon, he and the boys had moved the largest pieces of charred wood and fragments into a pile out of sight of the barnyard. At this rate, they would have the area cleared by the end of the day.

With so much already accomplished, CJ called for a break.

As if Mrs. Carson had been waiting for her cue, she exited the house with a tray filled with heaping plates of food. The moment the woman returned to the house, out came Molly carrying a pitcher of lemonade.

The simple pleasure of seeing her warmed CJ's heart. She set the pitcher on the table. Straightening, she reached up and absently anchored a hairpin in place.

It was then he remembered it was quilting bee day. He broke his silence with an innocuous question. "Are you working on a new quilt?"

He thought of the "decorative" blanket Hank Snowden had won at the Founder's Day celebration, and couldn't stop an amused smile from spreading across his face.

Molly drew in a sharp breath.

"We're not sewing today." Her voice sounded slightly

rusty. Because of him? CJ certainly hoped that was the case.

"We're...uh. We're sorting hammers, nails and all sorts of other hardware for the barn raising."

That made sense.

"Are the twins helping you?" He couldn't keep the skepticism out of his voice. The girls were awfully young for such work.

Molly's smile flashed. "They *were* helping us, but grew bored after about ten minutes. I left them inside playing jacks with Pauline Barlow."

"Now that," he said with amusement, "I believe."

Molly stared at him, hardly blinking. She seemed captured by the sight of him, freeing CJ to study her gorgeous, mesmerizing face. She was a study in femininity and he suddenly couldn't stand the distance between them, both figuratively and literally.

If only he knew what was keeping her from moving toward him. She liked him. She'd admitted as such.

Then what held her back? She had a huge capacity for love. He'd witnessed it in her relations with the twins, her family, her friends. Surely, there was room in her heart for both him and her deceased husband.

Aware they weren't alone, CJ kept his back to the boys, who were now digging into their lunch. Molly's beauty drew him a step closer.

He reached up, knuckled an errant curl off her forehead and tried to read her expression. All he saw was discomfort. That slayed him.

"Molly." He took her hand when she tried to turn away. "We still have unfinished business between us, namely our discussion about marria—"

"You can't possibly mean now."

"No, not now." CJ kept possession of her hand. "Soon.

This evening, or tomorrow morning. Definitely before the barn raising."

"I think that would be unwise. And unnecessary." She didn't quite meet his gaze. "You already know where I stand on the matter."

"I do." He released her hand. "However, until you give me a good reason for turning me down, I will keep asking the same question until I get the answer I want."

She gave him a quick, lovely smile. "You are certainly persistent."

"A flaw that has proved beneficial at times such as these."

When she shook her head in exasperation, her mask fell briefly. Barely concealed emotion showed on her face, giving her an exposed and defenseless air. She quickly schooled her features again, but not before CJ caught the hurt and grief swimming in her eyes. The emotions had been so strong and real he'd felt them with a jolt of awareness.

What terrible secret had she buried deep in her heart? What hidden hurt could possibly cause such a look of pain?

While he contemplated her sad, beautiful face, CJ had a terrifying moment of clarity. If someone didn't help Molly face her fear, she would continue turning within, slowly dying from the inside out until she became a broken shell.

As matters stood now, she was never going to share her secret with anyone, at least not on her own. If she had any chance of healing, someone would have to provide a safe environment where she could feel comfortable opening her heart.

Why not him?

CJ wanted—needed—to lighten Molly's cares, as she'd

done for him. He wanted to share her burdens in life. Not out of gratitude for all she'd done for him, but because he loved her.

He *loved* her?

Of course he did.

He'd always loved her, from their first meeting. Even when he hadn't known his own mind, his heart had known the truth. CJ would do whatever it took to gain Molly's trust and win her heart.

He'd never been more certain of anything in his life.

Molly noticed the change in CJ. It came in layers and tiers, much like the dawning of a new day. He'd gone from lighthearted, almost flirty, to thoughtful, then concerned, ultimately landing somewhere near grave and serious.

His eyes—oh, his eyes! They held such a depth of feeling—affection, adoration, something deeper still. Molly didn't quite know what to think.

She took a long breath, her inhalation pulling in the putrid scent of burned cinders that still lingered in the air. There was much work to be done, yet here the two of them stood. Staring.

He flashed her a smile. The real one not many people witnessed. Just Molly and the twins and...

Oh, my.

"Hey, CJ," Roy's voice called from behind him. "You gonna eat with us or stand there talking to my sister all afternoon?"

"On my way." He winked at Molly, then went to join the boys at the picnic table. In an assertive yet relaxed manner he sat down and took over the conversation. The youths hung on his every word.

Molly identified with their fascination. She liked being the center of CJ's attention. Liked it a bit too much. The man could charm the rattles off a snake, shift the stars in the sky and soften the hard blows of life with that boyish grin of his.

He can never be mine. The sense of defeat nearly dropped Molly to her knees.

With nothing more to do but despair, she went back inside the house. Instead of joining the other women, she indulged her melancholy a bit longer and stayed in the kitchen. A glutton for punishment, she moved to the window and watched CJ interacting with the tableful of boys.

He looked so comfortable, so capable. At one point, he reached over and ruffled Sean Gillen's hair.

In return, the boy, known for his churlish, surly nature, did the most extraordinary thing. He laughed.

The enormity of Sean's response wasn't lost on Molly. In just a single morning, CJ had turned the troubled, argumentative youth into a laughing, carefree boy.

Molly could only imagine what his influence on Sean's life would be after a few months, a year. CJ had taken on the role of a father figure as naturally as a fish swam in a stream.

Watching him with the boys, Molly had never admired him more. Nor had she felt closer to despair. CJ Thorn was meant to have that houseful of children he wanted.

The backs of her eyes burned with the prick of tears.

Battling for composure, she lifted her face to the ceiling, attempted to pray for guidance. Her mind remained empty of words. Several rogue tears ran hot and fast down her cheeks.

The day only needed this, she thought, as several more slipped from her eyes. She blinked—and blinked and blinked and blinked—until she had her emotions under control.

Lowering her head, she pushed away from the window

and made her way into the living room, where the women in her quilting bee were adding their collective effort to the rebuilding of the Carson family barn.

Eyes dry, she moved to her previously abandoned station and resumed sorting through a bucket of nails donated by their neighbors.

According to Molly's father, the more prepared they were before the raising, the smoother the day would go, hence the need for organizing the buckets-upon-buckets of nails by diameter and length. It was slow, tedious work that required concentration.

In the process, Molly eventually won the battle against her misery, but she feared she'd lost the war for her heart.

She was in love with CJ Thorn. She thought he might be in love with her, as well. It was the most wonderful, awful, hopeless feeling she'd ever experienced.

"Molly, dear, would you mind helping me fetch another couple of buckets of nails from the other room?" Her mother asked the question without looking at her, clearly assuming her daughter would follow without argument.

Molly headed out of the room, then paused to cast a glance at the twins. No longer playing with Pauline, they were now happily helping Lula May organize the stacks of donated plates, cups and pieces of cutlery that would be used to serve meals to the workers at the barn raising.

Smiling at them, Molly continued on.

The moment they were alone, her mother pulled her into a long, tight hug full of maternal love. "Oh, my dear, I have such wonderful news to share with you."

The older woman stepped back, and Molly was astonished to see her eyes glittered with tears—happy, unconstrained tears of joy.

Whatever could have put that jubilant expression on her face?

As soon as the question arose in her mind, Molly remembered another time her mother had looked like this. The day she'd told the family she was carrying Donny.

Was her mother with child again?

Something inside Molly shriveled and died. She was supposed to be happy, blissfully so. Helen Carson was a marvelous mother, a kind, gentle matriarch who showed her family unconditional love and support. She deserved as many children as the good Lord blessed her with.

All Molly could think was *I want a baby.*

If she let the thought continue she would break.

With her nerves in tattered threads, Molly braced herself for the blow that was sure to come. But, oh, how it would hurt. She forced a smile, an expression that didn't fool the other woman for a single moment.

"Molly. What is it?" Her mother touched her arm, whatever she'd been about to say forgotten. "What's wrong?"

"It is nothing."

"You've gone unnaturally pale."

"Please, Mother." Sliding her courage into place, wishing she could get this terrible moment over with quickly, she said in a wobbly voice, "I want to hear your news."

"It's not my news. It's yours."

"Mine?" Molly couldn't hide her confusion.

Eyes soft, her mother brushed her palm down Molly's sleeve in a gesture she remembered from her childhood. "CJ has asked your father for permission to court you."

"CJ…he *what*?"

Molly shook her head, hardly able to fathom what she'd heard come out of her mother's mouth. CJ had spoken with her father, about her. "When?" she asked. "When did he approach Papa? When did they have time to—"

She stopped, unable to go on, stricken into horrified

silence. Her legs didn't feel steady. Her breath froze in her lungs. Then came the joy, spreading warmth over the spears of ice.

"They spoke the morning after the fire."

CJ wanted to court her and had gone to her father seeking permission, as any honorable man would. It was so wonderful, so surreal, so impossible. Nevertheless, Molly found herself asking, "What did Papa say?"

"He gave his permission, of course." Her mother smiled. "We both approve."

"You approve? *Now* you approve?" Molly couldn't keep the resentment out of her voice. "When barely a week ago you were attempting to talk me out of serving his family? Why the sudden change of heart?"

"We have seen the kind of man he is. Strong, capable, someone others turn to for guidance."

CJ was all that her mother said and more.

"We have seen the way you are in his company. You smile often, and laugh, and seem at peace whenever he is near."

The chill had returned to her heart, causing Molly to shiver. She crossed her arms at her waist in an attempt to still the trembling.

"Well?" her mother asked. "Have you nothing to say?"

She pressed her hand to her forehead. "I don't know what to say."

"Do you care for him?"

The question echoed in her brain. There was only one way to answer: with the truth. "Yes."

The declaration stole the last of her air and she was forced to sit down in a nearby chair. For several moments, she studied her hands, as if they held the answer to her dilemma.

"Could you see yourself married to him?"

"Yes," she admitted, because she *could* see herself married to CJ. All she had to do was close her eyes and a thousand images of their life together appeared, nipping at Molly's resolve to protect him from the pain she'd inflicted on George.

"You will accept his suit?"

She could not allow CJ to court her. It would only give him hope where there was none. "No."

"Oh, my dear." Her mother knelt in front of her, placed her palms on her knees. "Why not?"

Misery lifted the ice from her heart and put it in her voice. "I cannot tell you."

If she revealed her reasons, her mother would try her best to understand. She would attempt to offer Molly words of comfort. But Helen Carson would never know the disappointment that came from an empty womb.

She would never know what it felt like to watch her husband's love and admiration diminish with each passing month she failed to conceive a child. And because she would never know those things, she could never truly understand her daughter's despair.

Molly jumped to her feet and, stifling a cry of pain, rushed out of the room.

Chapter Seventeen

Thoughts of Molly filled CJ's head for the next several days. Courting her was proving alarmingly difficult. Part of the problem was logistical, primarily due to the limited free time at his disposal. More cattle had gone missing, this time from Edmund's ranch. There was also the extensive prep work for the barn raising. Not to mention running the Triple-T.

All these things would have been surmountable, if not for the stubborn woman herself. Plain and simple, Molly was avoiding him. And not doing a very subtle job of it, either. She seemed determined to prevent spending time alone with him, resorting to any means possible. She consulted with Cookie every evening about how to make johnnycakes and other recipes that were her personal specialties.

She kept the girls close to her side, too close. She even pulled Roscoe into their inner circle, which pleased the cow dog to no end. It was as if Molly was intentionally raising barriers to prevent CJ from courting her.

On Sunday morning, the day of the first official meeting of local ranch owners, he woke from a fitful sleep. Groggy and feeling off balance, he was no longer confident he would succeed in his mission to win Molly's heart.

Giving his nieces his undivided attention that morning helped lighten his dark mood. CJ got them dressed, fed and loaded into one of the Triple-T wagons with minimum fuss, a far cry from the early days after Ned left home. Throughout each task their happy chattering rolled over him, eventually restoring his own joy.

With them flanking him on the bench, CJ drove into Little Horn for church service with his tenacity firmly in place. He would win Molly's affection.

Patience was his greatest weapon. He would wield it with the force of a mighty warrior.

"I can't wait to tell Miss Molly you made oatmeal this morning and didn't burn it even a little," Sarah announced in her sweet, little-girl voice. "She's going to be so proud of you."

Feeling rather proud of himself, he steered the wagon to a halt by the revival tent, set the brake and smiled down at his niece. "She'll not believe you."

"Yes, she will." Grinning broadly, she kissed him on the nose. "I love you, Unca Corny."

The last remnants of his gloominess disappeared. "I love you, too, buttercup."

As he assisted the child to the ground, then followed suit with her sister, he marveled at how far the three of them had come. He felt like a real father, rather than a temporary stand-in for Ned. CJ owed most of his success to Molly and would probably never tire of telling her just how grateful he was for her influence on his life.

Imagine how far we'll go as a family, how much happiness and joy we'll experience.

He and Molly would have a good life together, once the stubborn woman accepted his marriage proposal.

Laughing, Anna tossed her head, the ribbons in her hair fluttering in the wind, and motioned for CJ to come closer. As her sister had done seconds before, she kissed him on the nose, then said, "I love you, too, Unca Corny."

With no small amount of wonder, he hugged her close. "I love you, sweet pea."

Taking each child by the hand, he turned toward the tent, but paused after two steps and studied the distant sky. A wall of dark, menacing clouds churned in the west. The promise of a storm sounded in the distant rolling thunder. With the barn raising scheduled for the next day, CJ prayed the rain would blow through quickly and they could start construction as planned.

He hustled the twins toward the shelter of the tent.

"Hi, Miss Molly!" Anna waved at the lone figure standing by the tree where they met every Sunday— *their* tree, as CJ thought of it.

He briefly wondered if they would continue the tradition of sitting together during service if Molly refused his suit yet again. Nothing would be the same without her in his and the twins' lives.

He *must* win her hand.

Waving back at Sarah, a smile dancing in her eyes, Molly started toward them.

Impatient as always, the twins ran ahead to meet her.

CJ covered the distance at a slower rate. He could only stare at the beautiful picture Molly made, as striking in her Sunday best as she was in her everyday work clothes. She'd twisted her hair in some sort of complicated style atop her head and wore a dress in a pale, pretty blue that matched her eyes. To CJ's way of thinking, she looked like a dream come true.

His breath caught at the sight of Molly encircling the girls in her arms and pulling them close. She was so natural with them, so unconsciously affectionate. They were equally at ease with her. In a matter of weeks, she'd become the mother they'd been missing.

CJ shouldn't think of her that way. He shouldn't allow himself to feel this sense of amazement over a simple interaction he'd seen a dozen times in the weeks since Ned had taken off. Then again, why not?

She was going to be his wife one day. He was that determined.

Molly's feminine voice was musical this morning, capturing CJ's senses, running across his heart like a caress. He wasn't supposed to feel this connected to a woman who might never be his.

She could still turn you down again. It would be foolish of CJ to forget that Molly had already rejected him more than once. Anything between them was quite possibly doomed.

Yet she pulled at places in his soul no other woman had touched. CJ cared for Molly deeply. He cared so much it scared him. If she refused his next offer of marriage, he would ask again. And again. And again.

"You're sitting with us, aren't you, Miss Molly?"

"Of course I'm sitting with you, Sarah."

With that decided, the four of them stepped into the tent and found their usual seats in the back row. Only after they were settled, with CJ on one end of the small bench, Molly on the other, the twins in between, did he realize they were sitting in the same order as they had the last two Sundays. They'd fallen into a pattern.

As if they were a family.

Even more telling, neither Sarah nor Anna had asked about their father this morning. They'd rarely mentioned his name in the past week.

The girls were slowly forgetting Ned, or at least getting

over the loss of him in their daily lives. They were starting to turn to CJ. He swallowed back the well of emotion rising in his throat.

Thunder rumbled in the distance as Mrs. Hickey took her place at the piano and pounded out the first bars of the opening song. With her characteristic smile, Molly handed CJ a hymnal.

His voice rough as gravel, he thanked her.

Three hymns later, Brandon Stillwater took his place at the pulpit. Unusually somber, he looked out over the congregation, then began his sermon with a bang.

"Sin." A clap of thunder punctuated the word. Lips twisting at an ironic angle, he continued. "*Sin.* It has the power to devastate individual lives, divide families and ruin entire communities."

He paused, letting his words sink in. "Our God is merciful. He forgives sin, all sin, even the sins we keep secretly hidden in our hearts. However—and this is important, so lean in…" He waited a beat. "Though the Lord forgives, He does not always take away the consequences of our sin."

CJ shifted in his seat, glanced around the congregation. It was clear the preacher was calling out the cattle rustler and arsonist, as surely as if he'd pointed a finger at the culprit.

Out of the corner of his eye CJ saw Molly sit up straighter, her lips pressed tightly together. Apparently, she'd come to a similar conclusion.

"The Lord commands us to love one another and to do no harm. Thievery, deliberate acts of destruction, the abandonment of a loved one, these wicked acts hurt not just the victims but also our entire community."

A collective hush filled the area. This was serious talk and not everyone appeared comfortable.

"As we deal with the destruction that crime has brought to Little Horn, I urge all of us to consider our own actions. Think through the consequences of our sins, and what our choices mean to those around us."

He paused again, ran his gaze over the flock, stayed silent a moment.

CJ looked around the congregation again, wondering if the cattle thief was among them. The arsonist? He heard a rustle of material as Molly shifted in her seat. He caught her gaze over the children's heads. She gave him a sad, shaky smile.

After his short discourse on sin, the preacher turned the rest of his sermon to God's merciful capacity for forgiveness. "No sin is too great that it can't be forgiven. With our God, all things are possible."

Brandon continued speaking, urging the community to draw together in this difficult time. He then called for all able-bodied men and women to join in the effort to rebuild the Carsons' barn. He concluded the sermon with a prayer, or rather a petition for God to bring healing to their community.

The congregation rose to sing the closing hymn.

Having already worked it out with Molly that she would take the twins to her parents' ranch while he and Edmund conducted the cattlemen's meeting, CJ kissed each girl goodbye. Then he lifted his head and concentrated on Molly.

Her lips parted softly.

It took everything in him not to kiss her, too. He refrained, primarily because Constance Hickey was eyeing them from the crowd. He blessed the odious woman with a hard glare.

She didn't even flinch.

Shaking his head, CJ returned his attention to Molly.

"I'll meet you out at your parents' ranch later this afternoon."

He turned to go.

She stopped him with a brief touch to his forearm. "I'll be praying your meeting goes well."

"Appreciate that."

Two seconds later, he turned away. He caught Edmund's eye and angled his head toward the front of the tent. If all went according to plan, they would have a local ranchers' association before nightfall.

Molly watched CJ saunter to the front of the tent, where he met up with Edmund. She wanted to listen to what the two men had to say to the other ranchers. But CJ had left her in charge of his nieces and a meeting to discuss hunting down a cattle thief was no place for four-year-olds, especially ones already showing signs of restlessness.

Besides, there was a storm moving in. She'd be wise to hurry home.

Casting a final glance at the two men, she lifted up a prayer for success and then guided the girls away. Her constant supervision of Anna and Sarah no longer drew raised eyebrows from other Little Horn residents. Well, except for Mrs. Hickey's. That, Molly supposed, was to be expected. The woman lived for drumming up gossip.

Ignoring the woman's piercing scowl, Molly helped the girls into her family's wagon. Roy and Donny made room for them. She'd just gotten them settled when Lula May marched over. "Molly, a word, if you please."

With Daisy showing the girls her latest sewing creation, a lace cap with embroidered flowers around the edges, Molly stepped away from the wagon and approached her stone-faced friend. "Yes?"

"Do you have any idea what that meeting is about?" She looked pointedly toward the tent.

"I…" Molly blinked at her friend, wondering why she was distressed. "Well, yes, as a matter of fact, I do know. The men in our community are banding together to help the sheriff catch the cattle thief."

"Oh." Lula May's scowl disappeared. "That's actually a good idea."

Molly had thought the same thing when CJ had told her.

The meeting appeared to be under way, with CJ and Edmund doing all the talking, while the others found seats in the first two rows of benches. A clap of thunder had Molly and Lula May issuing each other a hasty farewell, then separating.

Molly lifted up one last prayer for the meeting's success before settling on the wagon's front seat with her mother.

After Edmund called the meeting to order, then explained the initial idea behind the association, CJ took over. "We hope to model our organization after the stockraisers' association in Graham. Due to their members' vigilance, cattle theft has dropped dramatically."

Bo Stillwater's hand went up. "How much?"

"Seventy-five percent."

"Impressive," Bo allowed.

Other ranchers nodded.

Clyde Parker raised his hand next. "You got a system in place for cataloging the ranches in the area and a description of each brand?"

"Not yet," CJ admitted. "But it's an important first step toward becoming an official association."

"I'll do it," Clyde offered, giving CJ a moment's pause.

For a man who'd initially fought the idea of an association, he certainly seemed eager to participate now.

"Thank you, Clyde. That would be a big help."

Men sitting near the crusty rancher added their thanks by way of hearty backslaps.

Out of the corner of his eye, CJ saw Lula May Barlow watching them from her wagon. He couldn't read her expression, so wasn't sure if she was upset or simply curious. CJ considered motioning her over.

Then he remembered that Edmund had insisted Lula May wouldn't be interested in joining an association of cattle ranchers. She owned only a few cows and focused most of her efforts on raising horses. With his thoughts consumed with other matters, CJ hadn't argued the point.

Now, he wasn't sure they should have excluded her.

Deciding to discuss the matter with Edmund again before their next meeting, *if* there was a next meeting, CJ returned to the subject at hand.

"It's become clear we have a cattle rustler in the area and possibly an arsonist. We're unsure if we're dealing with one man or several. Either way, we need to band together to fight this menace. Jeb—" he motioned the other man forward "—you want to take it from here?"

The sheriff laid out the need for policing the region and beating back the present threat of cattle theft. "I can't be in two places at the same time."

He went on to explain his ideas for keeping an eye on the various properties, which mostly amounted to neighbors watching out for neighbors. "Eventually, I'll want to train you on the finer points of peacekeeping."

"Why would we need to know something like that?" Cecil Sorenson asked.

"The association would assist in other ranch-related property loss aside from cattle," CJ explained, moving to stand next to Jeb. "On that note, I propose the rebuilding of the Carsons' barn be our first priority."

The ranchers gave their collective agreement.

"Preparations are already under way. I've enlisted help from some of the youth in town with the ground cleanup." He explained about his idea for a Young Ranchers program, then added, "Once we apprehend the cattle thief we'll get the boys out on the range and teach them some real ranching skills. But for now, it's important that you know I've been impressed with all five boys' commitment to working hard."

Pastor Stillwater offered his help with the program.

CJ thanked him for his support. "John," he said to Molly's father. "Can you fill us in on the preparations you've already done for the barn raising, and the tasks that still need completing?"

The older man stood. "The plans are drawn up and the materials purchased. The ground is cleared and the lumber laid in, with most of the hardware sorted, as well. CJ and I will do a walk-through this afternoon to make sure there's nothing we've missed."

The rest of the meeting was devoted to last-minute organizational issues. It took less than an hour for CJ to cover all the points. He appointed crew chiefs and assigned the critical jobs of joinery and dowelling to men with the necessary skills.

When he was finished, Edmund once again took over the meeting. "Now that we've presented our idea of an association and laid out the benefits, I'd like to see a show of hands. All those in favor of forming an official cattle raisers' association…?"

Every hand went up.

Edmund adjourned the meeting just as the first drops of rain hit the ground.

Chapter Eighteen

The morning of the barn raising arrived with a considerable amount of noise and commotion. Before the first light of dawn had barely staggered over the horizon, Molly heard the creak of wagon wheels slogging across the muddy land. Neighbors calling to one another accompanied the sound.

The work would soon begin.

Eager to add her effort to the cause, she dressed quickly and made her way downstairs. Momentarily forgoing her morning coffee, she stepped outside, and into what could only be described as controlled chaos.

So many people, she thought, *all here to help my family*.

She was quite literally stricken speechless by the outpouring of support.

Just last night, her father had claimed it would take the entire community pulling together to raise the barn in a single day. As wagons pulled up, and even more approached from the distance, Molly realized the entire community *had* shown up.

The rain from the day before had come in fierce and vicious, and had left with equal speed less than an hour later, giving the hot Texas sun hours to burn away some of the water, not all, and certainly not the scent of wet ash or soot.

The fragrance of freshly cut lumber, sawdust and iron, leather and tar, wafted over the putrid odor of charred wood. Molly leveled her shoulders, breathed in a lungful of the pungent air.

Having held out for an entire two and a half minutes, she searched for her first glimpse of CJ. She found him almost immediately, standing at the center of the activity, organizing the assembled men and boys into four groups. He then sent them off to build the side frames of the barn, or so Molly presumed.

He'd explained the building process to her yesterday afternoon, when he'd come inside the kitchen after completing a walk-through with her father. Molly had thought she'd understood the magnitude of the undertaking, but she hadn't. Not until she'd witnessed the organized teamwork herself.

She'd always known CJ was a man of action. From the first time she'd met him she'd admired his ability to focus on a task and see it through to the end.

When he made a promise, he stuck to it.

He would make some woman a wonderful husband.

More than ever she regretted that the woman would not be her.

Captured by the sight of him, she watched him a moment longer. He was big and skilled, larger than life and so dedicated to making sure the barn would be completed in a day.

How could she not adore him? How could she not *love* him?

Love? Something warm and soft moved through her. Of course she loved CJ. She'd always loved him, in vary-

ing degrees. Now, she felt the emotion with a depth of
maturity that would last a lifetime.

He noticed her watching him, and stopped in his
tracks, perfectly still for a moment. Then he grinned,
quickly and impulsively, and Molly forgot to breathe.

Out of self-preservation, she looked away.

Another wagon bounced across the land, this one
driven by Cookie. The twins sat on either side of him.
The flatbed was full of additional lumber, as well as pots
and pans he would deliver to the kitchen.

The girls squealed out a greeting to Molly.

She started toward them.

A lot had changed since Ned had left home. Though
her day-to-day existence had remained much the same,
Molly's life had taken a dramatic turn. Even her parents
had come around to a new way of thinking. Instead of
warning her against getting too close to the Thorn family,
they seemed to be pushing her in that direction.

Especially her mother, who all but shoved Molly out
of the house every morning, after extracting her promise
to tell that dear, sweet man and his lovely nieces hello
for her.

Cookie set the brake and took his time climbing to
the ground. "I'll haul these inside—" he motioned to the
pots and pans on top of the lumber "—and get to cooking right away."

"That would be wonderful." Molly reached for the
twins, setting Anna on the ground first.

Just as she reached for Sarah, another wagon pulled
in beside them, manned by Pastor Stillwater. Instead of
lumber in the flatbed, he carted the five boys from town
who'd helped Molly's brothers clear away the debris from
the fire.

Barely acknowledging her and the girls, they spilled out of the wagon and made a beeline for CJ.

Unaffected by the snub, Sarah looked out over the crowd. "This is so exciting," she declared. "Everyone came to help, just like Unca Corny said they would."

Brandon Stillwater stood in the back of his wagon and called for silence. "Please stop what you're doing and gather around." He waited for activity to cease. "I'd like to take a moment to lift up a word of prayer before we get too deeply involved in our individual tasks."

A hush fell over the crowd as they moved in closer.

"On behalf of the Carson family, I want to thank all of you for coming today." This earned him a nod of gratitude from Molly's parents. "Let us remember the value of helping our neighbors long after this day is over. As my earthly father taught my brother and me, what we do for ourselves dies with us. What we do for others remains forever. Let us pray."

All heads bowed.

"Father God, we humbly ask for Your blessing. Guide our hands as we rebuild the Carson barn. May we work quickly, efficiently and may the result be a sturdy structure that will last for decades. We pray this, Lord, in Your Son's name. Amen."

People separated off in groups.

Anna tapped Molly on the wrist. "Cookie said we can help him in the kitchen."

"Then we better get to work." Molly took their hands and guided the girls to the house.

At the door, she couldn't stop herself from sneaking a peek at CJ. He winked, and Molly couldn't help it; she sighed.

How could she not? The man was just so, well, sigh-worthy.

Oh, how she wanted to stay and watch him work. There was no time, of course. They had a long day ahead.

The barn was taking shape.

Somewhere around midafternoon, CJ set his hammer down and stepped away from the structure. The corner posts were in place and the cross braces set. The side frames had been raised and the rafters were set in place. Edmund led the team of men securing the roofing felt atop the sheathing.

Hank Snowden, acting once again as Lucas Bennett's proxy, directed his crew as they fastened pieces of siding along the exterior walls. The Gillen and Forester brothers worked alongside John Carson's sons. The boys mostly fetched supplies and water for the crews, small but necessary tasks so that the work could continue without interruption.

"We've made considerable progress." Satisfaction rang in John Carson's voice as he came to stand beside CJ. "We're on target to finish before dark."

"It's been a good day," CJ said. As if to punctuate the statement, the sound of hammers blended with the shouts and laughter of the men.

"I've been meaning to ask you." Speculation shifted into the other rancher's eyes. "How goes the campaign to win my daughter's heart?"

Caught off guard by the swift change of topic, CJ stared at him for a full three heartbeats.

"Not well," he said at last, hearing the weary resignation in his own voice. "She's proving stubborn."

"Don't despair, my boy." John clasped his shoulder briefly. "She'll come around."

CJ wasn't nearly as confident as Molly's father. "I can't

help thinking she's intentionally avoiding me," he admitted, needing to say the words out loud.

"Let me offer you a piece of advice I wish someone would have given me when I was courting her mother." The other man readjusted his stance, his gaze momentarily lost in some distant memory. "Strong women like Molly and my Helen need careful handling. You can't force them to your will, you have to guide them there—no different than taming a wild maverick."

"With all due respect, Molly is not a horse."

John chuckled. "I was speaking metaphorically. The theory still applies. My point is that a good horse trainer knows the power of walking away. If done at just the right moment, nine times out of ten the animal follows."

"You're telling me to give up on your daughter?"

"I'm telling you to be patient, treat her with respect and gentleness. Give her the chance to come to you."

As CJ considered the advice, a horse and rider appeared on the ridge. Squinting against the glare of the afternoon sun, he immediately recognized his foreman. Duke had stayed behind to keep an eye on the Triple-T while CJ and the other ranch hands attended the barn raising.

A terrible sense of foreboding had him stalking in Duke's direction. John Carson matched CJ step for step.

Duke skillfully maneuvered his horse around the various work crews. From the man's clenched jaw and the rigid set of his shoulders, it was clear something was wrong.

"What's happened?" CJ asked, looking up at him.

Duke's expression turned grave. "I spent the day riding the fence line. I found nothing out of the ordinary, until I went to check on the herd in the north pasture.

An entire section of the fence is missing and the herd is somewhat smaller."

A burning throb knotted in CJ's throat. "How much smaller?"

"By my estimation, we're missing at least twenty head, maybe more."

CJ experienced an empty feeling in the pit of his stomach. His first instinct was to charge out and investigate the ruined fence for himself. On the other hand, he was needed here. They were close to completing the barn. He hated leaving when they were so close to finishing the exterior.

John Carson solved the quandary for him. "Go on, CJ, see to your ranch." When he remained where he was, the older man added, "You've done more than your share of work today. We'll manage a few hours without you."

Still hesitant, CJ cast a glance in the direction of the barn. Under the expert guidance of the crew chiefs, the structure was already looking sound.

Satisfied that he wasn't leaving John Carson in the lurch, CJ made his decision. "I'll be back before dark."

"Whatever it takes." The man's lips curved. "We aren't going anywhere."

Tamping down the desire to let anger rule his actions, CJ retrieved his horse from one of the corrals. After securing the saddle strap and readjusting the rest of the tack, he mounted up and rode off, followed by Duke. Once they crossed on to Thorn land, CJ pushed his horse faster, and Duke matched his pace. They rode hard toward the northern property line.

After weaving among clumps of grazing cows, they finally came to a halt at the damaged fence.

CJ's temper flared when he saw the gaping hole and downed posts, all four of them. He studied the impressions left on the ground, a collection of horse and cow hoofprints. The pockmarks ran in a straight line across the spongy earth, starting in the pasture and leading over the first ridge five hundred feet beyond the fence line.

The thief was getting sloppier, not even bothering to cover his tracks.

Swiveling his attention back to the fence, CJ studied the damage with hard, narrowed eyes. It would take his entire crew to fix it properly. Even then, the job would take considerable effort.

"Let's get this fence repaired as best we can." He dismounted, slung his horse's reins over a portion of the fence not damaged. "We'll come back tomorrow and do the job properly."

A man of few words, Duke gave a nod and dismounted.

Two hours later, comfortable that the fence would hold the cows in until morning, CJ returned to the Carson ranch. His frustration disappeared at the sight of the progress made in his absence.

The exterior was nearly complete, with only the roofing left to finish. Most of the hammering now came from inside the barn, where crews labored over the animal stalls, grain bins, tack room and cleaning stations. The windows and doors would be installed last. At this rate, they would indeed be finished before nightfall.

Stopping at the corral, CJ dismounted, took care of his horse and then went in search of John Carson. He found him speaking with Lucas Bennett, the lone rancher who'd refused to attend their meeting.

Not exactly *refused*, CJ mentally amended, attempting to be fair. Lucas had agreed to be a founding member of the association, but had sent Hank to act as his proxy.

If pressed, CJ would admit that he didn't especially like Lucas. He never had. There was something about the rancher that set him on edge. His aversion for the man made little sense, however, especially when others considered him an upstanding member of their community.

"CJ." John greeted him with a handshake. "Your arrival gives me hope the damage to your fence wasn't as bad as your foreman led us to believe."

"We managed to repair the wire. But the entire section will to have to be replaced."

Lucas's eyebrows shot up. "You had trouble at your place?"

CJ explained about the stolen cattle.

"That's a real shame." The rancher's commiseration seemed sincere. "The loss of my cows was a real blow."

Only then did CJ recall that Lucas had been a victim of the cattle rustler, as well. Which begged the question, why was he so resistant to joining their association?

Before CJ could ask the question a movement at the back door of the main house had him looking over his shoulder. Molly stood in the sunlight, a large tray of food in her hands.

She set it on one of the many picnic tables scattered about, then glanced in CJ's direction.

Their gazes connected and something in him shifted, softened, then resettled in a way that reminded him of the important things in life. Family. Friends. Community.

Molly.

He needed a moment in her presence, a chance to wash away the taint of the last few hours. CJ started toward her.

John's voice followed after him. "Remember what I said, son. Patience."

CJ waved a hand over his head in acknowledgment of the advice.

Patience, he repeated in his head, knowing Molly's father was right. Unfortunately, the closer CJ drew to

Molly, the more *impatient* he became. He wanted to start their future together.

With her face full of concern, Molly met him at the edge of the eating area. "I heard about the trouble on your ranch."

The look in her eyes warmed him to the depths of his soul. "You worried about me, Molly?"

"Always."

The lack of hesitancy rendered him hopeful. CJ knew with a man's instinct that Molly cared for him—with the kind of caring he'd given up hope of ever winning from a woman like her. Molly had shattered his previous misconceptions with her open, giving nature.

Surely, with the proper amount of patience and persistence, CJ could shove past her barriers, help her face her fears and ultimately win her heart.

"I heard you lost twenty cows."

News traveled fast. "That's about right, give or take a few head."

Expelling a breath, Molly looked in the direction of his ranch. "How bad was the damage to the fence?"

She wanted to talk about the trouble on his spread? He supposed it was as good a topic as any, especially if it meant spending a few minutes in her company.

"Duke and I managed to temporarily fix the wiring. Tomorrow, we'll make more permanent repairs."

"Oh." Her eyes cut back to him. They were huge and sparkling in the afternoon sun. "Have you thought about enlisting the Young Ranchers' help?"

"That's not a bad idea."

"I'm happy you agree. I've come to like those boys. They're good kids." She paused and her features tightened.

An unexpected reaction. "Is there something about the boys I should know?"

"No. Well, actually, yes. They need masculine role models, but they also need…" Her words trailed off.

"What, Molly? What do they need?"

She opened her mouth, closed it, sighed heavily, then opened it again. "Food. I don't think they're fed on a regular basis."

CJ's heart filled with dread. "They tell you that?"

"It's just an impression. They gobble down their food like half-wild animals, which isn't necessarily all that odd. Growing boys always eat like that." She laughed softly, then shook her head and turned serious. "But those boys are overly enthusiastic in their gratitude for the food. That's what gives them away."

How had CJ missed that? Because he didn't think like a mother.

"Let me ask Brandon Stillwater to bring the boys to the ranch tomorrow. I'll put them to work, and you, Molly—" he took her hand, placed it briefly against his heart "—will feed them."

A slow smile curved her lips. "Now that's a plan I can easily get behind."

With the image of her beautiful smile playing in his mind, CJ went back to work on the barn.

Tomorrow, he decided, was going to be a very good day.

Chapter Nineteen

Everyone involved in the building project declared the barn raising a success. There were a few things that needed to be done yet—painting the exterior, a bit of specialty work on the inside. Nothing her father, brothers and the ranch hands couldn't complete in the coming weeks.

Molly knew the successful completion of the massive structure was due, in large part, to CJ. Her parents had thanked him profusely. CJ, being CJ, had deflected the praise back to every man, woman and child who'd shown up to do their part.

Was it any wonder Molly loved him?

Was there any way her time in his home would end without heartache?

As CJ promised, he'd spoken with Brandon Stillwater. The preacher had agreed to cart the Gillen and Forester brothers out to CJ's ranch the next morning.

Now, with the sun riding low in the afternoon sky, Molly and the twins stood on the porch, watching the men and boys returning from a long day on the range.

She lifted her hand in greeting.

The girls mimicked the move. "I can't wait to tell Unca

Corny that Anna and me made the johnnycakes," Sarah declared.

This is the life I want.

A spark of surety ignited deep within Molly, one she didn't dare fan into a flame. The man she loved wanted more than marriage. He wanted a large family.

Molly thought her heart might break for the family they would never have together. CJ needed someone to share his life with him, not just a friend, but a helpmate, someone who cared about him, who loved him. She could be that person, if only he didn't want children.

"…and it was really fun, digging our hands in the cornmeal. It felt gritty, but it wasn't too terrible."

Realizing Sarah had continued the conversation without her, Molly attempted to file through the information the child had imparted. "Sounds as if you like cooking."

"I love it."

"Me, too," Anna said.

Girls after her own heart.

Molly gathered them close. Instead of feeling comforted by their nearness, she felt bone-deep sorrow, because this moment felt like goodbye.

She was being overly dramatic, a trait she wouldn't normally attribute to herself. As she'd done so many times in the past three weeks, she locked away her fears, then chatted with the girls about the joy of cooking.

Near the corral, CJ showed the boys how to dismount properly and then guide their horses into the barn with a gentle hold on the reins. He was incredibly patient with the youths and was rewarded with their undivided attention.

Several minutes after disappearing into the barn, CJ exited, with boys flanking him on all sides. Their youthful laughter mingled with CJ's lower-pitched chuckles.

He chose that moment to look up. His piercing brown eyes turned serious and full of intent, a silent request for the one thing she couldn't give him—a yes to his marriage proposal.

Molly had never been this aware of a man. The sensation hurt. Oh, how it hurt.

"We made excellent progress today, mending not only the broken sections of the fence, but several other weak areas, as well." CJ came to a stop at the bottom of the porch steps and smiled up at her. "Thanks to these cowpokes, the Triple-T fence line is once again secure."

Looks of pride filled their faces.

"Well, then." Molly made eye contact with each of the five boys. "Let's get the cowpokes fed."

A cheer rose up from the group.

The next ten minutes went quickly. CJ took the boys to the well, where the six of them washed off the dirt from the day.

When they returned, the twins hovered around the boys like bees in a flower garden. Molly's smile came immediately as she watched their valiant effort to engage the boys in conversation, especially Sean.

Both girls stared up at the older boy with stars in their eyes.

Sean, for his part, seemed completely oblivious to their female interest. The tolerant pose he struck reminded Molly of the early days of her acquaintance with CJ. Had she looked at the handsome rancher in the same way his nieces stared up at Sean?

Molly had only a moment to ponder the question when the man himself came up beside her. His grin flashed and her heart fluttered at the romantic figure he made.

He was certainly pleasing to look at, tall, lean, muscular in all the right places, but his best features, at least in Molly's opinion, were his rock-solid character and his patience. He was a man of Christian integrity, who exuded quiet strength and confidence.

A woman could lean on him in good times and bad.

Anna caught sight of their uncle and rushed to him. Sarah soon followed, and so began a detailed accounting of what it took to make johnnycakes just the way he liked them.

Molly's heart filled with affection. The girls were unusually animated this afternoon, no doubt due to the presence of the Young Ranchers.

"I'll get the table set," she said, pleased her voice sounded even. "Then we'll eat."

Without another word, she went inside the house and shut the door behind her with a soft click.

CJ noticed the change in Molly the moment he and the children were sitting at the table, passing around full platters of food.

"Aren't you going to eat with us, Miss Molly?" one of the Gillen brothers asked her.

Her face went taut and, after a shake of her head, she made some excuse about needing to clean the kitchen. Her answer satisfied the boys.

It did not satisfy CJ. But he didn't think challenging her in front of the children was a wise idea.

Patience, her father had told him. At this point, CJ thought he could win awards for his fortitude.

As the meal progressed, Molly continued puttering around in the kitchen. She'd grown unnaturally quiet, almost withdrawn, as if intentionally holding a portion of herself separate from the rest of them. CJ couldn't think what had occurred to make her create such obvious distance, not only with him but with the girls, as well.

Thankfully, Anna and Sarah didn't notice. They were too busy mooning over the Gillen and Forester brothers.

Their obvious adoration was pretty cute. Wondering if Molly noticed, and hoping to share the humorous moment with her, CJ caught her eye.

She looked even more miserable than before.

Not for the first time, CJ wondered if her shift in mood had something to do with the children. Was she mourning not having a child with her deceased husband?

It was possible.

Though CJ could never replace George Langley, he would love Molly as well as any man could love a woman. She deserved a houseful of her own children. She would be a good, kind, loving mother. CJ couldn't wait to get started on their life together.

His patience had just run out.

"Molly, I'd like to speak with you a moment."

Before she could respond, the front door swung open, hitting the wall hard. Everyone in the room jumped at the sound, including CJ.

A second later, he was on his feet.

Duke stood in the doorway. "We have a problem—" he broke off, glanced at the children at the table "—in the, uh, barn. Come quick."

A sick feeling roiled in CJ's stomach.

"Right behind you." The scrape of chairs accompanied his words. "No," he told the boys. "I need you to stay here."

"What if it's something we can help with?" Sean asked.

"You're more help here, watching over Molly and the twins." He gave the youth a pointed look. "Understand?"

To his credit, the kid didn't argue. "We'll take care of them," he answered solemnly.

"Good man."

Out on the porch, Duke told CJ news that turned his blood to ice. "One of the ranch hands caught a man trying to steal one of your horses. We've got him cornered in the barn."

CJ's entire bearing went hard.

"Gage has a gun pointed to his head. Problem is he's got a gun trained on Terry's. The three are in a standoff, with the promise of bloodshed if one of them flinches."

CJ took off toward the barn.

Duke fell into step beside him.

"You get a look at his face?" he asked his foreman.

"Only his eyes. He's got a bandanna pulled up to his temples and the brim of his hat is pulled down low."

At the barn door, CJ shot out a hand to keep Duke from proceeding. "We do this right and go in smart."

He nodded.

"Give me one of your guns."

Without hesitation, his foreman pulled out a Colt 45 revolver from the holster on his hip, then retrieved the other one for himself.

CJ snapped open the barrel, checked the load and placement of the bullets. Satisfied the gun was fully loaded and in sound working order, he whipped the barrel back in place with a flick of his wrist. "Stay close."

They entered the barn shoulder to shoulder.

CJ's breathing came fast, his eyes gauging, searching. Hearing the gravelly voices and muttered oaths from the last stall on his right, he inched in the direction of the escalating standoff.

White-hot rage heightened his senses. Someone had come onto his land with evil intent and now held his men at gunpoint.

Slowly, very slowly, CJ raised his gun and entered the stall, Duke a step behind. "Drop your weapons."

As if he hadn't spoken, all three men stood rooted to the spot, guns raised.

"Gage, Terry, you okay?"

"Yeah, boss," Gage snarled. "We caught us a horse thief."

"So I hear." CJ inched a step closer to the dangerous stalemate. "There's four of us and one of you." He spoke in a calm, conversational tone. "The odds are not in your favor, cowboy."

The thief, covered in shadow, twisted his head to the right, then left, as if searching for a solution to his situation out of empty air.

"I'd suggest surrendering your weapon before someone, probably you, ends up hurt."

"You threatening me? When I have a gun pointed at your man's head?" The man growled the question in a deep, artificial tone that sounded vaguely familiar.

CJ narrowed his eyes at the dark form. "Just pointing out the complexities of the situation. You might take out one of us, but we'll *definitely* take you out."

"I'll do what you ask, but only if we keep this between you and me."

Something in the thief's stance was familiar, but one thing was clear: CJ wasn't staring at Ned. He would know his own brother. Relief surged. Ned wasn't the cattle rustler.

Then who was this man? "Everybody out."

"Boss, you sure this is wise?"

"If our friend here had plans to shoot, he would have done so by now." That didn't mean CJ was taking any chances with his men's life. He pulled back the hammer. "I expect you to be reasonable as my ranch hands leave."

The man nodded. There was enough light for CJ to make out red-rimmed, faded blue eyes. That sense of familiarity struck him again. He still couldn't pull up a name.

One by one, his ranch hands filed from the stall, Duke bringing up the rear. The foreman stopped beside CJ. "You want me to get the sheriff?"

CJ gave a quick, nearly imperceptible nod.

"Good enough." Duke continued out of the stall.

Once they were alone, CJ took a step toward the one remaining occupant. The man's identity was tucked in his memory but he couldn't seem to draw it into focus. "It's just you and me," he said. "Now drop your weapon."

The gun stayed pointed at CJ's chest. "This'll go better if you let me leave."

"You mean better for you." CJ kept his focus on the man's eyes. Any sudden move would show there first.

"I never meant for things to go this far." The quick, nervous speech was wrapped in a gruff, raspy voice that CJ didn't recognize.

However, the set of his shoulders reminded him of… someone. "I said lower your weapon."

With surprising cooperation, the shadowed figure did as ordered.

"Now, hand it over. Slowly. No, slower. Yes, that's it."

CJ sensed rather than saw the man's eyes narrow with intent. In a single, desperate move, he reversed the weapon in his grip, leaped forward and slammed the butt of the gun into CJ's head.

Reflexively, CJ swung to his left. Not fast enough. *Not fast enough.* Pain exploded behind his eyes. His feet gave out under him. As he crumpled to the ground, CJ thought of Molly and the twins.

Numbing darkness grabbed at him, urging him to let go. Just…let…go. He tried to call out to Duke. A swift kick in the ribs stole his ability to speak.

The shadowy figure stood over him, an unmistakable snarl in his voice. "Should have stayed out of it, CJ."

The thief knew him.

The thought barely had a chance to register before CJ's world went gray, growing darker, darker. He fought to keep his vision clear, but lost the battle almost immediately.

An image of Molly appeared behind his eyelids. He'd wasted so much time, time he could never get back. Life was too short, too fragile to let anything stand between them. Nothing else mattered in CJ's world without Molly in his life.

He'd had his chance years ago and had let her slip away.

Lord, if I survive this I'm never letting her go again.

The prayer brought a moment of utter peace. And then everything went black.

Chapter Twenty

Molly exited the house at the same moment a dark figure bolted out of the barn and took off running toward the eastern horizon. The Triple-T ranch hands followed after him, their shouts lifting on the air, their feet pounding hard on the ground.

Unfortunately, the fleeing figure had a considerable head start. Molly cataloged each of the men pursuing him and came up short by one.

Where was CJ?

He needs me. She knew it with the certainty of a woman hopelessly, desperately in love. From the moment he'd left the dinner table, she'd been unable to shake the notion that he was in trouble.

Now, with the girls still inside the house, Molly's blood turned cold, ice-cold. Fear punched like a brutal, white-knuckled fist.

Her feet were moving before her mind registered where they were taking her. As she swung open the barn door, she prayed to God for CJ's safety. She lifted up her requests with great fervor, asking the Holy Spirit for the words when her mind emptied of coherent thought.

She called out, "CJ. CJ, where are you?"

A masculine groan drew her to the back of the barn.

Following the sound of a second moan, she rushed inside the last stall and dropped to her knees beside CJ's prone form.

"CJ." She put all her love, worry, anger and affection in his name. "Talk to me."

There was a single, thready breath. Then his eyes opened. "Molly."

Her name sounded like both a caress and an apology.

Gulping through the storm of emotion rising in her throat, she cupped his face. "Are you hurt?"

"No idea." He struggled to sit up.

"Slowly now." Molly braced a hand behind his shoulder, urging him along, patient but persistent. All the while she ran her eyes over him, head to toe, toe to head, searching for injury. Other than the lump forming on the right side of his head, he appeared unharmed.

Once he was in an upright position, she investigated the injury with gentle, probing fingers, then searched for other wounds. Finding none, she let out a relieved sigh, moving her fingers over his scalp a moment longer. "That is one nasty bump."

When she pressed a little harder, he winced.

"Should have seen the blow coming." The muscles in his jaw flexed. "He caught me by surprise."

"You're going to have a monstrous headache."

"Already do." He raised a tentative hand to his skull, flinched when he touched his injury. "It could have been worse. He could have shot me."

A gasp flew out of Molly's lips. "Are you telling me you faced down a man with a loaded gun?"

He slanted her a look, one she couldn't quite read.

"Molly, my beautiful, lovely, Molly." CJ reached up

and hooked a tendril of her hair around his finger. "Are you worried about me?"

He'd asked her a similar question yesterday. Her answer was the same, if somewhat escalated. "Terrified."

Despite his obvious pain, his well-cut lips spread into a boyish smile. "I like having you worry about me."

"Well, I don't like it. Not one bit."

It frightened her to realize how easily she could have lost him. She had a chilling moment, barely the length of a heartbeat, when she saw what her days would be like without him in the world. "You scared ten years off my life."

The twins rushed into the stall, eyes wild. They were frantic, out of breath, tears streaking down their puffy cheeks. They skidded to a stop when their eyes landed on CJ.

"Unca Corny!" Anna screeched in a frightened, panicked voice. The sound was so high-pitched both CJ and Molly winced.

The girls fell to their knees beside Molly, their faces leached of color.

"I'm okay," he told them, pulling them close. "Nothing to worry about."

With the brutal honesty of a child, Sarah eyed him suspiciously. "Then how come you look like you're going to be sick?"

The question had him climbing hastily to his feet. "I'm fine, really."

No, he wasn't, not if his pinched lips and bunched shoulders were anything to go by. He managed to stand, though he was swaying like a sapling in a stiff wind.

Molly reached for him, thinking to steady him, but he warded her off with a wave of his arm.

Stubborn, wonderful man.

Molly took the girls' hands and tugged them back a few steps to give him room to find his balance.

Masculine shouts came from the barn door. Within minutes the stall was full of people. First came the Gillen brothers. The Foresters spilled in next, followed by the Triple-T ranch hands. The only people missing were Cookie and Duke.

Breathing hard, his gaze darting between CJ and the other ranch hands, Gage delivered the bad news. "He got away."

CJ absently rubbed at his temples as if to relieve a shard of unexpected pain. "You get a look at his face?"

"Afraid not."

"Me, either."

Cookie appeared at the edge of the stall a beat later, scowling and barking at everyone to move aside. "I mean it," he growled. "Out of my way."

A path immediately formed.

One look at CJ's face and Cookie was back to issuing orders in rapid-fire succession. "Everybody out, now, all but Miss Molly and the twins."

Verbally flinging more threats, all but bodily shoving the men and boys out of the stall, Cookie managed to clear the area as quickly as it had filled up.

Now that the danger was over, Molly started shaking. She hated giving in to the weakness, but it couldn't be helped. She cared for CJ too much, *loved* him too much.

"Molly." CJ reached for her. She nearly went into his arms, but her hands were still busy holding on to the twins.

They broke away and ran to their uncle a second time. He sank to his haunches and tugged them into his embrace.

"I'm glad you're okay," Sarah whispered into his shoulder.

Anna seconded the remark and then added, "You can't leave us, Unca Corny, not ever."

"Not ever," he promised.

Cookie's mild blue eyes locked with Molly's. "Girls, I baked a cake for our Young Ranchers. Want to help me serve it?"

"Will you give us a piece, too?"

"Absolutely."

Lured by the promise of cake, Anna and Sarah deserted their uncle. Cookie hustled them along with a gentle hand at their backs.

"You know where to find us," he said over his shoulder.

And then...

There were two.

CJ, eyes on Molly, only her, opened his arms in silent appeal.

Refusing to argue with herself any longer, Molly drew in a shuddering breath and went to him. He buried his face in her hair and breathed in slowly.

Cocooned in his embrace, she spoke her greatest fears aloud. "You could have been killed."

His arms tightened ever so slightly, a sure sign he wasn't as steady as he pretended. "I'm safe now."

"Yes." She forced herself to step back. Away from the man she loved.

Away from the future she wanted. It was time to let him go.

"CJ—"

"Molly—"

They shared an awkward laugh.

Eyes tender, he brushed a hand down her arm, the move casual yet powerful in its simplicity.

"Molly," he began again. "After the blow came to my head, right before the world went black, I realized just how fragile life really is and how quickly it can be snuffed out."

She closed her eyes against the image of him lying flat on the stall floor. "If you're trying to scare me you're doing a remarkably fine job."

"I'm not trying to scare you. I'm trying to reveal the contents of my heart."

No, she wanted to scream. He couldn't love her. *Please, Lord, don't let him love me.* Anything but that. It would be so much harder to walk away.

Smiling sadly, he took her hand, cupped it protectively in his. "I'm no longer sorry Ned left. I should be, but I'm not. He gave me the greatest gift. Two beautiful daughters and you, Molly."

"Me?"

"Had my brother stayed home I might have missed the blessing right under my nose. You and me…" He wagged a finger between them. "There's always been something between us. I felt it five years ago. I still feel it today."

He was declaring himself. And breaking her heart at the same time. She tried to pull free of his grip. He refused to let her go.

"I love you, Molly. When you're near me everything makes sense. I want to marry you as soon as possible." He lowered himself to one knee. "Will you marry me?"

A hot, blistering wave of regret threatened to push her to the ground. CJ loved her. He wanted to marry her. She couldn't think of anything more remarkable and yet simultaneously awful. "Oh, CJ."

Remaining on one knee, he pressed his lips to her

knuckles. "You're a good woman, the best I've ever known. When I'm with you I'm a better man." He rose to his feet. "Say yes. Say you'll be my wife."

"I'm sorry, CJ." There was only one way out of this mess, only one way to ensure he didn't continue pursuing her once she gave her answer. "I could never marry a man like you."

"A man like me." He repeated the words in a fast, rough cadence. Behind his eyes, she saw the confusion, the disbelief and the pain. Pain she'd caused by letting him think he was unworthy.

She'd made a tactical error. In her attempt to protect CJ from the resentment that would eventually fill their home if she married him, she'd hurt him.

She was a horrible, awful person.

"What kind of man am I, Molly?"

Kind, loving, born to be a father. "We would never suit," she said, evading a direct answer. "We want different things in life."

Turning away from her, he paced the perimeter of the stall. "Are you honestly telling me you don't want a home of your own?"

"That's not what I said."

He returned to her side. His eyes, a deep troubled brown, searched her face. "Do you not want children?"

She wanted to tell him the truth, needed to tell him the truth, tried to tell him the truth. "No, I don't."

"You're lying." His eyes narrowed on hers, his gaze so intense she was sure he could see all the way into her soul. "You want children. You just don't want them with me." His mouth was set and firm, matched only by the severity of his pained expression.

"I would give you a dozen babies, if I could. But I can't." Her heart ached for him. For her. For them both.

"One day, you'll thank me for turning down your proposal."

"I'm supposed to believe you're somehow doing me a favor by rejecting me?"

"It has to be this way." Her voice broke over the words and she pressed a hand to her mouth.

Instead of judgment, or condemnation, or even anger, she saw compassion in his eyes. "Tell me what has you so afraid to take a chance on me, on us?"

Unable to stand the spiral of anguish descending upon her, and too ashamed to tell CJ the truth, Molly took the coward's way out. "Goodbye."

She muttered one last request for forgiveness, then spun on her heel and ran out of the stall. Blinded with unshed tears, she clambered onto Sadie's back and rode hard toward the Rolling Hills ranch.

Her time with the Thorn family was over. The dream of a life with CJ and the twins was no longer within her grasp. She would find a way to say goodbye to the twins properly. Not yet. Not until she could do so without breaking down.

Her heart was shattering. All that was left was the crying.

She gave in to her sorrow with big, choking sobs.

Be patient and give Molly the chance to come to you.

Against every instinct, CJ followed John Carson's advice. Instead of going after Molly, he let her leave the ranch. He was questioning his decision when Jeb Fuller arrived at the Triple-T. CJ gave the sheriff his statement, including his suspicions concerning the man's identity.

"So you think it's someone local?"

"There was something about him that felt familiar."

After that, he had to focus on getting the twins calmed

down and in bed. They were confused over why Molly wasn't there to tuck them in. CJ made up an excuse for her, knowing she would never intentionally hurt the girls. She'd done so only because he'd pushed her too hard. He should have taken her father's advice.

Unable to sleep, he paced through the house all night. Somewhere in the early morning hours, after dissecting every portion of his conversation with Molly, CJ realized where he'd went wrong. He shouldn't have let her leave the ranch.

She'd been close to telling him the real reason behind her refusal to his proposal. *I would give you a dozen babies if I could...*

The answer had been right in front of him and he'd missed it. Thinking back over their first conversation about marriage, CJ remembered Molly's vulnerable expression. He'd assumed the look meant she was still in love with her dead husband and mourning his loss.

Now he wondered.

He remembered the sorrow that came and went in her eyes whenever she looked at the twins, the wistful longing whenever CJ spoke of having children.

In the privacy of his mind, he reviewed his original marriage proposal. That had been when the subject of children had first come up. CJ had mentioned wanting a houseful of kids.

Her response hadn't struck him as odd at the time. *I always thought two was a nice number.*

She'd looked so shocked when he'd said eight was even better. After he'd amended the number to six she'd turned down his marriage proposal.

Guilt pushed its way through him.

He'd been a selfish fool, thinking only of himself and what marriage to Molly would mean to him.

A horse whinny cut through his troubled thoughts. He looked out the window, noted that the sun was already peeking over the horizon. A new day beckoned. CJ's ambition for the immediate future had one focus. Make things right with Molly.

He hustled to meet her, hesitated a fraction of a second when he saw the young woman atop the mare. "Good morning, Daisy."

Molly's sister yawned behind her hand. "Morning."

"I see Molly sent you to take care of the twins." It was a statement, not a question.

"Nothing gets past you."

"She give you a reason?"

Daisy stifled another yawn. "Said she's not feeling well."

Molly was ill? Panic hammered down on him. Suddenly, the world felt too small, the air too stifling. "Have your parents sent for a doctor?"

"She's not that kind of sick." Perfectly calm, as if they were discussing the Texas heat, the young woman dismounted and swung her horse's reins over the porch rail. "She was up all night crying."

His heart slammed against his ribs. He needed to get to Molly. Daisy moved into his path, barring his way. "What did you do to my sister?"

"I asked her to marry me."

"Oh." She angled her head and studied his face. "You must be really terrible with words."

"You have no idea," he muttered.

"Maybe you should try asking her again, only this time try using pretty, complimentary words. Women like those."

He felt his lips twitch. "I'll take that under advisement."

"Flowers couldn't hurt, either." She patted him on the shoulder, held his stare. "Don't mess this up, CJ. I think I'd like you as a brother-in-law."

He gave in to the laugh bubbling in his throat. "I *know* I'd like you as a sister-in-law."

"Then go reconcile your differences with Molly."

Coiled like a spring, he covered the ground between the Triple-T and the Carson ranch as fast as he dared push his horse. As if drawn by some unknown force, he bypassed the main house and hiked down to the stream that fed into Kettle Creek.

His feet halted at the sight of the lone figure sitting on a rock overlooking the water. With her knees drawn up and caged in the circle of her arms, Molly looked so alone, so lost.

He knew she was hurting. CJ hurt for her, because he knew the cause of her sorrow was something that pretty, complimentary words couldn't fix.

That didn't mean he wasn't going to try. He vowed to do anything, say anything, sacrifice everything to ease her pain.

With no specific plan in mind, he navigated the rocky bank with as much speed as he dared.

"Molly."

She looked over her shoulder and he saw the tears in her eyes. Her sadness was a living, breathing thing. He hated that he'd caused a portion of her pain. *Lord, give me the words to convince her to take a leap of faith with me.*

Wiping furiously at her cheeks, she slowly gained her feet. "You shouldn't be here, CJ."

She was perfectly polite, her voice steady, her gaze tracking everywhere, yet landing nowhere. The wild glancing about made her look small and vulnerable.

"I'm exactly where I want to be, Molly." He stretched out his hand.

For a moment, the world seemed to slow down and wait. Would she answer his silent call?

She took a tentative step toward him. Then stopped.

CJ wanted to push past her composure, whatever it took to break through all that female resistance and uncover the frightened woman underneath. He needed to soothe her fears. But she had to admit to them first.

"I have one question," he said, lowering his hand. "Do you love me?"

Her calm vanished. "Yes. I love you." Her face showed nothing but misery. "With all my heart."

"But you won't marry me." With slow, gentle movements he swept a lock of hair off her cheek. "Tell me why."

"I..." She lowered her head. "I don't know how."

He took her trembling chin in his hand and gently urged her to look at him. "Trust me with your secret pain."

"I can't." A tear slipped from the corner of her eye. "You will think less of me."

"That will never happen."

"I..." She lifted her chin and did as he suggested, blurting out the cause of her pain. "I'm barren."

"There, that wasn't so hard."

Her eyes widened. "That's all you have to say?"

"Oh, I have a lot to say, starting with I love you. I love you, Molly," he said again. "I want to marry you and spend the rest of my life with you by my side."

"But..." She shook her head. "Did you not hear what I said?"

"I heard. You can't bear children."

"And you want a houseful of them. That's why marriage between us would never work."

Patience, he reminded himself. "You once said that two was a nice number. Now that I've had time to think on it, I find I agree."

"Oh, CJ, you're just saying that to make me feel better."

"I'm saying it because it's true."

The tempered hope in her eyes was nearly his undoing. "You want a large family."

Though she continued to argue with him, he could hear the quiet desperation in her voice. She needed convincing. And he needed to convince her.

Patience.

"We have the twins and we have each other. That's enough for me."

"You should know the rest."

"All right, I'm listening."

In halting terms, she told him her failure to bear a child had created resentment in her home. By the end of her speech, her shoulders had slumped, making her appear beaten down and defeated. "So you see, there's no reason to hope for something that will never happen."

"Let me hope for us both." He guided her into his arms. "No, Molly, don't pull away. Let me hold you a moment."

Slowly, in increments, she relaxed against him. Progress. "Just because you never had children with your first husband doesn't mean you won't have them with me."

"Why won't you accept that I can't marry you?"

"Because you *can* marry me. All you have to do is say yes. The rest will fall into place."

She shoved herself out of his arms. "I'm done talking.

Go away now." She was trying to look as chilly as her words sounded, but CJ saw past the facade.

"I'm not going anywhere until you accept that I want you, Molly. You, not your womb."

Something precariously close to hope flashed in her eyes. "I want you to be happy, CJ."

"I can never be happy without you in my life."

"I think you really mean that."

"With everything that I am. I love you. You love me. I need you. And, Molly—" he took her face in his hands "—you need me."

"I do. Oh, CJ, I do love you. And I do need you. But—"

He pressed his lips to hers.

After a moment, he stepped back.

The next move was up to her.

"You really want to marry me? Still? Even knowing how little I have to bring to a marriage?"

"If you need me to demonstrate just how deep my affections run, I will give it another go." Allowing her no chance to protest, he dragged her back into his arms and kissed her again.

After a considerable amount of persuasion on his part, he released his hold. "Well?"

"Yes, CJ." This time, *she* reached up and cupped *his* face. "It would be my great honor and privilege to become your wife."

Epilogue

CJ and Molly were married a week later, one day after a fortuitous letter from Ned arrived at the Triple T. There hadn't been a single ounce of sentiment in the hastily scrawled words, only news that Ned was heading to the Alaskan territory to start his life anew.

CJ had been understandably angry for the girls' sake, then disappointed, then resigned. "Their father may have abandoned them," he'd said, unspeakable sorrow sounding in his tone, "but they will not go a day in this house without knowing they are loved."

Molly had echoed his vow with equal conviction.

Their life as a family began today.

Brandon Stillwater officiated at the ceremony beneath the revival tent in Little Horn. Molly would remember her wedding day as a happy, blessed gathering of family, friends and neighbors.

A month ago, she'd been lost, alone, and didn't know where she belonged.

Now, as she stood before the preacher, looking into the eyes of her handsome groom, she knew she was right where she was supposed to be.

She saw the future when she looked into CJ's eyes.

She also saw strength of character and, most of all, a man who would love her through the good times and the bad, whether she was able to bear him a child or not.

They would raise the twins as their own, and guide troubled boys to become men of sound integrity.

The Lord had blessed Molly with children, after all.

"Molly, wilt thou have this man to be thy wedded husband to live together after God's ordinance in the holy estate of matrimony? Wilt thou love him? Comfort him, honor and keep him, in sickness and in health, and forsaking all others, keep thee only unto him as long as you both shall live?"

"I will."

CJ was presented with the same question. "I will."

Oh, how she adored this man. He looked especially handsome in his black coat, black pants and crisp white shirt.

As he slid a simple gold ring on her finger, Molly cast a glance at the children standing on either side of him. Sarah and Anna were full of smiles and behaving beautifully.

Of course, the very moment she had the thought, Sarah began fidgeting. Molly couldn't blame the little girl. The ceremony must seem impossibly long to a child her age.

At last, the wedding came to an end. The preacher smiled at Molly, then CJ, then said, "I now pronounce you husband and wife."

CJ let out a whoop, pulled her into his arms and kissed her soundly on the mouth. "I love you, Mrs. Thorn."

"I love you, Mr. Thorn." She smiled into her husband's beautiful brown eyes and kissed him back, taking her time. From the front row, her father cleared his throat, and she and CJ laughingly broke apart.

Constance Hickey's gasp of outrage was its own reward.

As one, CJ and Molly turned to face the rather large gathering. As they had that first Sunday after Ned left town, they took the twins' hands and the four of them walked down the aisle.

Each step pulled Molly away from her sad, barren past and closer toward a fruitful future, one she would share with her handsome husband and two little girls she loved as her own. They were her family now. All the family she would ever need.

Smiling at Molly in a way that nearly made her swoon, CJ led her to the cottonwood tree and kissed her again. When he finally pulled away, his eyes were full of promises. Promises she knew he would keep.

They might never have children together, but with faith, hope and God's loving hand guiding their way they would have a good marriage and a happy life.

What more could a woman ask?

* * * * *

Dear Reader,

Thank you for joining me in Little Horn, Texas. I enjoyed exploring this fictional town nestled in the beautiful Texas Hill Country. I have a confession to make. I'm a city girl at heart. But, there's something compelling about a cowboy with a swagger. Even more so if he's attempting to do the right thing in a situation far removed from his wheelhouse. Although this book is my nineteenth title with Love Inspired, *Stand-In Rancher Daddy* was my first fish-out-of-water story.

Poor CJ, I certainly didn't make it easy for him. I especially had fun writing the scenes where he interacted with Sarah and Anna, each with varying degrees of success. As a twin myself, telling the girls' story was a sweet trip down memory lane. I remember my own father, a single dad, trying to make breakfast for my sister and me, *once*. After that, the three of us went out to eat, *a lot*.

I have many more stories left to write. Keep checking my website www.reneeryan.com and Facebook page for future titles. In the meantime, HAPPY READING!

Renee

REQUEST YOUR FREE BOOKS!

2 FREE INSPIRATIONAL NOVELS
PLUS 2 *FREE* MYSTERY GIFTS

Love Inspired HISTORICAL

SPECIAL EXCERPT FROM

Love Inspired **HISTORICAL**

*With her uncle trying to claim her ranch, widow
Lula May Barlow has no time to worry about romance.
But can she resist Edmund McKay—the handsome
cowboy next door—when he helps her fight for her
land...and when her children start playing matchmaker?*

*Read on for a sneak preview of
A FAMILY FOR THE RANCHER,
the heartwarming continuation of the series
LONE STAR COWBOY LEAGUE:
THE FOUNDING YEARS*

"Just wanted to return your book."

Book?

Lula May saw her children slinking out of the barn,
guilty looks on their faces. So that's why they'd made such
nuisances of themselves out at the pasture. They'd wanted
her to send them off to play so they could take the book to
Edmund. And she knew exactly why. Those little rascals
were full-out matchmaking! Casting a look at Edmund,
she faced the inevitable, which wasn't really all that bad.
"Will you come in for coffee?"

He tilted his hat back to reveal his broad forehead, where
dark blond curls clustered and made him look younger
than his thirty-three years. "Coffee would be good."

Lula May led him in through the back door. To her
horror, Uncle sat at the kitchen table hungrily eyeing
the cake she'd made for Edmund...and almost forgotten
about. Now she'd have no excuse for not introducing them
before she figured out how to get rid of Floyd.

"Edmund, this is Floyd Jones." She forced herself to add,
"My uncle. Floyd, this is my neighbor, Edmund McKay."

As the children had noted last week when Edmund first

stepped into her kitchen, he took up a good portion of the room. Even Uncle seemed a bit unsettled by his presence. While the men chatted about the weather, however, Lula May could see the old wiliness and false charm creeping into Uncle's words and facial expressions. She recognized the old man's attempt to figure Edmund out so he could control him.

Pauline and Daniel worked at the sink, urgent whispers going back and forth. Why had they become so bold in their matchmaking? Was it possible they sensed the danger of Uncle's presence and wanted to lure Edmund over here to protect her? She wouldn't have any of that. She'd find a solution without any help from anybody, especially not her neighbor. Her only regret was that she hadn't been able to protect the children from realizing Uncle wasn't a good man. If she could have found a way to be nicer to him... No, that wasn't possible. Not when he'd come here for the distinct purpose of seizing everything she owned.

The men enjoyed their coffee and cake, after which Edmund suggested they take a walk around the property to build up an appetite for supper.

"We'd like to go for a walk with you, Mr. McKay," Pauline said. "May we, Mama?"

Lula May hesitated. Let them continue their matchmaking or make them spend time with Uncle? Neither option pleased her. When had she lost control of her household? About a week before Uncle arrived, that was when, the day when Edmund had walked into her kitchen and invited himself into her...or rather, her eldest son's life.

"You may go, but don't pester Mr. McKay." She gave the children a narrow-eyed look of warning.

Their innocent blinks did nothing to reassure her.

Don't miss
A FAMILY FOR THE RANCHER
by Louise M. Gouge, available August 2016 wherever
Love Inspired® Historical books and ebooks are sold.

www.LoveInspired.com

LIHEXP0716